This Year's Christmas Present

SANDRA HILL
"Few authors can fuse erotica
and drop-dead humor like Hill."
—*Publishers Weekly*

NINA BANGS
"Bangs's wacky tales never disappoint and her
offbeat characters face danger with flair."
—*RT BOOKreviews*

DARA JOY
"A bright, shining star."
—*RT BOOKreviews*

SANDRA HILL
NINA BANGS
DARA JOY

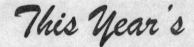

This Year's Christmas Present

LOVE SPELL NEW YORK CITY

LOVE SPELL®

October 2008

Published by

Dorchester Publishing Co., Inc.
200 Madison Avenue
New York, NY 10016

ISBN 10: 0-505-52790-1
ISBN 13: 978-0-505-52790-5

Visit us on the web at www.dorchesterpub.com.

This Year's Christmas Present

TABLE OF CONTENTS

SANDRA HILL

Fever

To my Aunt Catherine Conklin, who passed away last year:
Oh, the Christmas memories she brings to mind.
Angel hair on the tree, children's laughter, delicious scents
from her warm kitchen, but most of all, love.

I will always miss you, Aunt Catherine, but especially at
Christmas.

CHAPTER ONE

"Oh, my gawd! It's George Strait."

"Where? Where? Ooh, ooh! I swear, Mabel, I'm so excited I'm gonna pee my pants."

Clayton Jessup III, was about to enter his hotel suite when he heard the high-pitched squeals of the two blue-haired ladies in matching neon pink ELVIS LIVES sweat-shirts.

He glanced over his shoulder to see who was generating so much excitement and saw no one. *Uh-oh!* In an instant, he realized that they thought he was the George person . . . probably some Memphis celebrity. Even worse, they were pep-stepping briskly toward him with huge smiles plastered across their expectant faces and autograph books drawn and at the ready.

"Open the damn door," he snarled at the wizened old bellhop, whose liver-spotted hands were fumbling with the key.

"I'm tryin', I'm tryin'. You don't wanna get caught by any of these country music fanatics. Last week over on Beale Street, they tore off every bit of a construction worker's clothes for souvenirs, right down to his BVDs, just 'cause they thought he was Billy Dean."

"Who the hell is Billy Dean?"

"You're kidding, right?" the bellhop said, casting him a sideways once-over of disbelief.

Clay grabbed the key out of the bellhop's hand and
inserted it himself. Just before the women were ready
to pounce, gushing, "Oooh, George. Yoo-hoo!" the door
swung open and they escaped. Leaning against the closed
door, he exhaled with a loud whoosh of relief.

He heard one of the women say, "Mabel, I don't think
that was George. He wasn't wearing a cowboy hat, and
George never goes anywhere without his trademark wide-
brimmed cowboy hat."

"Maybe you're right, Mildred," Mabel said.

"Besides, he was too skinny to be George. He looked
more like that Richard Gere."

Richard Gere? Me? Mildred needs a new set of bifocals.

"Richard Gere," Mabel swooned. "Hmmm. Is it
possible . . . ? Nah. That guy was taller and leaner than
Richard Gere. Besides, Richard Gere is more likely to be
off in Tibet with the Dolly Lay-ma, not in Memphis."

"At least we saw Elvis's ghost at Graceland today."

Their voices were fading now, so Clay knew they were
walking away.

Dropping his briefcase to the floor, he opened his closed
eyes . . . and almost had a heart attack. "What is this?" he
asked the bellhop.

"The Roustabout Suite," the bellhop said proudly, shifting from foot to foot with excitement. The dingbat looked
absolutely ridiculous in his old-fashioned red bellhop outfit, complete with a pillbox hat. "It's the best one in the
Original Heartbreak Hotel, next to the Viva Las Vegas and
the Blue Hawaii suites, of course. Families with children
love it."

"I do not have children," Clay gritted out.

"Aaahh, that's too bad. Some folks think the spirit of
Elvis lives in this hotel. Seen 'im myself a time or two.

Maybe if you pray to the Elvis spirit, he'll intercede with the good Lord to rev up your sperm count. Or if the problem is with the little lady, you could . . . uh, why is your face turnin' purple?"

"I do not have children. I am not married. Mind your own damn business."

"Oops!" the bellhop said, ducking his head sheepishly. "Sometimes I talk a mite too much, but I'm a firm believer in Southern hospitality. Yep. Better to be friendly and take a chance than . . ." The fool blathered on endlessly without a care for whether Clay was listening or not. Really, he should be home in a rocking chair, instead of parading around a hotel like an organ grinder's monkey. Another "to do" item to add to his itinerary: check the hotel's retirement policy.

Clay turned his back on the rambling old man . . . and groaned inwardly as he recognized that his view from this angle wasn't any better. *The Roustabout Suite. Hell!*

The split-level suite had a miniature merry-go-round in the sitting room. As the carousel horses circled, a pipe organ blasted out carnival music. A cotton candy machine was set up in one corner, and the blasted thing actually worked, if the sickly sweet odor was any indication. Candy apples lay on the bar counter beside a Slurpee dispenser in the small kitchenette. The walls were papered with movie posters from the Elvis movie *Roustabout*, and the bed was an enlarged version of a tunnel-of-love car. On the bedside table were a clown lamp and a clock in the shape of a Ferris wheel. Up and down went the clown's blinking eyes. Round and round went the clock's illuminated dial. Mixed in with this eclectic collection were quality pieces of furniture, no doubt from the original hotel furnishings.

If Clay didn't have a headache already, this room would surely give him the mother of all migraines. "You can't seriously think I'd stay in this . . . this three-ring circus."

"Well, it was the best we could do on such short notice," the bellhop said, clearly affronted.

"Hee-haw! Hee-haw! Baaaa! Baaaa! Hee-haw!"

For a moment Clay lowered his head, not sure he wanted to know what those sounds were coming from outside. Walking briskly across the room, he glanced out the second-floor window . . . then did an amazed double take.

"Oh! Aren't they cute?" the bellhop commented behind him.

"Humph!" Clay grumbled in disagreement. Pulling his electronic pocket organizer from his suit, he clicked to the Memphis directory, where he typed in his observations, punctuated by several more "Humphs." It was a word that seemed to slip out of his mouth a lot lately . . . a word his father had used all the time. *Am I turning into a negative, stuffy version of my father now? Is that what I've come to?*

"Hee-haw! Hee-haw! Baaaa! Baaaa! Hee-haw!"

"Oh, good Lord!" The headache that had been building all day finally exploded behind his eyes—a headache the size of his bizarre "inheritance" he'd come to Tennessee to investigate. Raking his fingers through his close-clipped hair, he gazed incredulously at the scene unfolding on the vacant lot below . . . a property that he now happened to own, along with this corny hotel. Neither was his idea of good fortune.

"Hee-haw! Hee-haw! Baaaa! Baaaa! Hee-haw!"

"What the hell is going on?" he asked the bellhop, who was now standing in the walk-in closet hanging Clay's garment bag.

"A live Nativity scene."

"Humph!" Clay arched a brow skeptically. It didn't resemble any Nativity scene he'd ever witnessed.

"Did you say humbug?" the bellhop inquired.

"No, I didn't say humbug," he snapped, making a mental note to add an observation in the hotel file of his pocket organizer about the attitude of the staff. *What does the imbecile think I am? A crotchety old man out of a Dickens novel? Hell, I'm only thirty years old. I'm not crotchety. My father was crotchety. I'm not.* "I said 'humph.' That's an expression that denotes . . . Oh, never mind."

He peered outside again. The bellhop was right. Five men, one woman, a baby, a donkey, and two sheep were setting up shop in a scene reminiscent of a Monty Python parody, or a bad "Saturday Night Live" skit. The only thing missing was a camel or two.

Please, God. No camels, Clay prayed quickly, just in case. He wasn't sure how many more shocks he could take today.

The trip this morning from his home in Princeton had been uneventful. He'd managed to clear a backlog of paperwork while his driver transported him in the smooth-riding, oversize Mercedes sedan to Newark Airport. He'd been thinking about ditching the gas guzzler ever since his father died six months ago, but now he had second thoughts. The first-class, airline accommodations had been quiet, too, and conducive to work.

The nightmare had begun once he entered the Memphis International Airport terminal. Every refined, well-bred cell in his body had been assaulted by the raucous sounds of tasteless music and by the even more tasteless souvenirs of every conceivable Elvis item in the world . . . everything from "Barbie Loves Elvis" dolls to "authentic" plastic miniflasks of Elvis sweat.

The worst was to come, however.

When Clay had arrived at the hotel to investigate the last of his sizable inheritance, consisting mostly of blue-chip stocks and bonds, he'd found the Original Heartbreak Hotel. How could his father . . . a conservative Wall Street investment banker, longtime supporter of the symphony, connoisseur of old master paintings . . . have bought a hotel named Heartbreak Hotel? And why, for God's sake? More important, why had he kept it a secret since its purchase thirty-one years ago?

But that was beside the point now. His most immediate problem was the yahoos setting up camp outside. He hesitated to ask the impertinent bellhop another question, which was ridiculous. He was in essence his employee. "Who are they?"

The bellhop ambled over next to him. "The Fallons."

"Are they entertainers?"

The bellhop laughed. "Nah. They're dairy farmers."

Dairy farmers? Don't ask. You'll get another stupid nonanswer. "Well, they're trespassing on my property. Tell the management when you go down to the lobby to evict them immediately."

"Now, now, sir, don't be actin' hastily. They're just poor orphans tryin' to make a living, and—"

"Orphans? They're a little old to be orphans," he scoffed.

"—and besides, it was my idea."

"Your idea?" Clay snorted. Really, he felt as if he'd fallen down some garden hole and landed on another planet.

"Yep. Last week, Annie Fallon was sittin' in the Hound Dog Café, havin' a cup of coffee, lookin' fer all the world like she lost her best friend. She just came from the monthly Holstein Association meeting across the street. You know what Holsteins are, dontcha?"

"Of course I do," he said with a sniff. *They're cows, aren't they?*

"Turns out Annie and her five brothers are in dire financial straits," the bellhop rambled on, "and it occurred to me, and I tol' her so, too, that with five brothers and a new baby . . . her brother Chet's girlfriend *dropped* their sweet little boy in his lap, so to speak . . . well, they had just enough folks fer a Nativity scene, it bein' Christmas and all. I can't figure how the idea came to me. Like a miracle, it was . . . an idea straight out of heaven, if ya ask me." The old man took a deep, wheezy breath, then concluded, "You wouldn't begrudge them a little enterprise like this, wouldja, especially at Christmastime?"

Clay didn't believe in Christmas, never had, but that was none of this yokel's business. "I don't care if it's the Fourth of July. Those . . . those squatters had better be gone by the time I get down there, or someone is going to pay. Look at them," he said, sputtering with outrage. "Bad enough they're planting themselves on private land, but they have the nerve to act as if they own the damn place." Hauling wooden frames off a pickup truck, they were now erecting a three-sided shed, then strewing about the ground hay from two bales.

That wasn't the worst part, though. All of the characters were made up as Elvis versions—*What else!*—of the Nativity figures, complete with fluffed-up hair and sideburns.

The three wise men were tall, lean men in their late teens or early twenties wearing long satin robes in jewel-tone colors, covered by short shoulder capes with high stand-up collars. Their garish attire was adorned with enough sequins and glitter to do the tackiest Vegas sideshow proud. They moved efficiently about their jobs in well-worn leather cowboy boots, except for the shepherd in duct-taped sneakers. Belts with huge buckles, like rodeo cowboys usually wore, tucked in their trim waists.

The shepherd, about thirteen years old, wore a knee-high, one-piece sheepskin affair, also belted with a shiny clasp the size of a hubcap. Even the sleeping baby, placed carefully in a rough manger, had its hair slicked up into an Elvis curl, artfully arranged over its forehead.

Joseph was a glowering man in his mid-twenties, wearing a gem-studded burlap gown, a rope belt with the requisite buckle, and scruffy boots. Since he kept checking the infant every couple of minutes, Clay assumed he must be the father.

"Hee-haw! Hee-haw! Baaaa! Baaaa! Hee-haw!"

Clay's attention was diverted to an animal trailer, parked behind the pickup truck, where one of the wise men was leading the braying donkey and two sheep, none of which appeared happy to participate in the blessed event. In fact, the donkey dug in its hooves stubbornly—*Do donkeys have hooves?*—as the now-cursing wise man yanked on the lead rope. The donkey got in the last word by marking the site with a spray of urine, barely missing the boot of the Wise Man who danced away at the last moment. The sheep deposited their own Nativity gifts.

Clay would have laughed if he weren't so angry.

Then he noticed the woman.

Lordy, did he notice the woman!

A peculiar heat swept over him then, burning his face, raising hairs on the back of his neck and forearms, even along his thighs and calves, lodging smack-dab in his gut, and lower. *How odd!* It must be anger, he concluded, because he sure as hell wasn't attracted to the woman. Not by a Wall Street long shot!

She was tall—at least five-foot-nine—and skinny as a rail. He could see that, even under her plain blue, ankle-length gown . . . well, as plain as it could be with its overabundant studding of pearls. In tune with her outrageous ensemble, she sported the biggest hair he'd ever seen outside a fifties-movie retrospective. The long brunette strands had been teased and arranged into an enormous bowl shape that flipped up on the ends— probably in imitation of Elvis's wife. *What was her name? Patricia? Phyllis? No. Priscilla, that was it.* She must have depleted the entire ozone layer over Tennessee to hold that monstrosity in place. Even from this distance he could see that her eyelids were covered with a tawdry plastering of blue eyeshadow and weighted down with false eyelashes, à la Tammie Faye Baker. Madonna she was not . . . neither the heavenly one, nor the rock star with the cone-shaped bra.

Still, a strange heat pulsed through his body as he gazed at her.

Does she realize how ridiculous she looks?

Does she care?

Do I care?

Damn straight I do! he answered himself as the woman, leader of the motley biblical crew, waved her hands dictatorially, wagged her forefinger, and steered the others into their places. Within minutes, they posed statuelike in a Memphis version of the Nativity scene. The only one un- frozen was the shepherd, whose clear, adolescent voice rang out clearly with "O, Holy Night."

Already tourists passing by were pausing, oohing and ahhing, and dropping coins and paper money into the iron kettle set in the front. It was only noon, but it was clear to Clay that by the end of the day this group was going to make a bundle.

"Not on my property!" Clay vowed, grabbing his overcoat and making for the door. At the last minute, he
paused and handed the clearly disapproving bellhop a
five-dollar bill.

For some reason, the scowling man made him feel
like . . . well, Scrooge . . . and he hadn't even said
"Humph!" again. It was absurd to feel guilty. He was
a businessman . . . an investment banker specializing in
venture capital. He had every right to make a business
decision.

"Thank you for your service," he said coolly. "I'm sure
I'll be seeing you again during my stay here in Memphis."
Clay intended to remain only long enough to complete
arrangements for the razing of the hotel and the erection
of a strip mall on this site and the adjoining property. He
expected to complete his work here before the holidays
and catch the Christmas Eve shuttle back to New Jersey
on Thursday. Not that he had any particular plans that
demanded a swift return to Princeton. On the contrary.
There was no one waiting for him in his big empty mansion, except for Doris and George Benson, the longtime
cook/housekeeper and gardener/driver. No Christmas par-
ties he would mind missing. No personal relationships
that would suffer in his absence.

Clay blinked with surprise at his out-of-character,
maudlin musings. This hokey Elvis-mania that pervaded
Memphis must be invading his brain, like a virus. *The
Elvis virus. Ha, ha, ha!*

The bellhop's eyes bored into him, then softened, as if
seeing his thoughts.

Clay didn't like the uncomfortable feeling he got under the bellhop's intense stare.

"You really plannin' on kicking the Fallons off your

property? At Christmastime?" the bellhop inquired in a condemning tone of voice.

"Damn straight."

"Even the iciest heart can be melted."

Now what the hell does that mean? "Yeah, well, it's going to take a monumental fever in my case, because I have plans for that property." *This is the craziest conversation in the world. Why am I even talking to this kook?*

"You know what they say about the best-laid plans?"

"Am I supposed to understand that?" *Shut up, Jessup. Just ignore him.*

"Sometimes God sticks out his big toe and trips us humans. You might just be in for a big stumble."

God? Big toe? The man is nuts. "Lock up on your way out," Clay advised, opening the hallway door. *Time to put a stop to this nonsense . . . the bellhop, the hotel, the Nativity scene, the whole freakin' mess.*

But damned if the impertinent old fart didn't begin humming "Fever" as Clay closed the door behind him, thus getting in the last word.

"This is the dumbest damn thing you've ever conned us into, Annie."

"Tsk-tsk," Annie told her brother Chet in stiff-lipped sotto voce. "We're supposed to be statues. No talking. Furthermore, St. Joseph should *not* be swearing."

A flush crept up the face of her oldest brother, who was handsome even with the exaggerated Elvis hairdo. Chet was the kind of guy who would probably make a young girl's heart stop even if he were bald.

Good looks aside, her heart went out to Chet. He was twenty-five, only three years younger than she, and so very solemn for his age. Well, he had good reason, she supposed. He'd certainly never hesitated over taking responsibility for raising his baby, Jason, when his girlfriend Emmy Lou abandoned the infant to his care a month ago. Even before that, he'd tried hard to be the man of the family ever since their parents had died in a car accident ten years ago, changing overnight from a carefree teenager to a weary adult.

Well, they'd all changed with that tragedy. No use dwelling on what couldn't be helped.

"There's no one around now," Chet pointed out defensively.

That was true. It was lunch hour and a Sunday, so only a few people had straggled by thus far. But tourist sidewalk traffic past their panorama on Blues Street, just off the famous Beale Street, should pick up soon. Yesterday, their first day trying out this enterprise, had brought in an amazing $700 in tips between eleven A.M. and five P.M. Annie was hoping that in the five days remaining before Christmas they would be able to earn another $3500, enough to save the farm, so to speak.

"I feel like an absolute fool," Chet grumbled.

"Me, too," her other four brothers concurred with a unified groan.

"Wayne keeps trying to bite my butt," Johnny added. "I swear he's the meanest donkey in the entire world. Pure one-hundred-proof jackass, if you ask me."

"He is *not* mean," Jerry Lee argued. The only one Wayne could abide was Jerry Lee, who'd bred him for a 4-H project five years ago. "Wayne senses that you don't like him, and he's trying to get your attention."

"By biting my butt?"

Everyone laughed at that.

"I had a girl once who bit my butt—" Roy started to say.

Annie gasped. "Roy Fallon! If you say one more word,

I swear I'll soap your mouth out when we get home. I don't care if you are twenty-two years old."

Everyone laughed some more. Except for Annie.

"Your sheep keep nuzzling this fleece outfit you made me wear," Johnny continued to gripe. He directed his complaint now at Annie. "I think they think I'm one of their cousins."

Ethel and Lucy were Annie's pets. She'd won them when they were only baby lambs in a grange raffle two years ago.

"Stop your whining, boys," she snapped. "Do you think *I'm* enjoying myself? My scalp itches. My skin is probably breaking out in zits like a popcorn machine. I'm surely straining some muscles in my eyelids with these false eyelashes. And I'm just praying that the barn roof doesn't cave in before we earn enough money for its repair. Or that the price of milk doesn't drop again. Or that we'll be able to afford this semester at vet school for Roy. And—"

"Don't blame this sideshow on me," Roy chimed in. "It's not my fault the government cut the student-aid program."

"Oh, Roy, don't get your sideburns in a dither," she said, already regretting her sharp words.

"Or get your duck's-ass hairdo in a backwind," Hank taunted.

Annie shot Hank a scowl, and continued, "No one's to blame, Roy. Our problems have been piling up for a long time."

"Well, I'll tell you one thing. If anyone from school comes by, I'm outta here, barn roof or no barn roof," Jerry Lee asserted. At fifteen, peer approval was critical, and dressing up as an Elvis wise man probably didn't score many points with the cheerleading squad.

"You're just worried that Sally Sue Sorenson will see you," Hank teased.

"Am not," Jerry Lee argued, despite his red face.

"Shhhh," Annie cautioned.

A group of tourists approached, and Annie's family froze into their respective parts. Johnny, her youngest brother—*God bless him*—broke loose with an absolutely angelic version of "Silent Night." He must have inherited his singing talent from their parents, who'd been unsuccessful Grand Ole Opry wanna-bes. The rest of them could barely carry a tune.

In appreciation, the group, which included a man, a woman, and three young children, waited through the entire song, then dropped a five-dollar bill into the kettle, while several couples following in their wake donated a bunch of dollar bills each, along with some change. Thank God for the Christmas spirit.

After they passed by, Roy picked up on their interrupted conversation. "Actually, Jerry Lee, don't be too quick to discount the appeal of this Elvis stuff. Being an Elvis look-alike could be a real chick magnet for some babes."

"You've been hanging around barns too long," Jerry Lee scoffed, but there was a note of uncertainty in his voice. Roy was a first-year vet student and graduate of Memphis State. Jerry Lee wasn't totally sure his big brother, at twenty-two, hadn't picked up a few bits of male-female wisdom.

"He's bullshittin' you," Hank interjected with a laugh, ignoring the glare Annie flashed his way for the coarse language. Hank was a high school senior, a football player, and the self-proclaimed stud of the family.

Jerry Lee gave Roy a dirty look for his ill advice. Obviously, Hank ranked as the better "chick" expert.

"What do you think, Annie?" Roy asked, chuckling at Jerry Lee's gullibility.

"How would I know what attracts women? I haven't had a date in two years. Then it was with Frankie Wilks, the milk-tank driver."

"And he resembles the back end of a hound dog more than Elvis," Hank remarked with a hoot of laughter at his own joke.

"That was unkind, Hank," Annie chastised, "just because he's a little . . . hairy."

They all made snorting sounds of ridicule.

Frankie Wilks had a bushy beard and mustache and a huge mop of frizzy hair. Masses of hair covered his forearms and even peeked out at the neck of his milk company uniform. *Hirsute* would be an understatement.

"You could go out with guys if you wanted to," Chet offered softly. "You don't have to give up your life for us or the farm. It was different when we were younger, but—"

"Uh-oh!" Roy said.

Everyone stopped talking and stiffened to attention.

A man was stomping down the sidewalk toward them, having emerged from the hotel entrance. He wore a conservative black business suit, so finely cut it must have been custom-made, with a snow white shirt and a dark-striped tie, spit-shined wing-tip shoes, and a black cashmere overcoat that probably cost as much as a new barn roof.

He was a taller, leaner version of Richard Gere, with the same short-clipped dark hair. He would have been heart-stoppingly handsome if it weren't for the frown lines that seemed to be etched permanently about his flaming eyes and tight-set mouth. How could a man so young be so disagreeable in appearance?

Despite his demeanor, Annie felt a strange heat rush

through her just gazing at him. It was embarrassment, of course. What woman enjoyed looking like a tart in front of a gorgeous man?

Unfortunately, Annie suspected that the flame in his eyes was directed toward them. And she had a pretty good idea who he was, too. Clayton Jessup III, the new owner of the Original Heartbreak Hotel and the vacant lot where they had set up their Nativity scene.

The kindly couple who managed the hotel, David and Marion Bloom, had given them permission for the Nativity scene when Annie had asked several days ago. "After all, the lot has been vacant for more than thirty years," Marion had remarked. "It's about time someone made use of it."

But when Annie and Chet had stopped in the hotel a short time ago, where David and Marion had also been nice enough to let them use an anteroom for changing Jason, they soon realized that everyone at the hotel was in an uproar. The new owner had arrived, unannounced, and he intended to raze the site and erect a strip shopping mall. As if Memphis needed another mall!

Didn't the man recognize the sentimental value of the hotel and this lot? No, she guessed, a man like him wouldn't. Money would be his bottom line.

Just before Mr. Jessup got to them, some tourists paused and listened with "oohs" and "ahhs" of appreciation, dropping more paper money and change into their kettle. The boys stood rock still, but Annie saw the gleam of interest in their eyes at a petite blonde in gray wool slacks and a cardigan over a peach-colored turtleneck who stood staring at them for a long time. There was a hopeless sag to her shoulders until Hank winked at her, and she burst out with a little laugh.

Drawing the sides of his overcoat back, and planting

his hands on slim hips, Mr. Jessup glared at them, his lips curling with disdain upon getting a close-up view of their attire. At least he had the courtesy to wait till the tourists passed by before snarling, "What the hell are you doing on my property?"

The baby's eyes shot open, and he began to whimper at the harsh voice.

"We have permission," Chet said, his voice as frosty as Mr. Jessup's as he leaned over and soothed his child. "Hush, now. Back to sleep, son," he crooned, rocking the manger slightly.

Annie tried to explain, "Mr. and Mrs. Bloom told us it would be all right. We'll only be here for a few days, and—"

He put up a hand to halt her words. "You won't be here for even a few more hours." He peered down at his watch—probably one of those Rolex things, equal in value to the mortgage on their farm—and grated, "You have exactly fifteen minutes to vacate these premises, or I'll have the police evict you forcibly. So stop fluttering those ridiculous eyelashes at me."

"I was not fluttering."

"Hey, it's not necessary to yell at our sister," Roy yelled. He, Hank, Jerry Lee, and Johnny were coming up behind Annie to form a protective flank. Chet had taken Jason out of the manger and was holding him to his shoulder, as if Mr. Jessup might do the infant bodily harm.

"Furthermore, those animals had better not have done any damage," Mr. Jessup continued, and proceeded to walk toward the shed where Wayne was hee-hawing and the sheep were bleating, as if sensing some disaster in progress.

"No! Don't!" they all shouted in warning.

Too late.

Mr. Jessup slipped on a pile of sheep dung. Righting

himself, he noticed Wayne's back leg shoot out. To avoid the kick, he spun on his ankle. Annie could almost hear the tendons tearing as his ankle twisted. His expensive shoes, now soiled, went out from under him, and the man went down hard, on his back, with his head hitting a small rock with an ominous crack.

"I'm going to sue your eyelashes off," Mr. Jessup said on a moan, just before he passed out.

CHAPTER TWO

He was drunk . . . as a skunk.

Well, not actually drunk. More like under the influence of painkillers. But the effect was the same. Three sheets to the Memphis wind.

"Oh, I wish I was *not* in the land of Dixie," Mr. Jessup belted out. He'd been singing nonstop for the past five minutes.

Annie and the emergency room intern exchanged a look.

Annie tried to get him to lie down on the table. "Mr. Jessup, you really should settle—"

"Call me Clay." He flashed her a lopsided grin, accompanied by the most amazing, utterly adorable dimples. Then he resumed his rendition of "Dixie" with a stanza ending, ". . . *strange* folks there are not forgoooootten."

Geez!

"I wish I'd bought that t-shirt I saw at the airport." Mr. Jessup . . . rather, Clay . . . stopped singing for a moment to inject that seemingly irrelevant thought. "It said, 'Elvis Is Dead, And I'm Not Feelin' So Good Myself.' Ha, ha, ha!"

"He's having a rather . . . um, strange allergic reaction. Or perhaps I just gave him a little too much Darvon," the young doctor mumbled, casting a sheepish glance toward the other busy cubicles to see if any of his colleagues had overheard.

"No kidding, Ben Casey!" Annie remarked. Clay was now leading an orchestra in his own version of "Flight of the Bumble bee." She didn't think Rimsky-Korsakov had actual buzzing sounds in his original opera containing that music.

"You have biiiiig hair," he observed to Annie then, cocking his head this way and that to get just the right angle in studying its huge contours. "Does it hurt?"

"No."

"Does your boyfriend like it?"

"I don't have a boyfriend."

He nodded his head, as if that was a given. "A man couldn't get close enough to kiss you. Or other things," he noted, jiggling his eyebrows at her.

The man was going to hate himself tomorrow if he remembered any of this.

Annie was already hating herself . . . because, for some reason, the word *kiss* coming from his lips—*who knew they would be so full and sensual when not pressed together into a thin line of disapproval?*—prompted all kinds of erotic images to flicker in her underused libido. She pressed a palm to her forehead. "Boy, is it hot in here!"

"I'll second that. I'm burning up." Clay twisted his head from side to side, massaging the nape of his neck with one hand. Then, before she could protest, he loosened the string tie at the back of his shoulders and let his hospital gown slide to the floor. He wore nothing but a pair of boring white boxer shorts.

Boring, hell! He was sexy as sin.

Annie's mouth gaped open, and her temperature shot up another notch or two at all that skin. And muscle. And dark, silky hair.

Funny how hair on Frankie Wilks seemed repulsive. But with this man, she had to practically hold her hand back for fear she'd run her fingertips through his chest hairs. Or forearm hairs. Or—*lordy, lordy*—thigh hairs.

How could a man so stodgy and mean be so primitively attractive? She'd gotten to know just how stodgy and mean he could be on the ride over here. And how did a man who presumably worked at a desk all day long maintain such a flat, muscle-planed stomach?

Startled, she clicked her jaw shut.

"It's not warm in here," the doctor pointed out, intruding into her thoughts. *Thank God!* "Perhaps you both have a fever. But, no, I checked your temperature, Mr. Jessup. It's normal."

Normal? There's nothing normal about the steam heat rising in this room.

Clay glared at Annie accusingly. Was he going to blame her for a fever, too? To her horror, he broke out with the husky, intimate lyrics, "You give me fever." He was staring at her the whole time.

Oh, mercy! Who would have thought he even knew an Elvis lyric? It had probably seeped into his unconscious over the years through some sort of Muzak osmosis.

"The medication will wear off in a couple of hours," the doctor was saying. "After that, we'll switch to Tylenol with codeine. Considering his reaction, I would suggest you give him only half a tablet."

"Me? Me?" *Hey, I've got to get back to the Nativity scene. Without my supervision, who knows what my brothers are doing? Probably a Macarena version of "Away In a Manger." I wouldn't put it past Roy and Hank to be flirting with passersby, too.*

The doctor finished wrapping Clay's sprained ankle tightly and took on what he'd probably practiced in front of a mirror as a serious medical demeanor. "The goose egg on the back of your head is just a hard knock, but you should be watched closely for the next twenty-four hours. I don't like the way you reacted to the Darvon. Do you have family nearby to keep an eye on you?"

"I have no family," Clay declared woefully.

He's not married. Annie did a mental high-five, though why, she couldn't imagine. Her heart would have gone out to the man at that poignant comment if it weren't for the fact that he was back to glowering at her. She tried to understand why he directed all his hostility toward her. No doubt it stemmed from the fact that he'd been *really* angry about the accident and blamed it all on her family. "You and your crazy brothers are going to pay," he'd informed her repeatedly on the drive to the hospital, during the long wait in the emergency room, throughout the examination, right up until the painkillers had performed their miraculous transformation. Good thing she'd talked her brothers into manning the Nativity scene, minus a Blessed Virgin, till she returned. They would have belted Clay for his surliness!

She was hoping he'd meant the threat figuratively. She was hoping it had only been the pain speaking. She was hoping God listened to the prayers of Blessed Mother impersonators.

They couldn't afford a new barn roof *and* a lawsuit.

"Well, then, perhaps we should admit you," the doctor told him. "At least overnight . . . for observation."

"I'm going back to my hotel room," Clay argued, shimmying forward to get off the examining table and stand. In the process, his boxers rode high, giving Annie an eyeful, from the side, of a tight buttock.

And her temperature cranked up another notch.

Who knew? Who could have guessed?

"Ouch." He groaned as his feet hit the floor. He staggered woozily and braced himself against the wall.

"You could stay at the farm with us for a few days," Annie surprised herself by offering. The fever that had overcome her on first viewing this infuriating tyrant must have gone to her brain. "Aunt Liza can help care for you. . . ." *While we're in the city doing our Nativity scene.* "It'll be more comfortable than a hotel room." *And you wouldn't see us on your property.*

"That's a good idea," the doctor offered, obviously anxious to end this case and move on to the next cubicle.

"Okeydokey," Clay slurred out, the time-release medication apparently kicking in again. He was leaning against the wall, bemusedly rubbing his fingertips across his lips, as if they felt numb. Then he idly scratched his stomach . . . his *flat* stomach . . . in an utterly male gesture his lordliness probably never indulged in back at the manor house.

Her heart practically stopped as the significance of his quick agreement sank in. *Criminy! I'm bringing Donald Trump home with me. What possessed me to make such an offer? My brothers will kill me. But no. It really is a good idea. Get him on home turf where we can talk down his anger. Perhaps convince him to let us continue our Nativity scene the rest of the week. Take advantage of his weakened state. Heck, we might even persuade him to change his plans about razing the hotel.*

On the other hand, Elvis might be alive and living in the refrigerator at Pizza Hut.

"A farm? I've never been on a real farm before." A grin tugged at his frowning lips, and he winked at her. "Eeii, eeii, oh, Daisy Mae."

Holy cow! The grin, combined with the sexy wink, kicked up the heat in her already feverish body still another notch. Even worse, the man appeared to have a sense of humor buried under all that starch. It just wasn't fair. Annie didn't stand a chance.

"Uh-oh." His brow creased with sudden worry. "Do you have outhouses? I don't think I want to live on a farm if I have to use an outhouse."

Live? Who said anything about "live"? We're talking visit here. A day . . . two at the most. But Annie couldn't help but smile at his silly concern.

"Hey, you're not so bad-looking when you smile." Clay cocked his head to one side, studying her.

"Thanks a bunch, your smoothness," she retorted. "And, no, we don't have outhouses."

"Do you have cows and horses and chickens and stuff?" he asked with a boyish enthusiasm he probably hadn't exhibited in twenty-five years . . . if ever.

"Yep. Even a goat."

"Oh, boy!" he said.

As the implications of her impetuous offer hit Annie— Mr. GQ Wall Street on their humble farm—she echoed his sentiment; *Oh, boy!*

"Did you ever make love in a hayloft?" he asked bluntly.

"No!" She lifted her chin indignantly, appalled that he would even ask her such an intimate question. Despite her indignation, though, unwelcome images flickered into Annie's brain, and her fever flared into a full-blown inferno.

"Neither have I," Clay noted, as he stared her straight in the eye and let loose with the slowest, sexiest grin she'd seen since Elvis died.

At the sign, SWEET HOLLOW FARM, Annie swerved the pickup truck off the highway and onto the washboard-rough dirt lane that meandered for a quarter mile up to the house.

Tears filled her eyes on viewing her property, as they often did when she'd been away, even if only for a few hours. She loved this land . . . the smell of its rich soil, the feel of the crisp breeze coming down from the Blue Ridge Mountains, the taste of its wholesome bounty. It had been a real struggle these past ten years, but she prided herself on not having sold off even one parcel from the 120-acre family legacy.

"Oh, darn!" she muttered when she hit one of the many potholes. The eight-year-old vehicle, with its virtually nonexistent springs, went up in the air and down hard.

She worriedly contemplated her sleeping passenger, who groaned, then rubbed the back of his aching head. His eyelids drifted open slowly, and Annie could see the disorientation that hazed their deep blue depths. As his brain slowly cleared, he sat straighter and glanced at the pasture on the right, where sixty milk cows, bearing the traditional black-and-white markings of the Holstein breed, grazed contentedly, along with an equal number of heifers and a half dozen new calves.

"Holy hell!" Clay muttered. "Cows!"

Geez! You'd think they didn't have dairy herds in New Jersey.

Slowly, he turned his head forward, taking in the clapboard farmhouse up ahead, which must be a stark contrast to his own Princeton home. She knew she was correct in her assessment when he murmured, "The Waltons! I've landed in John Boy Central."

His slow survey continued, now to the left, where he flinched visibly on seeing her . . . still adorned in all her Priscilla/Madonna garishness.

His forehead furrowing with confusion, he loosened his tie and unbuttoned the top button of his dress shirt. Then his fingers fluttered in an unconscious sweep down his body, hesitating for the briefest second over his groin.

Annie understood his bewilderment, even if he didn't. For some reason, an odd heat—of an erotic nature, not the body-temperature type—was generated when they were in each other's presence. She empathized with his consternation. Clayton Jessup III was a gorgeous hunk . . . when he wasn't frowning, that was. He, on the other hand, would find it unbelievable that he could be attracted to a tasteless caricature of the Virgin Mary.

"Can you turn down the heat?" he asked testily.

"There is no heat. The thermostat broke last winter."

"Humph!" he commented as he rolled down the window on his side. "Pee-yew!" He immediately rolled it back up. "How can you stand that smell?"

"What smell? Oh, you mean the cows." She shrugged. "You get used to it after a while. Actually, I like the scent. It spells good country living to me."

"Humph! It spells cow crap to me."

Clay's condescending attitude was starting to irk Annie. She had liked him a whole lot better when he was under the influence.

"Am I being kidnapped?" he inquired hesitantly.

"What?" *Where did that insane idea come from? Oh, I see.* His gaze was riveted now on his far left, where Chet's hunting rifle rested in the gun rack above the bench seat. "Of course not."

"Where am I?"

"Don't you remember? You fell outside the hotel. I took you to the hospital emergency room. Oh, don't look so alarmed. You just have a sprained ankle and a goose egg on your head. The doctor said you need special care for a day or two because of the reaction you had to the Darvon, and I offered to bring you out to the farm. We're about a half hour outside Memphis."

"I agreed to stay on a . . . *farm?*" His eyes, which were

really quite beautiful—a deep blue framed by thick black lashes—went wide with disbelief.

"Yes," she said in a voice stiff with affront.

"Why, for heaven's sake?"

Yep, his superiority complex was annoying the heck out of her. "Maybe because you were under the influence of drugs."

"I don't take drugs."

"You did today, buddy."

"Take me back to the hotel."

She let loose with a long sigh. "We've already been through this before. You need special care. Since you have no family, I volunteered—out of the goodness of my heart, I might add—and do I get any thanks? No, sirree."

"Who said I have no family?"

"You did!"

"I . . . did . . . not!" His face flushed with embarrassment.

Geez, why would he be uncomfortable over revealing that he had no family? It only made him appear human. *Ha!* Maybe that was the key. He didn't want to be human.

"I don't discuss my personal life with . . . strangers."

Bingo! "Well, you did this time."

His eyelids fluttered with sleepiness even as he spoke. "What elsh did I saaaay?"

The little demons on the wrong side of Annie's brain did a victory dance at Clay's question. Here was the perfect opportunity for her to get even for his patronizing comments.

"Well, you did a lot of singing."

His eyes shot open. "Me? In public?"

"Hmmm. Do you consider the emergency room a public place?"

"That's impossible."

"And, of course, there was your remark about haylofts . . ."

"Huh?"

Annie could see that the poor guy was fighting sleep. Still, she couldn't keep herself from adding, ". . . and making love."

"Making love in a hayloft? I said *that*?" Clay murmured skeptically. "With *you*? Humph! I couldn't have been *that* much out of my mind."

Before she could correct his misconception that he'd associated making love in a hayloft with her, his head fell back. Good thing, too, because Annie was about to give him a matching goose egg on his insulting noggin. "Did you say humbug?"

"No! Why does everyone think I'm a Scrooge?" he said drowsily, following with a lusty yawn.

"Maybe because you are."

"I said humph," he mumbled in his sleep. Then a small snore escaped from his parted lips.

"Humph you, you egotistical bozo."

Clay awakened groggily from a deep sleep to find it was dark outside. He must have slept a good four hours or more.

For several moments, he didn't move from his position on the high maple poster bed, where he lay on his stomach, presumably to protect the back of his aching head. He burrowed deeper beneath the warm cocoon of a homemade patchwork quilt and smiled to himself. *So this is how it feels to be one of the Waltons.*

By the light of a bedside hurricane lamp, he studied his surroundings. It was a cozy room, with its slanted dormer ceiling—hardly bigger than his walk-in closet at home. The only furniture, besides the bed, was a matching maple dresser and a blanket chest under the low double windows facing the front of the house. A well-worn easy chair of faded blue upholstery sat in one corner, flanked on one side by a floor lamp and on the other by a small sidetable on which sat a paperback book and a pile of magazines. A few photographs, which he couldn't decipher from here, a high school pennant, and some cheaply framed prints of cows—*What else!*—adorned the pink rose–papered walls.

It had to belong to the Blessed Virgin bimbo who'd brought him here. Unless the collection of teddy bears on the chest and the toiletries on the bureau belonged to one of her brothers. Somehow, though, he didn't think any of the strapping young men he'd seen in that wacky Nativity scene were gay farmers.

Clay should have felt outrage at finding himself in this predicament. Instead, a strange sense of well-being filled him, as if he'd been running a marathon for a long, long time, and finally he'd reached the finish line.

Slowly he came fully awake as the sounds of the house, which had been deathly quiet before, seeped into his consciousness. The slamming of a door. The clomp, clomp, clomp of boots on hardwood floors. Laughter and male voices. Water running. The never-ending blare of Elvis music, "You ain't nothin' but a hound dog . . ." *Good Lord! People have the nerve to call that caterwauling music. Humph!*

The cry of a baby emerged from down the hall—from one of the other second-floor bedrooms, he presumed—mixed with the soft crooning voice of an adult male, a mixture of lullaby and words of comfort. "Shhh, Jason. You've had a long day. What a good boy you were! Just let me finish with this diaper; then you can have your bottle. Aaah, I know, I know. You're sleepy." Gradually, the crying died down to a slow whimper, then silence, except for the creak, creak, creak of a rocker.

From the deep recesses of Clay's memory, an image emerged . . . flickering and ethereal. A woman sitting in a high-backed rocking chair, holding an infant in her tender embrace. He even imagined the scent of baby powder mixed with a flowery substance. Perfume? The woman was singing a sweet, silly song to the baby about a sandman coming with his bag of magic sleepytime dust.

A lump formed in Clay's throat, and he could barely breathe.

Could it have been his mother . . . and him? No! His mother had left when he was barely one year old. It was impossible that he could recall something from that age. Wasn't it?

With a snort of disgust, Clay tossed the quilt aside and sat up on the edge of the bed. He gritted his teeth to fight off the wooziness that accompanied waves of pain assaulting him from both the back of his head and his bandaged ankle. Once the worst of the pain passed, he took in the fact that he was clothed only in boxers. Had he undressed himself? No, it had been the woman, Annie Fallon, and her Aunt Liza, a wiry, more ancient version of the grandma on *The Waltons. God, I've got a thing about the Waltons today.* They'd helped him remove his clothing, then encouraged him to take half a pill before tucking him into the big bed.

In fact, Clay had a distinct recollection of the old buzzard eyeballing his near-nude body, cackling her appreciation, then telling Annie, "Not bad for a city slicker!"

He also had a distinct recollection of Annie's response. "Don't go there, Aunt Liza. He's an egotistical bozo with ice in his veins and a Scrooge personality disorder."

"Scrooge-smoodge. You could melt him down, sweetie. Might be a nifty idea for our Christmas good deed this year."

Annie had giggled. "I can see it now. The Fallon family Christmas good deed, 1998: bring a Scrooge home for the holidays."

I am not a Scrooge. Not, not, not! I'm not icy, either. In fact, I'm hot, hot, hot . . . at least when the Tennessee tart is around. Furthermore, nobody—especially not a bunch of hayseed farmers—had better make me their good deed. I am not a pity case.

Clay wanted nothing more than to be back home, where his life was orderly and sane. He was going to sue the pants off these crackpots, but he had more important things on his mind right now. An empty stomach—which rumbled at the delicious scents wafting up from downstairs—and a full bladder.

First things first. Clay pulled on his suit pants gingerly, and made his way into the hall, using one crutch to avoid putting full weight on his injured ankle. Across the corridor, a boy of about thirteen—the one who'd been a shepherd in the Nativity scene—was propped against the pillows on one of the twin beds in the room, reading a biology book and writing in a class notebook. He wore jeans and a T-shirt that proclaimed, FARMERS HAVE LONG HOES. His hair was wet from a recent shower and no longer sported the high pouf on top or duck's tail in the back. It was from a stereo at the side of his bed where the Elvis music was blasting.

When he noticed Clay in the doorway, the boy set his schoolbooks aside and turned down the volume. "You're up. Finally."

"Where's the bathroom?"

"Gotta take a leak, huh?" the boy inquired. "My name's Johnny," he informed him cheerily. "You're Clay, right? Annie says you're gonna stay with us for a while. Cool. Do you like Elvis?" The boy never waited for answers to his questions, just chattered away as he led the way to the end of the hall.

By the time they got there, Clay was practically crossing his legs—not an easy feat when walking with a sprained ankle. Was there only one bathroom to serve more than a half dozen people? There were eight bathrooms in his home, and he was the sole inhabitant these days, except for Doris and George, and they lived over the old carriage house.

Clay soon found himself in the small bathroom with an old-fashioned claw-footed tub and porcelain pedestal sink. No shower stall here, just a showerhead and plastic curtain that hung from an oval aluminum rod, suspended from the ceiling and surrounding the tub on all sides. At least there was a toilet, Clay thought, releasing a long sigh of near-ecstasy after relieving himself.

He'd barely zipped up his pants when there was a knock on the door. "You decent?" a male voice called out.

Define decent. Hobbling around barefooted, decent? Wearing nothing but a knot on my head the size of a fist and a pair of wrinkled slacks, decent? Caught practically midleak, decent? Under the influence of drugs, decent? "Yeah, I'm decent."

The door creaked open and the oldest brother, the father of the baby, stuck his head inside. He apparently hadn't showered yet because he still had the Elvis hairdo, though the St. Joseph outfit was gone, in favor of jeans and a sweatshirt. "Hi. My name's Chet. Annie told me to give you these." He shoved a pair of jeans, a white undershirt, a blue plaid flannel shirt, socks, and raggedy sneakers at him. "You look about the same size as me."

Clay took the items hesitantly. He was about to tell him that he wouldn't need them, since he intended to go back to the hotel, ASAP. And call his lawyer. Before he could speak, though, the man—about twenty-five years old—asked with genuine concern, "How ya feelin'? Your body must feel like a bulldozer ran over it."

"Do you mean your sister?"

Chet threw his head back and laughed. "Annie does have that effect sometimes, doesn't she? No, I meant the boink to your head and your twisted ankle."

Clay shrugged. "I'll be all right."

Just then Clay noticed the black satin bra hanging on the doorknob. The cups were full and feminine to the nth degree. He was pretty sure the wispy undergarment didn't belong to Aunt Liza. Hmmm. It would seem the scarecrow Madonna was hiding something under her virginly robes.

"Hey, that's my sister you're having indecent thoughts about," Chet protested, interrupting his reverie.

"I was not," Clay lied, hoping his flushed face didn't betray him.

"Yeah, right. Anyhow, dinner's almost ready. Do you want me to bring a tray upstairs? Or can you make it downstairs?"

Clay debated briefly whether to eat here or wait till he got back to the hotel. The embarrassing rumble in his gut decided for him. Clay told him he'd be down shortly and went back to the bedroom to change clothes while Chet made use of the shower.

A short time later, he sat at the huge oak trestle table in the kitchen waiting for Annie to come in from the barn with two of her brothers, Roy, a twenty-two-year-old vet student, and Hank, a high school senior. They were completing the second milking of the day for the dairy herd. All this information was relayed by Aunt Liza. That was what the woman had demanded that he call her after he'd addressed her as "ma'am" one too many times.

Had he ever eaten dinner in a kitchen? He didn't think so.

Did he have a personal acquaintance with anyone who had ever milked a cow? He was fairly certain he didn't.

Aunt Liza wore an apron that fit over her shoulders and hung to her knees, where flesh-colored support hose bagged conspicuously under her housedress. She hustled about the commercial-size stove off to one side of the kitchen. Sitting on benches that lined both sides of the table, chatting amiably with him as if it were perfectly normal for him to be there, were Chet, Johnny, whom he had already met, and Jerry Lee, a fifteen-year-old. This family bred kids like rabbits, apparently. The baby was up in his crib, down for the night, Chet said hopefully.

A radio sitting on a counter was set on a twenty-four-hour country music station. *Surprise, surprise.*

"Do you people honestly like that music?" Clay asked. It was probably a rude question to ask when he was in someone else's home, but he really would like to understand the attraction this crap held for the masses.

"Yeah," Chet, Jerry Lee, Johnny, and Aunt Liza said as one.

"But it's so . . . so hokey," Clay argued. "Listen to that one. 'I Changed Her Oil, She Changed My Life.'"

They all laughed.

"That's just it. Country music makes you feel good. You could be in a funky mood, and it makes you smile." Jerry Lee thought about what he'd said for a moment, then chuckled. "One of my favorites is 'She Got the Ring, I Got the Finger.'"

"Jerry Lee Fallon, I told you about using such vulgarities in this house," Aunt Liza admonished. Then she chuckled, too. "I'm partial to 'You Done Tore Out My Heart and Stomped that Sucker Flat.'"

"I like 'I Would Have Wrote You a Letter but I Couldn't Spell Yuck,'" Johnny said.

"Well, the all-time best one," Chet offered, "is 'Get Your Tongue Outta My Mouth 'Cause I'm Kissing You Good-Bye.'"

Some of the other titles tossed out then by one Fallon family member after another were: "How Can I Miss You if You Won't Go Away," "I've Been Flushed from the Bathroom of Your Heart," "If I Can't Be Number One in Your Life, Then Number Two on You," "You Can't Have Your Cake and Edith Too," and the one they all agreed was best, "I Shaved My Legs for *This?*"

Despite himself, Clay found himself laughing with the whole crazy bunch.

Just then, the back door could be heard opening into a mudroom. Voices rang out with teasing banter.

"You'd better not have mooned any passersby, Hank. That's all we need is a police citation on top of everything else," Annie was chastising her brother.

"I didn't say he mooned the girl," another male said. It must be Roy, the vet student. "I said he was mooning *over* her."

There was the sound of laughter then and running water as they presumably washed their hands in a utility sink.

Seconds later, two males entered the room, rubbing their hands briskly against the outside chill, which they carried in with them. They nodded at him in greeting and sat down on the benches, maneuvering their long legs awkwardly under the table.

Only then did Clay notice the woman who stepped through the doorway. She was tall and thin. Her long, *looong* legs that went from here to the Texas panhandle were encased in soft, faded jeans, which were tucked into a pair of work boots. An oversize denim shirt—probably belonging to one of her brothers—covered her on the top, hanging down to her knees with its sleeves rolled up to the elbows. A swath of brunette hair lay straight and thick to her shoulders. Not a lick of makeup covered her clear complexion. Even so, her lips were full—almost too full for her thin face—and parted over large, even, white teeth. She resembled a thinner, more beautiful version of Julia Roberts.

Clay put his forehead down on the table and groaned.

He knew everyone was probably gawking at him as if he'd lost his mind, but he couldn't help himself. He knew even before the fever flooded his face and arms and legs and that particular hot zone in between . . . he knew exactly who this stranger was. It was, unbelievably, Annie Fallon.

He cracked his eyes open a bit, still with his face in his plate, and glanced sideways at her where she still stood, equally stunned, in the doorway. Neither of them seemed to notice the hooting voices surrounding them.

How could he have been so blind?

How could he not have seen what was happening here?

How could he not have listened to the cautionary voice of the bellhop who'd warned of destiny and God's big toe?

All the pieces fit together now in the puzzle that had plagued Clay since he'd arrived in Memphis. God's big toe had apparently delivered him a holy kick in the pants. Not to mention the fever He'd apparently sent to thaw his icy heart.

Clay, a sophisticated, wealthy venture capitalist, was falling head over heels in love with a farmer. Old McAnnie.

Donald Trump and Daisy Mae.

Hell! It will never work.

Will it?

He raised his head and took a longer look at the woman who was frozen in place, staring at him with equal incredulity. It was a sign of the madness that had over-come them both that the laughter rippling around them failed to penetrate their numbed consciousness.

He knew for sure that he was lost when a traitorous thought slipped out, and he actually spoke it aloud.

"Where's the hayloft, honey?"

CHAPTER THREE

Clay felt as if he'd landed smack-dab in the middle of the Mad Hatter's party. It was debatable who was the mad one, though—him or the rest of the inmates in this bucolic asylum.

Love? Me? Impossible!

Music blared in the background—ironically, "Can't Help Falling in Love"—and everyone talked at once, each louder than the other in order to be heard. A half dozen strains of dialogue were going on simultaneously, but no one seemed to notice. Good thing, too. It gave him a chance to speculate in private over his monumental discovery of just a few moments ago.

I'm falling in love.

Impossible! Uh-uh, none of this falling business for me.

What other explanation is there for this fever that overtakes me every time I look at her? And, man, she is so beautiful. Well, not beautiful. Just perfect. Well, not perfect-perfect. Hell, the woman makes my knees sweat, just looking at her.

Maybe it's not love. I've never been in love before. How do I know it's love? Maybe it's just lust.

Love, lust, whatever. I'm a goner.

But a farmer? A farmer?

"How come you and Annie keep googly-eyeing each other?" Johnny asked.

"Shut your teeth and eat," Aunt Liza responded, whacking Johnny on the shoulder with a long-handled wooden spoon.

"Ouch!"

Meanwhile, a myriad of platters and bowls were being set on the table. Aunt Liza assured him this was an everyday meal, not a special spread on his behalf.

Pot roast—about ten pounds, give or take a hindquarter—cut into half-inch slabs. Mashed potatoes. Gravy. Thick noodles cooked in beef broth. Creamed spinach. Pickled beets. Succotash—whatever the hell that was! Chowchow—whatever the hell that was, too! Tossed salad. Coleslaw. Homemade biscuits and butter. Pitchers of cold, unhomogenized milk at either end of the table sporting a two-inch head of real cream. Canned pears. Chocolate layer cake and vanilla ice cream.

There were enough calories and fat grams on this table to fatten up the entire nation of Bosnia. Yet, amazingly, everyone here was whip-thin. Either they'd all inherited good genetic metabolisms, or they engaged in a massive amount of physical labor. He suspected it was a combination of both.

"Do you think it's a good idea to eat so much red meat and dairy?" Clay made the mistake of inquiring.

"Bite your tongue," everyone declared at once.

For a moment, Clay had forgotten that these were dairy farmers whose livelihood depended on milk products. Plus, they had about a hundred thousand pounds of beef on the hoof in their own backyard.

Clay rubbed a forefinger over his upper lip, pondering all that had happened to him so far this day. In the midst of the conversations swirling around him now, he felt as if he were having a personal epiphany. Not just the monumental discovery that, for the first time in his life, he was falling in love; it was much more than that. He'd never realized till this moment how much he'd missed having a family. He never would have described himself as a lonely man—a loner, perhaps, but not *lonely*. Now he knew that he'd been lonely for a long time.

And that wacky bellhop had been right this morning about his coldness. Over the years, he must have built up an icy crust around his heart. *Just like my father.* Little by little, it was melting now. Every time he came within a few feet of Annie, a strange fever enveloped him, and his chest tightened with emotions too new to understand. He yearned so much. For what exactly, he didn't know.

In a daze, he reached for a biscuit, but Chet coughed meaningfully and Aunt Liza glared stonily at him. Once he sheepishly put the roll back, Annie took his hand on one side, and Jerry Lee on the other. All around the table, everyone bowed their heads and joined hands, including Aunt Liza and Chet, who sat in the end chairs, on either side. Then Annie said softly, "Lord, bless this food and all the poor people in the world who have less than we do, and even the rich people who have less than we do. For this bounty, we give you thanks. Amen."

Everyone dug in heartily then, passing the bowls and platters around the table as they chattered away. Clay soon found himself with an unbelievable amount of high-cholesterol food on his plate, and enjoying it immensely. He practically sighed at the almost sinful flavor of melt-in-your-mouth potatoes mixing on his palate with rich beef gravy.

"Frankie Wilks called when you were in the barn." Jerry Lee bobbed his eyebrows at Annie. "Said something about wantin' you to go to the Christmas Eve candlelight service with him."

"Oooooh! Oooooh!" several of her brothers taunted, meanwhile shoveling down food like monks after a Lent-long fast.

"Who's Frankie Wilks?" Clay's voice rose with more consternation than he had any right to exhibit. *Yet.*

"The milkman," Annie said, scowling at Jerry Lee. She had a hearty appetite, too, Clay noticed, though you wouldn't know it from her thin frame. Probably came from riding herd on her cows.

Did they ride herd on cows?

Then Annie's words sank in. *The milkman? The milkman? I have a five-million-dollar portfolio, I'm not a bad-looking guy, attracting women has never been a problem for me, and my competition is . . . a milkman?*

Competition? Whoa! Slow down this runaway testosterone train.

"Don't you be sittin' there, gloatin' like a pig in heat, Chet," Aunt Liza interjected as she put another slab of beef onto Clay's plate, despite his raised hand of protest. His mouth was too full to speak. "You got a phone call to-day, too, Chet."

Everyone at the table turned in tandem to stare at Chet.

"Emmy Lou?" Chet didn't appear very happy as he asked the question.

"Yep. She was callin' from London. Said she won't be home before Christmas to pick up the baby, after all."

"Stupid damn girl," Annie cursed under her breath. Clay suspected *damn* was not a word she used lightly.

"You drove her away, if you ask me," Hank accused, reaching for his dessert, which Aunt Liza shoved out of the way, pushing more salad his way first.

"Who asked you, mush-for-brains?" Chet snapped.

"All you had to do was tell her you looooovvvve her,"

Roy teased. He waved a forkful of potatoes in the air as he spoke.

"I offered to marry her, didn't I?"

"*Offered?* Sometimes, Chet, you are dumber than pig spit," Annie remarked. "Have some pickled beets," she added as an aside to Clay.

Chet's face, which was solemn to begin with, went rigid with anger, but he said nothing.

"Is this Lilith?" Annie addressed Aunt Liza as she chewed on a bite of pot roast.

"Yep. Nice and tender, ain't she?" Aunt Liza answered. "Thank God we got rid of the last of Alicia in the stew Friday night. She was tougher than cow hide."

They name the cows they eat? Will they eat those two sheep that were in the Nativity scene, too? Or—God forbid—the donkey? Bile rose in Clay's throat, and he discreetly pushed the remainder of his pot roast to the side of his plate.

"Speaking of cows, I noticed this morning that Mirabelle's vulva is swollen and red," Johnny interjected. "We better breed her soon."

"I'll do it tomorrow night."

Clay choked on the pot roast still remaining in his mouth. A thirteen-year-old kid was discussing vulvae at the dinner table, and no one blinked an eye. Even worse, Annie—*his* Annie—was going to breed a cow. "Can I watch?"

"Huh? Oh, sure," she said and resumed eating. Clay liked to watch Annie eat. Her full lips moved sensuously as she relished each morsel, no matter if it was a beet or the chocolate cake. He about lost it when her tongue darted out to lick a speck of chocolate icing off the edge of her bottom lip. "If you're sure you want to. Some people get kind of squeamish."

"I can handle it," he asserted. Heck, he'd probably seen worse in Grand Central Station. But, hot damn, Annie had just-like-that agreed to let him observe her breeding a cow. And she wasn't even embarrassed.

"Are you rich?" Roy asked.

"Rooooy!" Annie and Aunt Liza chastised.

"Yes."

"Yes?" Everyone at the table put down their eating utensils and gaped at him. Except Annie. Her face fell in disappointment. Could she be falling in love with him, too? He didn't have time to ponder for long. He just kicked into damage control. "Well, not *rich*-rich."

"How rich?" Annie demanded to know.

Before he could respond, Hank commented, "Betcha draw a bunch of chicks, having heaps of money and all."

"At least a bunch," Clay said dryly.

Annie flashed Hank a glower, which the teen ignored, smiling widely. "Man, if I had a little extra cash, and a hot car, I would be the biggest chick magnet in the whole United States. I'm already the best in the South."

His brothers hooted in reaction to his high self-opinion.

"If you'd get your mind off the girls once in a while," Aunt Liza reprimanded, "maybe you'd pass that cow-cue-lust."

Everyone laughed at her mispronunciation of the word *calculus*, except Annie. "And, by the way, where is your second-term report card, Mr. I-Am-the-Stud?"

"Uh-oh," Johnny and Jerry Lee groaned at the same time.

"You had to remind her," Johnny added.

Clay's lips twitched with suppressed mirth. Being in a family was kind of fun.

But Jerry Lee was back on his case again. "Do you have a chauffeur?"

Clay felt his face turn red. "Benson—George Benson—doubles as my *driver* and gardener. His wife Doris is my cook and housekeeper."

"You have a gardener!" Annie wailed. You'd think he had told her he employed an ax murderer. "And a house-keeper!"

"Do you live in a mansion?" Johnny's young face was rapt with interest.

"No, he lives in a trailer, you dweeb," Hank remarked, nudging Johnny in the ribs with an elbow.

"No. Definitely not. Uh-uh. I do *not* live in a mansion." This was the most incredible conversation Clay had ever experienced. Why was he trying to downplay his lifestyle?

To make Annie more comfortable, that was why.

Annie's eyes narrowed. "How big is this nonmansion?"

"Tweytfllrms," he mumbled.

"What?"

"Twenty-two rooms. But it's not a mansion."

"Twenty-two rooms! And you live there alone?" She appeared as if she might cry. "You probably have caviar for breakfast and—"

He shook his head quickly. "Toast, fresh-squeezed orange juice, and black coffee, that's what I have. Every day. I don't even like caviar."

"—gold faucets in your bathrooms and—"

"They're only gold plated. Cheap gold plating. And brass. I'm pretty sure some of them are brass."

"—and date movie stars—"

"The only movie star I ever dated was Brooke Shields, and that was because she and I are both Princeton alumni. And it wasn't really a date, just brunch at—"

"Brooke Shields!" five males at the table exclaimed.

Annie honed in on another irrelevant fact. "He eats brunch. *Brunch*. Oh, God! He must think he's landed on Welfare Row. *Better Slums and Gardens*."

"Who's Brooke Shields?" Aunt Liza wanted to know. "Is she one of those *Melrose Place* hussies Roy watches all the time?"

Before anyone could explain, Annie sighed loudly and declared, "Maybe I'd better take you back to your hotel tonight."

"Annie!" Johnny whined. "You promised we would put up the Christmas tree tonight."

"Yeah, Annie," Jerry Lee chimed in. "We would have had it up by now if it wasn't for your dumb Nativity scene idea."

"Well, actually . . . uh, I'm not feeling so good," Clay surprised himself by saying. He was in a sudden panic. If he went back to the hotel, he'd have no opportunity to study this fever thing with Annie . . . or this falling in . . . uh, whatever. He could easily conduct business on his pocket cell phone from the farm, for a day or two anyhow.

"You aren't?" Annie was immediately concerned.

"Maybe coming downstairs was too much for you." Aunt Liza got up and walked to his end of the table, then put a hand to his forehead to check his temperature. "Yep, he's got a fever."

No kidding! What else is new?

"I'll help you back up the steps," Chet offered.

"No, that's all right. I think I could sit in a chair and watch you put up your tree." *I am shameless. Pathetic, even.* Then, before he had a chance to bite his tongue, he blurted out, "I've never had a Christmas tree."

Everyone stared at him as if he'd just arrived from Mars. Or New Jersey.

"My father didn't believe in commercial holidays," he

disclosed, a defensive edge to his voice. *Put a zipper on it, Jessup. You don't want pity. You want . . . well, something else.*

"That settles it, then," Aunt Liza said, tears welling in her eyes.

Yep, pity.

Annie reached under the table and took his hand in hers.

On the other hand, I can stomach a little pity.

Immediately, a warm feeling of absolute rightness filled him almost to overflowing. He knew then that he'd made the right decision in forestalling his return to the city. Besides, he'd just remembered something important.

He hadn't checked out the hayloft yet.

Annie Fallon had thought she had troubles this morning before she ever left for Memphis. Little had she known that her troubles would quadruple by nightfall.

In fact, she'd brought trouble home with her, willingly, and it sat big as you please right now on her living room sofa, with one extended leg propped up on an ottoman, gazing at her with smoldering eyes that promised . . . well, trouble.

Clayton Jessup III had looked handsome this morning when Annie had seen him for the first time in his cashmere overcoat and custom-made suit. But now, sporting a nighttime shadow of whiskers, dressed in tight, faded jeans, a white T-shirt, and an unbuttoned blue plaid flannel shirt that brought out the midnight blue of his eyes, the man was drop-dead gorgeous, testosterone-oozing, hot-hot-hot trouble-on-the-hoof, with a capital *T*.

"I need to talk with you . . . *alone*," he whispered when Annie stepped close to get the popcorn and cranberry strings he'd been working on for the past two hours. When Aunt Liza had first suggested that he help make the homemade decorations, he'd revealed with an endearing bashfulness, "My father would have been appalled to see me performing this mundane chore. 'Time is money,' was his favorite motto. Over and over he used to tell me, 'You're wasting time, boy. Delegate, delegate, delegate.'" Then Clay had ruined the effect of his shy revelation by asking Aunt Liza the crass question, "Don't you think it would be cheaper, timewise, to buy these garlands already strung?"

Clucking with disapproval, Aunt Liza had shoved the darning needle, a ball of string, and bowls of popcorn and cranberries in his lap. "You can't put a price tag on tradition, boy."

Along the same line, he'd observed, "I never realized Christmas trees could be so messy." Her brothers had just dragged in the seven-foot blue spruce from the porch, leaving a trail of fresh needles on the hardwood floors. "Wouldn't an artificial tree be a better investment in the long run?"

They'd all looked at him as if he'd committed some great sacrilege. Which, of course, he had. An artificial tree? Never! Couldn't he smell the rich Tennessee forest in the pine scent that permeated the air? Couldn't he understand that bringing a live tree into the house was like bringing a bit of God's bounty inside, a direct link between the upcoming celebration of Christ's birth and the world's ongoing rejuvenation of life?

"Think with your heart, not your brain, sonny," Aunt Liza urged.

Now the tree decorating was almost complete, except for the star—which had been in the family for three generations—the garlands, and the last of the handcrafted ornaments made by Fallon children for the past twenty-five or so years. And all Annie could think about was the fact that the man had said he wanted to talk with her, *alone*. About two thousand red flags of warning went up in Annie's already muddled senses. "If it's about your threat to sue, well, you can see we don't have much."

The Fallons were a proud family, but her brothers were trusting souls, and in the course of the evening they'd casually divulged their dire need for a new barn roof, the money crunch caused by lower milk prices, and Roy's tuition woes. They'd even discussed at length how every year at Christmastime the Fallons performed one good deed, no matter how tight they were for money. One year it had been a contribution to a local farm family whose house had burned down. Another year they made up two dozen baskets for a food bank in Memphis, complete with fresh turkeys, home-canned fruits, vegetables and preserves, crisp apples, and pure maple syrup. Still another year, when the till was bone-dry, they'd donated ten hours each to Habitat for Humanity. This year, they hadn't yet come up with any ideas. But they would before Christmas Eve. Tradition demanded it.

"You can sue us if you want, but it's obvious that we barely have two dimes to spare. I'll fight you to the death if you try to take our farm."

"What in God's name gave you the idea that I want your farm?" he snapped. Then his voice lowered. "It's not your farm I'm interested in, Annie."

Annie loved the way he said her name, soft and special. But there was no way in the world she would ask what he meant by that enigmatic remark. "Perhaps we could pay for your medical expenses over a period of time."

He shook his head slowly. "I'm insured."

Okay, he's insured, but he didn't say he wouldn't sue us. Should I ask, or assume that he won't? Hmmm. Better to let sleeping dogs lie. "I hope you're not going to stop us from doing our Nativity scene for the rest of the week. You've got to know it's our last chance. And—"

He put up a halting hand. "I'd rather you didn't go back to that sideshow again, but that's not why I want to talk with you."

"It's not?" Annie's heart was beating so fast she was afraid he might hear it.

"It's not."

"What do you want from us, then?"

"From your family . . ."—he shrugged—"nothing."

She reflected on his words. "From me?" she squeaked out.

A slow grin crept across his lips, causing those incredible dimples to emerge. Annie had to clench her fists against the compulsion to touch each of the tiny indentations, to trace the outline of those kiss-me lips, to—

A low, masculine chuckle emerged from said lips. "If you don't stop looking at me like that, Annie, love," he said in a husky undertone, "I'll *show* you what I want."

Annie, love? Mercy! "I don't know what you mean," she said huffily, and backed away before he could tell her exactly how she'd been ogling him and what he would show her.

"You know what I mean, Annie," he commented to her back. "You know."

She didn't know, not for sure, but her imagination kicked in big-time. It was the fever, of course—that strange malady that seemed to affect only the two of them when they were in the same room. Hadn't they complained of the heat all night? And they both knew it had nothing to do with the roaring fire in the fireplace. It was a fire of another kind entirely.

After that, in the midst of their decorating efforts, Clay helped Hank with his calculus homework. No one was surprised that a man with his financial background could actually perform the complicated equations. Then Jerry Lee expressed a curiosity about Clay's electronic planner gadget. He showed him its various gee-whiz functions and answered questions about the stock market. Annie had never realized that Jerry Lee was even interested in the investment world.

Throughout the evening, Aunt Liza coddled them all by bringing out trays of hot chocolate and her latest batch of Christmas sugar cookies. "Have another," she kept urging Clay, who swore his jeans were going to unsnap.

Now that was a picture Annie tried to avoid.

Finally, the tree decorating was complete.

"Turn off the lamps and flick on the tree lights," Aunt Liza advised. The darkened room looked beautiful under the sheen of the multicolored lights. There was a communal sigh of appreciation from everyone in the room, even Clay.

"Is everyone ready?" Johnny asked, reaching over to turn up the volume on the old-fashioned stereo record player. It had been pumping out Elvis Christmas songs all night.

Her family began singing along with "Blue Christmas" . . . a less than harmonic but poignant custom that always brought tears to Annie's eyes. It reminded her of her parents, now gone, and the yuletide rituals they'd started that would be carried on by Fallons forevermore. In some ways, it was as if, at times like this, their parents were still with them.

Annie glanced over at Clay to see how he was reacting to what he must consider a sappy custom. By the glow of the tree lights and the burning logs in the fireplace, she noticed no condescending smirk on his face. He seemed stunned.

Moving to the front of the sofa and leaning forward, she inquired, "What do you think of your first Christmas tree?"

Before Annie could blink, he grabbed her by the wrist and pulled her down to the sofa at his side. One of her brothers chuckled midstanza, but Annie couldn't bother about that. Clay had tucked her close with an arm locked around her shoulder and her hip pressed tight against his. Only then did he answer . . . a husky whisper breathed against her ear.

"This is a Christmas I will never forget, Annie, love."

They were alone at last.

And Clay had plans.

Big plans.

Aunt Liza had gone to her bedroom on the first floor off of the kitchen after wishing everyone Merry Christmas and giving each a good-night kiss on the cheek, including Clay, who felt a tightening in his throat at being included in the family. Hank had put another log on the fire for them, winked, then hit the telephone for a long chat with his latest girlfriend. Roy and Jerry Lee had gone out to the barn for a final check of the farm animals. Chet was upstairs giving his baby a last nighttime bottle. Johnny was probably asleep already, being among those who'd gotten up by four A.M. today to do farm chores before going into Memphis. Even Elvis had shut down for the night.

Clay turned to Annie, almost overwhelmed with all the new emotions assailing him. "What's happening here?" he asked in a hoarse voice that surely tipped her off to his sorry condition.

"I don't know," she answered, not even having to ask him what he meant, "but it scares me."

"Me, too," he said, nodding. "Me, too."

"I never really believed in all that instant-attraction stuff. It's the kind of thing you see in sappy movies, or read about in romance novels. Not real life."

"I thought it—the instant . . . uh, attraction stuff—was a woman thing . . . some half-baked idea women dream up to snare men."

Neither of them said the word, but it was there, hovering between them . . . a wonderful-horrible possibility.

Then, unable to resist any longer, he relaxed the arm that had been wrapped around her shoulder, holding her immobile. His hand crept under her silky hair to clasp the bare nape of her neck. His other hand briefly traced the line of her jaw and her full, parted lips before tunneling into her hair, caressing her scalp.

She moaned. But she didn't pull away. She, too, must sense the inevitable . . . the impending kiss, and so much more.

"Oh, Annie, I've been waiting to do this for hours."

"I've been waiting, too," she confessed, turning slightly so he could see her better. "For a long, long time."

He wasn't sure if she referred to a kiss or this bigger thing looming between them. By the expression of fear on her face, it was probably the latter. Hell, he was scared, too.

At first, he just settled his lips over hers, testing. With barely any pressure at all, he shifted from side to side till they fit perfectly. Then, deepening the kiss, he persuaded her to open for him. The first tentative thrust of his tongue inside her mouth brought stars behind his closed lids and another moan from Annie. He pulled back and whispered against her moist lips, "You taste like candy canes."

She smiled against his lips and whispered back, "You taste like popcorn. All buttery and salty and movie-balcony naughty."

Chuckling, he cut her off, kissing her in earnest now, long, drugging kisses that went on and on. He couldn't get enough. She seemed to feel the same way.

"Annie, love," he cautioned after what appeared an hour, but was probably only a few minutes, "your brothers are back." The clomp of heavy boots could be heard on the back porch by the kitchen.

They both sat up straighter, their clasped hands their only body contact.

"G'night," Roy and Jerry Lee said as they passed through the living room on their way to the stairs. There was a snicker in Roy's tone, but thankfully he said nothing more.

"Were they kissin'?" he heard Jerry Lee ask in an undertone once they were in the upper hall.

"Do pigs grunt?" Roy answered.

"Annie? Our Annie? Yech!"

"What? You didn't think she knew how to kiss?"

"Sure . . . I mean, I guess so. It's just . . . I never saw her lookin' so pink and flustery. And Clay, he looks guilty as sin."

"Better not be too guilty, or too sinful," Roy growled.

Their muted voices faded to nothing.

Annie put her face in her hands and groaned. "Pink and flustery! I'll never hear the end of this. Never. By tomorrow morning, my brothers will be making pink jokes. 'What's pink and goes squawk-squawk?' 'A flustered Annie chicken.' Ha, ha, ha."

Clay barely suppressed a smile. Her embarrassment was endearing. "Annie, that's not a joke. It's not even funny."

She raised her head. "Since when do my brothers' jokes have to be funny? And don't think you're going to escape their teasing either. Uh-uh. You are in for it, bigtime. How about, 'What's got a scratchy jaw and googly eyes?'"

"Annie," he warned.

"'A Princeton hog in rut.'" At his gaping mouth, she nodded her head vigorously. "See. That's what you can expect."

Is she saying I have googly eyes . . . whatever the hell googly eyes are? Clay lowered his lashes to half-mast and pulled Annie into his embrace again, fitting her face into the curve of his neck. He kissed the top of her head, murmuring, "Oh, Annie. It doesn't matter what they say when this feels so right."

She sighed, which he took for a nonverbal sign of agreement, and nestled closer. "I suppose you want to sleep with me."

Whoa! That got his attention. "Where did that come from? We were just kissing, Annie." *Not that other parts of my body weren't headed in that direction. But, geez! Talk about getting right to the point!*

Annie put her hands on his chest and shoved away slightly so she could look at him directly. "Are you saying you don't want to make love with me?"

"Hell, no."

He reached for her, but she squirmed back, keeping her distance.

"Me, too."

Me, too? What does that mean? Oh, my God! Did she just say she wants to make love with me? "Annie, this is going a bit fast, don't you think? I mean, I'm not sure it's a good idea making love on your living room couch where anyone could barge in at any moment." *Me, too? Son of a gun! I do like a woman who can make up her mind. No games with my Annie. No, sirree.*

She made a snorting sound of disgust, waving a hand in the air. "That's not what I meant, you dolt."

His spirits immediately deflated. *Damn!*

"I'm just trying to tell you that . . . uh . . . um . . ."

"What?" he prodded. This was the most disarming, confusing conversation he'd ever had with a woman, and if it got any hotter in this room he was going to explode.

As if mirroring his thoughts, Annie wiped her forehead with the back of one hand and began to unbutton her flannel shirt, revealing a tight white T-shirt underneath.

He refused to look *there*.

He was not going to look.

He was looking.

Man, oh, man!

That had been her bra in the bathroom, all right. Her breasts pushed against the thin material, full and uptilted, the nipples puckered into hard peaks. It wasn't that she was big busted, but because she was so thin, it appeared that way. Good thing she didn't look like that in her Blessed Mother outfit or she'd have had men propositioning her right there in the Nativity scene. Or else she'd get some super tips.

"Stop looking at me like that."

"Like what?" he choked out.

"Like you're . . . like you're . . ."

". . . interested?" He couldn't stop the grin that twitched at his lips.

"Stop smirking. I'm trying to tell you something."

"Oh?" he said, trying his damnedest not to look at her chest and not to grin with pure, unadulterated anticipation. As a final measure, he clenched his fists at his sides to keep from grabbing for her.

"I'm a virgin."

That was the last thing Clay had expected to hear.

"A virgin?" he squeaked out. A *twenty-eight-year-old virgin?*

"Yeah, isn't that the biggest joke of all?"

She was actually embarrassed by her virginity. Well, it did put a new light on their making love. Not that he didn't still want her, but it sure as hell wouldn't take place on a sofa with broken springs in a houseful of gun-toting brothers and an aunt who wielded a wicked spoon. "Annie, why tell me this now?"

"You have a right to know . . . if I'm reading that glimmer in your eye the right way."

She is. Clay lowered his lashes and tried his best to curb that "glimmer" in his eye.

"You probably think I'm repressed or gay or ultrareligious. But it's just that I haven't had time for dating since my parents died. And Prince Charming doesn't come riding his charger down the lane to a dairy farm real often."

"So I'm the first prince to come your way?" he asked with a laugh.

She slanted him a Behave-yourself glare and went on, "Now that you know, I suppose you don't want me anymore." She glanced at him shyly and looked away.

He took her chin in his hand and turned her face back to him. Kissing her lips lightly, he murmured, "I still want you."

A slow, wicked smile spread across her lips. "Stand up, then," she ordered.

Huh? With his brow furrowing in confusion, he got up cautiously, bracing himself on one crutch. At the same time, the stereo suddenly came on with Elvis wailing, "It's Now or Never."

He jerked back at the unexpected noise and Annie laughed.

"The stereo does that sometimes. There's a short in its circuit, I guess."

He thought about telling her that was a safety hazard,

but decided he had more important things on his mind right now. Like why she'd wanted him to stand, and why she was staring at him, arms folded across her chest, with that odd expression on her face. She was probably afraid, being a virgin and all. It was sweet of her, actually.

"Don't be afraid, Annie. I won't do anything to hurt you."

She laughed, a joyous, rippling sound mingling with Elvis's husky now-or-never warning.

That was probably nervous laughter, Clay concluded. Still, he tilted his head to the side, questioning. "Annie?"

"Take off your shirt, Clay. Please."

Her softly spoken words ambushed him. With a quick intake of breath, he almost swallowed his tongue.

"Reeeaal slow."

CHAPTER FOUR

Annie could see that she'd shocked Clay, but she didn't care. This was her big chance.

Just because she was a virgin didn't mean she was a dried-up old spinster with no needs. As she'd told him before, there weren't many princes who ambled on down the farm lane. And when one not-so-perfect specimen accidentally rode in, well, heck, she'd be a fool not to drag him down off his destrier and have her way with him.

"I have needs," she told him matter-of-factly.

"Needs?" he choked out. Geez, the man looked as if he were choking on his own tongue. Where was the suave, cool-as-a-hybrid-cucumber man who could cut a person off at the knees with a single icy stare?

Okay, sometimes Annie forgot that city people didn't understand the plain speaking of farm folks who lived with the facts of life on a daily basis. Those who worked with the land and animals tended to be more earthy, more accepting of the forces of nature. Sex was just another of the physical urges God gave all animals, nothing to be embarrassed about. At least, that was what she told herself. If she didn't justify her behavior in that way, she'd have to admit she was a lust-driven hussy with a compulsion to jump this poor prince's royal bones.

"Yep. Needs," she answered with more bravado than she really felt. If he rejected her, she was going to crawl in a hole and never come out. "So shuck that shirt, honey. I've been having indecent thoughts ever since I saw you in the emergency room in those cute little boxer shorts."

Stains of scarlet bloomed on his face at her mention of his boxers. Or was it her needs turning up his internal thermometer?

"This is a joke, right?" Clay said, backing up a bit.

Oh, swell! I'm scaring him. Slow down, Annie. Play it cool. Pretend he's just hairy old Frankie Wilks.

Ha!

"No joke, Clay. You have a chest that would cause a cloistered nun to melt, and I already have a fever to begin with. So take off the darn shirt, for crying out loud." Her voice had turned shrill at the end.

"All right, all right," he said, raising a palm in surrender. "Let's backtrack to step one. You want me to take off my shirt because you like my chest?"

"Yes."

He smiled then, one of those glorious affairs that bared his even white teeth and caused those irresistible dimples to play peekaboo with her heart. "What if someone walks in . . . like your aunt?"

She pooh-poohed that idea. "Do you think Aunt Liza hasn't seen a man's chest before? In a house with five males?"

"But Annie," Clay explained with exaggerated patience. "If you want me to take off my shirt, I'm pretty sure I'll be wanting you to take off your shirt." He flashed her a So-there grin.

"Oh." Delicious images swam in Annie's head at that suggestion. "Well, I guess I forgot to mention that Aunt Liza is dead to the world once her head hits the pillow. Her alarm clock, set religiously for four A.M., is the only thing that will awaken her now."

"Yes, you did forget to mention that fact." His grin didn't waver at all. "And your brothers?"

"The same. Besides, there's an unwritten rule in the Fallon house. Nobody walks in unannounced on a courting couple . . . not that you and I are courting, mind you. Don't get your feathers all ruffled in that regard. I'm not out to trap you."

"My feathers aren't ruffled," he protested indignantly. Then, understanding that they wouldn't be interrupted, he immediately pulled off the flannel shirt and raised the T-shirt over his head. Superman couldn't have done it faster. After that, standing still, he waited for her to make the next move.

He wasn't smiling now.

He was so beautiful. Wide shoulders. Narrow waist and hips. A thin frame, but not too thin. Muscles delineating his upper arms and forearms and the planes of his chest and abdomen—not a muscle-builder's puffed-up flesh, just healthy, fit male muscle. Dark, silky hairs peppered his chest, leading down in a vee to the low-riding jeans.

Under her sweeping appraisal, he never once lowered his eyes. Women faltered under such close scrutiny, but not men . . . not this man.

"Can I touch you?" she whispered.

She saw the hard ridges of his stomach muscles lurch.

Heat curled in her stomach.

At first, he closed his eyes and a low, strangled sound emerged from his lips. He appeared to be out of breath, panting. When he lifted his eyelids, Annie almost staggered backward under the onslaught of blue fire. "If you *don't* touch me, I think I'll go up in smoke," he whispered back.

Well, that sounds encouraging. She stepped closer and put her hands on his shoulders. He tried to take her in his arms, but Annie swatted his hands away. She wanted to do this herself, with no distractions. "Let me . . . I want . . ." she murmured, her brain reeling with feverish urgency. "I want to do things to you. So many things." *Things? What things? Where are these outlandish thoughts coming from? And how am I getting up the nerve to say them aloud?*

"Annie . . ." he started to say, then paused, lost for words. "You take my breath away."

"Don't move," she ordered, and ran her fingertips down both sides of his tension-corded neck, over his shoulders, skimming over the light fur on his arms to his hands, where she twined their fingers for one brief moment, raising the knuckles of one hand, then the other for a brief kiss. She released his hands then, setting them back at his side.

Smoothing the palms of her hands across his chest, she felt his heartbeat thud. She watched in fascination as the flat male nipples hardened and elongated.

Clay gritted out one crude word between clenched teeth.

Annie decided to take the expletive as a compliment.

She couldn't resist then. Lowering her head, she licked one nipple, sucked it into her mouth, rolled it between her lips.

"Omigod, omigod, omigod!" Clay exclaimed, snaking out a hand to grasp her nape, then lifting her into an embrace where her hips cradled his erection. Alternately kissing her with a devouring hunger and growling into the curve of her neck, he ended up cupping her buttocks and rocking her against him. All the time he was overcome with a violent shiver.

Incredibly, Annie felt herself approaching climax. It was way too soon for that, and not the way she wanted it to happen.

It was Clay who slowed the action. Setting her away from him, he said in a gravelly rasp, "Do you know what I want, Annie, love?"

She cocked her head to the side. "I think so."

"Not *that*, silly girl. I mean, yes, I want *that*, but not now. What I really want is to feel your skin against mine."

It took several moments for his words to sink in. When they did, Annie felt a thrill of excitement ripple through her already oversensitized body. She jerked off her flannel shirt, then drew the T-shirt up and over her head, leaving only a plain, white nylon bra. Through its thin fabric, her small nipples stood out with stiff, pale rose peaks, aching for his touch.

His eyes studied her with apparent appreciation. He licked his lips as he waited for her final unveiling. When the wispy bra fell to the floor, his eyes seemed to water up. "Oh, Annie, you are so beautiful."

She wasn't beautiful; Annie knew that. But it was nice that he found her appealing. She wanted to be beautiful for him.

"It's your turn now, sweetheart. Don't move," he said then, giving equal attention to her body, murmuring compliments to each part examined by his tantalizing fingers and feathery kisses. When he came to her breasts, Annie's heart stood still. First he raised them up in the palms of his hands, then skimmed both nipples with the pads of his thumbs. By the time he angled his head down to wet one, then the other with his lips and tongue, and finally suckled rhythmically, Annie was mewling in an increasing frenzy.

Recognizing her spiraling passion, Clay eased backward toward the couch, taking Annie with him. But he lost his balance and fell onto his back, half reclining, with one leg extended out to the floor. Annie tripped, too, and ended up plopped on top of him. When she raised herself up, she found herself, amazingly, straddling him, jean-clad groin to jean-clad groin.

Clay groaned, a long, husky sound of pain emitted through clenched teeth.

Immediately, Annie remembered Clay's injuries. It was a sign of her fevered brain that she'd forgotten to begin with. "Oh, my God! Did I hurt you? Is it your head? Or your ankle?"

Clay tried to laugh, but it came out strangled. "That's not where I'm hurting, Annie." He rolled his hips from side to side against Annie's widespread thighs, and Annie felt the clear delineation of the ridge pressing against her with an urgency that matched her own.

"Oh," she said.

Clay chuckled. " 'Oh' about says it, darling." Then he chucked her under the chin.

"I've shocked you, haven't I?" she asked, belatedly shy.

Shocked would be the understatement of the year, Clay decided. *Who knew when I woke up this morning, a cold, dreary day in Princeton, that my evening would end with such unexpected manna from heaven? But wait a minute.* He didn't like the look creeping onto Annie's face. "Don't go shy on me now, Annie."

"I've never behaved this way before . . . so forward and uninhibited," she confessed, hiding her face in her hands.

"Your eagerness excites me. Tremendously. Don't you dare stop now," he said in a suffocated whisper, prying her fingers away. "I have plans for you that require a major dose of forwardness and uninhibitedness."

"You do?"

Was that hope in her voice? "Absolutely. Are you afraid?"

"No. Are you?"

He laughed outright. God, how he loved her openness.

"Listen, Annie—stop, you witch . . . I can't think when you do that." She was leaning forward, her hair a thick swatch curtaining his face, as she still straddled him. Back and forth, she was brushing her breasts across his chest hairs.

"That's the point, isn't it? Not to think?"

He leaned up and gave her a quick kiss. "You don't act like any virgin I've ever known." *Not that I've known very many . . . or any, for that matter, that I can recall.*

"Just because I didn't do *that*, doesn't mean I didn't do anything," she said, meanwhile kissing a little line from one end of his jaw to the other.

Clay fought against the roil of jealousy that ripped through him at the thought of any other man touching his Annie in any way. Had it been the milkman, or someone else? How many someone elses? "Annie, you're driving me mad. Be still for one moment. Please."

Surprisingly, she did as he asked. Of course, when she stilled, she also sat upright, square on his already overeager, overengorged erection. He closed his eyes for one second, to keep them from bulging clear out of his head. Finally, when he managed to speak above a squeak, he said, "We're not going to make love tonight, Annie."

She stiffened at once, and her face went beet red. "You don't want me?"

"Of course I want you, but I refuse to make love with you on an uncomfortable sofa, out in the open, with a houseful of people . . . no matter what you say about sleeping patterns or rules for . . . uh, courting."

She pondered his words, then seemed to accept their logic. "So, we're not going to make love *tonight*? Will we ever?"

"Oh, for sure, darling. For sure."

She smiled widely at that.

"And there's another thing, Annie, love. We have to talk about this thing that's happening with us."

"It is . . . strange."

"Strange, overpowering, confusing. I have an idea, Annie. Let's go out tomorrow night. Slow down this runaway train. See where this relationship is going."

"I like the sound of that."

He took a breast in each hand then and admired the contrast of the firm, white mounds against his darker skin. "I love your breasts. I love the way they aren't big, but appear to be so because of your thin frame." He stretched his head forward to savor one of them with his mouth.

She made a keening sound low in her throat, halfway between a purr and a cry for mercy. "I thought we weren't going to make love," she gasped out.

"True. We're not going to make love. But we can make out. A little."

"Oh, goody," she cooed. Before he knew what she was about, Annie slid a hand between them and caressed his tumescence. "Does this count as making love or making out?"

He about shot off the couch. And all he could think was, *Who the hell cares?*

"Whoa, whoa, whoa, Annie." Very carefully, he dislodged her grasp and placed both her hands at her sides and held them there. "You've been running the show for much too long in your family. It's time for you to sit back and let someone else take over."

Her chin went up.

"All right?"

After a long pause of hesitation, she nodded.

He proceeded then to unbutton her jeans.

Her eyebrows shot up in surprise, but she didn't protest.

"Lift up a little, honey, and lean forward," he advised. When she did, he slid a hand inside the waistband of her panties, down between her legs. The warm wetness he met there caused him to sigh with pleasure. "Oh, Annie, love, you feel so good."

"Clay," she cried out, unsure whether she wanted him to touch her there.

Before she had a chance to think further, he inserted a long middle finger inside her tightness and rested a pulsing thumb against the swollen bud. "Now, Annie," he encouraged her with a guttural hoarseness, "you ride . . . you set the pace."

"I . . . I don't think I can," she whimpered.

"Yes, you can, darling."

And she did.

With each forward thrust, she brushed the ridge of his erection. They were separated by denim material, but the sensation was still intense. With each withdrawal, that part of his body yearned for her next stroke. It didn't last long. Probably only minutes. But when Annie began to spasm around his finger and melt onto him, he held her fast by the hips, leaned forward to kiss her with a devouring hunger, and bucked upward . . . once, twice, three times.

"Annie, love," he whispered into her hair a short time later. She was nestled at his side, both of them stretched out full-length on the sofa.

"Hmmm?" She was half-asleep and sated.

Clay couldn't have been prouder if he'd pulled off a million-dollar investment deal. You'd think he was personally responsible for having made the world move. Well, he had, actually. For both of them.

"Clay?" she prodded.

"I think I'm falling in love with you," he disclosed. He hadn't intended to tell her . . . not yet. But his senses were on overload, brimming with so much joy. He couldn't contain it all.

"I already know I'm in love with you. I think I fell the minute I saw you storming across that vacant lot looking like Scrooge himself."

He poked her playfully in the ribs at that insult, but inside he felt such a triumphant sense of elation. *Annie loves me. Annie loves me. Annie loves me.* It was all so new and strange and confusing. Not what he'd come to Memphis to find. It would pose all kinds of problems in his life. But what a wonderful, wonderful thing. *Annie loves me.*

Annie worried her bottom lip with her teeth then. Obviously, she had something on her mind. Finally, she blurted out, "When will you know for sure?"

Clay chuckled and said, "Maybe after we check out the hayloft."

I love her.

It was Clay's first thought when he awakened the next morning to bright sunlight warming the cozy bedroom. You'd think it was springtime, instead of four days before Christmas. But then, Clay recalled, he was in Tennessee . . . almost the Deep South.

With an openmouthed yawn, he stretched widely, becoming immediately aware of the ache in his ankle and at the back of his head. He glanced to the side, saw the bedside clock, and jolted upright, causing the dull pain to intensify. *Ten o'clock!* He hadn't slept beyond six A.M. in the past twenty years.

Oh, well! First he would take a shower. Afterward he had at least a dozen calls to make, first to check with his office in New York, then to set the hotel sale in motion here in Memphis.

But there was only one thought that kept ringing through his head. *I love Annie.* Clay was not a whimsical person. If anyone had told him a few days ago that he would believe in love at first sight or romantic destiny, he would have scoffed heartily. He didn't know how it had happened or why, though he suspected, illogically, that it involved that dingbat bellhop and God's big toe and Elvis's spirit. He'd been fated to come to Memphis. Not to sell the blasted hotel, though he would do that as soon as possible, but to find Annie. *Amazing!*

It would take some doing to get Annie moved to Princeton. Probably they'd have to wait till after the holidays. Oh, he knew it would be hard for her to leave the farm, but she had Chet and her brothers here to take over for her. And her Aunt Liza would care for the boys. Hell, he'd hire a live-in housekeeper to help Aunt Liza if necessary. Or the whole gang could come live with him, though he couldn't imagine that ever happening. It would be like the Clampetts moving to Princeton. All he knew was that it was time someone took care of Annie, and Clay thanked God it was going to be him.

Would they get married?

Of course. There was no way her family would allow her to live with a man without the bonds of matrimony. And Annie would want that, too, Clay was sure.

How did he feel about marriage? *Hmmm.* A few days ago, he would have balked. But now . . . Clay smiled. Now the idea of marrying Annie seemed ordained. Perfect.

So everything was all set. He and Annie would go out

tonight on a date. He would propose. She would accept. They'd make plans for the wedding and the move to Princeton. And a honeymoon . . . they'd fit a honeymoon in there, too. Perfect.

The only problem was that Clay kept hearing the oddest thing. Somewhere in the house, a radio was playing that old Elvis song, "Blue Suede Shoes," but every time Elvis would belt out a stanza that was supposed to end in a warning not to step on "my blue suede shoes," Clay kept hearing, ". . . don't you step on *God's big toe*."

If Clay was a superstitious man, he would have considered it a premonition.

"You've got to be kidding!"

Clay had showered and shaved with a disposable razor he'd found in the bathroom. Then he'd unhesitatingly entered Chet's room, where he borrowed a clean set of clothes, including a pair of new underwear straight from the package. This family owed him that, at least. Okay, he owed them a lot, too, he was beginning to realize . . . like a new life.

But now, Aunt Liza had forced him into a chair at the kitchen table, where she'd placed in front of him a half dozen platters heaped with bacon and sausage, hotcakes dripping with butter and maple syrup, scrambled eggs and leftover biscuits from last night (also dripping with butter), slices of scrapple (which he feared contained pork unmentionables, like noses and things), black pudding (which Aunt Liza told him without blinking was blood sausage), coffee, orange juice, and a glass of cold milk with a head of pure cream.

"All I ever have for breakfast is coffee, juice, and an English muffin or toast," he demurred.

"Well, you ain't in New Jersey now, boy. So eat up. I got some oatmeal cookin' on the stove, too, to warm up your innards."

He groaned. "If I eat all this, I won't be able to move."

"You ain't goin' anywhere anyhow, sonny. You're stuck here on the farm with a gimp leg, in case you hadn't noticed."

"But I have work to do . . . calls to make—"

She slapped a couple of pig-nose slabs on his plate and glared at him till he finally gave in. He pushed the pig-nose slabs to the side, though, and gave himself modest helpings of eggs and biscuits, one sausage link, two slices of bacon, and one hotcake, but before he knew it his plate was overflowing.

Despite all his protests, the food was mouthwateringly delicious, and he told Aunt Liza so. She smiled graciously at the compliment and sat down at the table with him, sipping a cup of coffee.

"When did everyone leave for Memphis?" he asked as he ate . . . and ate . . . and ate.

"'Bout nine," Aunt Liza said, nibbling on a buttered biscuit slathered with strawberry jam, while she continued to drink her coffee. "They wanted to get an early start today . . . hopin' the Christmas shoppers and tourists will be out early."

Clay nodded. "Why didn't they leave Jason here with you?"

Aunt Liza's shoulders slumped, and her parchment cheeks pinkened. "I can't be on my feet too long. Gotta take lots of naps. And sometimes I don't hear the baby when he cries."

Clay wished he hadn't asked when he saw the shame on her wrinkled face. He decided silence was a better route to take . . . to shut his big mouth. So he tentatively tasted a piece of the black pudding, which was surprisingly palatable.

"So when you gonna make an honest woman of our Annie?" Aunt Liza asked unexpectedly.

His milk went down the wrong pipe and he sputtered. He probably had a cream mustache, to boot. "I haven't done anything to make Annie *dis*honest," he asserted, wiping at his mouth with a napkin.

Aunt Liza gave him a sidelong glance of skepticism. "That whisker burn she was sportin' on her cheeks this mornin' didn't come from a close shave, honey. Besides, Roy and Jerry Lee was sayin' somethin' 'bout 'pink and flustery' and 'guilty as sin.' Don't suppose you know what they was talkin' about?"

Clay hated the fact that his face was heating up, but he wasn't about to cower under the old buzzard's insinuations. He raised his chin obstinately and refused to rise to her bait.

"We got one loose chick hatched on this place, and I don't want no more," Aunt Liza went on. "Randy roosters and footloose hens are runnin' rampant these days."

Clay didn't have the faintest idea what she was talking about. Roosters and hens and chicks?

"Now I don't countenance loose behavior none, but you'd best be keepin' these," she said, pulling a small box out of her apron pocket and shoving it his way, "just in case the devil sits on your shoulder sometime soon."

"Wh-what?" Clay stammered as he realized that Aunt Liza had handed him a box of condoms. *Oh, man! A woman old enough to be my grandmother is giving me condoms.* "Where did you get these?"

"The supermarket."

"You . . . you went into a supermarket and bought condoms?"

"Yep. Durn tootin', I did. 'Bout caused ol' Charlie Good, the manager, to swallow his false teeth."

"You bought condoms *for me*? But . . . but I just got here yesterday." Clay's head was reeling with confusion.

"Don't be an idjit, boy. 'Tweren't you I bought those suckers for." Aunt Liza took another sip of coffee, ignoring the fact that he was waiting, slack jawed, for her next bombshell. "Chet learned his lesson good, I reckon, with that little chick of his. But I was figurin' on havin' a talk with Hank. That boy's headed on the road to ruination sure as God made Jezebels and hot-blooded roosters."

Hank? She bought the condoms for Hank? That makes sense. I guess. Whew!

"This whole generation's goin' to hell in a handbasket, if you ask me." Aunt Liza made a *tsk*ing sound, piercing him with a stare that included him in the wild bunch. "I blame it all on the tongue business."

The tongue business? Don't ask. Don't ask. "What tongue business?"

"Tongue kissin'. What tongue business didja think I was gabbin' about?" she answered tartly, as if he should have known better. "When courtin' couples start tongue kissin', the trouble begins. Next thing ya know they're buyin' Pampers by the gross."

She narrowed her eyes at Clay, and he just knew Aunt Liza was going to ask him if he'd been giving Annie tongue. Before she could speak, he put up a halting hand. Time to put some brakes on this outrageous conversation.

"Aunt Liza," Clay said in the calmest voice he could muster, without breaking out in laughter, "Annie and I have not had sex." *Yet.* "But even if we had, whatever happened or didn't happen or is about to happen is between me and Annie."

"Well, that may very well be, Mr. Hoity-Toity City

Feller, but if there's a weddin' to be planned, I gotta commence makin' a menu, and preparin' food. Everyone in the whole county will wanna come to Annie Fallon's weddin', that's for sure. I don't wanna be goin' to all that trouble for a bride with a belly what looks like she swallowed a watermelon seed nine months past."

I'm going insane. I just discovered I'm falling in love, and already she has me making babies and walking up the aisle, in that order. And, good Lord, does she think we would get married in a farmhouse? With pigs' noses and cows' blood and other equally distasteful stuff on the wedding menu?

Now that was unkind. She's only being concerned. You really are being hoity-toity, if that means the same as poker-up-your-butt snobbish. C'mon, Jessup, stop acting like you're in Princeton.

"Aunt Liza, if and when Annie and I decide to marry, you'll be the first to know."

"Oh, I know, all right," she said, leveling him with a scrutiny that saw right through his facade. "I knew the minute Annie brung you through that door yesterday. I knew when the radio kept bopping on and off all day with Elvis's music that his spirit has come into the house. I knew when you gawked at Annie all durin' dinner last night, and couldn't keep the love out of your eyes. I knew—"

"Enough!" he said with a laugh of surrender. "Pass me the pigs' noses."

CHAPTER FIVE

Clay was waiting on the front porch when Annie got home at five.

She felt the now familiar feverish heat envelop her the minute he came into view. It was the strangest, most wonderful, scariest feeling in the world to drive up in the pickup and see this man she'd come to love in such a short time, just standing there waiting for her to come home.

Leaning against a porch post, he was dressed in his neatly pressed suit, the sides of his jacket pulled back over his slim hips by hands that were tucked into the pockets of his slacks. One crutch was propped beside him. It was a casual pose, but Annie could see he was as nervous and excited as she was.

"Hi," she said breathlessly, coming up the steps.

"Hi," he said back, his eyes crinkling with amusement as they skimmed over her, from bouffant hair to Blessed Mary robe.

She stopped midway up the steps, an attack of timidity overcoming her. All day she'd been thinking about him, the wicked things he'd done to her last night, how he'd made her feel. Now, all the thoughts she'd wanted to share with him stuck in her throat. What if he'd changed his mind? What if his heart wasn't racing as madly as hers?

What if he didn't really want to take her out tonight? What if he didn't love her?

Clay uncoiled himself from his leaning position and stepped forward, slowly. One hand snaked out to grasp her by the nape and draw her closer. "I missed you," he said in a husky voice.

"Oh, God, I missed you, too. But I look awful," she said, waggling her fingers in a flustery fashion to indicate her caricature appearance. *Flustery? I'm probably pink, too. Roy and Jerry Lee were right. Flustery and pink.*

Clay chuckled. "Just shows how far gone I am. You're beginning to look good even as a sixties Madonna." He dragged her close and lowered his head toward hers. Annie watched, mesmerized, as his eyelids fluttered closed and his lips parted.

Then she forgot everything, too engrossed in the kiss, which seared her already feverish body to her very soul. When he slipped his tongue inside her mouth, she felt his heat, and knew the fever had overtaken him as well.

She moaned against his open mouth.

He moaned back.

A sharp rapping noise jarred them both from their kiss, ending it far too soon. It was Aunt Liza, using her wooden spoon to knock a warning on the kitchen window, which looked out over the porch. "There'd better not be any tongue business goin' on," Aunt Liza called out. "Remember what I told you, young man."

Annie leaned back, still in the circle of Clay's arms, and peered questioningly up at him.

He laughed. "You don't want to know."

"Hey, Clay," Chet greeted him. Still dressed in his Elvis/

St. Joseph gear and high, duck-tail hairdo, Chet had

just come from the pickup truck, where he must have been gathering the baby's paraphernalia, which was looped over one shoulder. The baby, which he held in the other arm, was wide-awake and gurgling happily, swatting at Chet's nose with a rattle. Chet must have heard Aunt Liza, because he waggled his eyebrows in commiseration and commented, "Aunt Liza gave you the tongue lecture, right?"

"Oh, no!" Annie groaned, putting her face in her hands.

"We made eight hundred dollars today," Johnny informed him cheerily as he skipped up the steps, Elvis hair bouncing up and down. His sheepskin shepherd outfit was in sharp contrast to his duct-taped sneakers. "Annie says I can get a new pair of athletic shoes for Christmas if we keep going at this clip. And see, Annie? I didn't say one single word about 'pink and flustery,' just like you warned."

"Where do you think you're going?" Annie asked Johnny. "There's milking to be done."

"I know, I know. Don't get your dander up. I have to go to the bathroom first. They can start without me," he whined, pointing at his brothers.

Roy, Hank, and Jerry Lee, still dolled up as Elvis wise men, were unloading the donkey and two sheep from the animal van, alternately smirking toward him and Annie and trying to get the stubborn donkey to move. At one point, Roy and Jerry Lee were shoving the donkey's butt while Hank pulled on a lead rope. The only thing they accomplished was a load of donkey manure barely missing their feet.

"I swear, Annie, I'm butchering this donkey come Christmas," Roy vowed.

Clay tasted bile rising in his throat. They wouldn't really eat donkey, would they? Hell, they ate beef blood and pigs' noses. Why not donkey? "Hurry and shower so we can go out," he whispered to Annie. "I have big plans for tonight."

"Big plans? Oh, my! I certainly hope so."

"Before you shower, we'd better go out to the barn and breed Mirabelle. She's not gonna be in heat much longer. I don't think we wanna wait another twenty-one days for her to go in heat again." Clay hadn't realized that Chet still stood on the porch, behind them. "Here," Chet added, handing the baby to Clay, "take him in the house for me. We'll be back in a half hour or so."

"What? Who? Me?" Clay said, staring at the wide-eyed baby who gaped at him as if his father had just delivered him to King Kong. Clay was holding the kid gingerly with hands under both his armpits. Just when Clay thought the baby was going to let loose with a wail of outrage, Jason gave him a slobbery smile and belted him on the forehead with a rattle.

Clay could swear he heard Aunt Liza giggling on the other side of the kitchen window. She probably considered it just payment for tongue.

A half hour later, Annie hadn't returned to the house. Aunt Liza had changed baby Jason after Clay had performed the amazing feat of feeding him a bottle. The kid, who was really quite precious, was now cooing contentedly from his infant seat in the kitchen, where he was pulverizing a piece of melba toast.

Clay decided to check out this cow-breeding business.

What he saw when he entered the huge barn stunned him. First of all, there was the overpowering smell: cow manure, the hot earthy scent of animal flesh, and fresh milk. A cow belched near him and he almost jumped out of his wing-tips. The sweet reek of the cow's breath that drifted toward him on the wake of the bovine burp was not unpleasant, but strange. Very strange.

There was a center aisle with about sixty black-and-white cows lined up in stalls on both sides. Jerry Lee was washing down cow udders and stimulating teats, while Roy was hooking the teats up to automated milking contraptions, six cows at a time.

Hank was shoveling feed in the troughs for the big cows, which must have weighed about 1500 pounds, at the same time ministering to the sixty or so young stock at the far end of the barn. The whole time he was addressing the cows by name. Florence. Sweet Caroline. Aggie. Winona. Rosie Posie. Lucille. Pamela Lee. On and on, he chatted with the cows. How he ever remembered all the names, Clay didn't know.

Johnny was sitting off to the side, bottle-feeding a half dozen baby calves. "Hey, Clay, wanna help me?" he asked.

"Uh . . . I don't think I'm dressed for that," he declined. Besides, he wanted to see what Annie was doing at the other end of the barn. She and Chet were in a separate, larger stall with one humongous cow about the size of a minivan. That must be the breeding section.

"Where's the bull?" he inquired casually, as if he strolled through barns every day to view cow sex.

Chet and Annie jerked to attention. Apparently they hadn't heard him come up behind them. Well, no wonder. With all these cows mooing, he could barely hear anything himself.

"We don't have any bulls," Annie answered. "We butcher or sell off all the male stock."

"Why?"

"Bulls are too darn ornery, that's why," Chet answered. "They're not worth the trouble, believe me."

"But . . . but how do you breed the cows then?"

"Artificial insemination," Chet informed him. "This is the nineties, man."

It was only then that he noticed Chet was holding the cow still, even though it was tied by a loose rope to the front of the stall. Annie, on the other hand, stood there with a big brown apron covering her Virgin Mary gown. On one arm, she wore a plastic glove that reached all the way to the shoulder. In the other hand, she held a huge syringe-type affair, more like a twenty-inch caulking gun. *My Lord!*

"You'd better step back," Chet warned him.

Clay's eyes bugged and his mouth dropped open at what he saw then. Almost immediately, he spun on his heels and rushed outside . . . where he proceeded to hurl the contents of his stomach, which Aunt Liza had taken great pains to stuff all day long.

I wonder where this ranks in the God's-big-toe category?

Clay had almost botched things, big-time.

At first, it had seemed as if their blooming relationship had been slam-dunked back to step one, or zero, with his disastrous reaction to that scene in the barn. He still shivered with distaste at what he'd seen, but he was doing his shivering internally. The sooner he could erase that picture from his mind, the better. In time—maybe ten or twenty years—he would, no doubt, forget it totally.

Annie had appeared crushed when she'd followed him out. He could understand that. Farm work, in all its crude aspects, was what Annie did for a living—her identity. It had been obvious that Annie thought he was repulsed by *her*. But it wasn't her, it was what she'd been doing. But Clay hadn't dared say that. Instead, he'd lied, "My stomach has been upset all day. It must be the aftereffects of those painkillers, or something I ate."

She'd stared at him dubiously. "Maybe it's not such a good idea for us to go out on a date. Things have been happening too fast. We haven't stopped to consider our differences. It's probably a good idea for us to slow down and count to ten—"

Reconsider? Count to ten? No way! We're not even counting to two. Oh, God! She's going to dump us. He'd backpedaled then and convinced her to give him another chance. At what, he wasn't sure. He only knew he loved her, cow breeding or no cow breeding. And he didn't want to blow the best thing that had ever happened to him.

Now, strolling down Memphis's famous Beale Street, he was getting yet another view of his Annie. This one he liked a whole lot better than all the rest. So far, he'd had the Priscilla Virgin Mary, the jeans-and-flannel farm girl—he was still waiting for the Daisy Mae outfit, darn it!—and the cow breeder to the bovine stars. Now Annie wore an ankle-length floral print skirt of some crinkled gauze material over a satin lining. It was robin's egg blue with gold flowers. On top was a long-sleeved, matching blue sweater of softest angora, which reached to her hips and was belted at the waist. The gold flowers of the skirt were picked up in embroidery around the sweater's neckline. On her legs she wore sheer stockings and old-fashioned, lace-up ankle boots. Her lustrous brown hair was pulled off her face by gold clips and hung in disarray to her shoulders. She'd even used some makeup for the first time since the day Clay had met her—a little blush, mascara, and lip gloss, as far as he could tell. She looked smart and sexy. Sort of like Julia Roberts, but better, to his mind. No wonder he'd fallen head over heels in love with her.

Clay couldn't stop looking at her.

And she couldn't stop looking at him.

She smiled at him.

He smiled back.

He was using one crutch to keep his full weight off his sprained ankle, which was almost better today. With his free hand, Clay twined Annie's fingers in his.

She swung their clasped hands.

Clay couldn't understand how he got so much pleasure from just holding hands with a woman and hobbling slowly down the street. Annie had been giving him a running commentary on the history of Memphis.

"Are you sure you don't want to eat yet?" she inquired. "It's almost eight o'clock."

He shook his head. They'd already passed up hot tamales and greasy burgers at the Blues City Café, where Tom Cruise had filmed a scene for the movie *The Firm*, as well as ribs, catfish, and world-famous fried dill pickles, the specialties at B. B. King's club.

"How about this?" Annie had stopped in front of Lansky Brothers/Center for Southern Folklore. "This museum is dedicated to preserving the legends and folklore of the entire South, but especially Memphis. They have an excellent photography collection here."

"My mother was a photographer," Clay revealed. *Now, why did I mention that? I never talk about my mother.*

"Really? Did she use her maiden name or her married name?" Annie was already tugging him by the hand to enter the small museum, where a plaque informed him it was the site of the former Lansky Brothers Clothing Store where Elvis, B. B. King, Jerry Lee Lewis, Carl Perkins, and

others had purchased their clothes. *Well, that impresses the
hell out of me. I'd want to buy my boxers in the same store as
Elvis, for sure. Geez!*

But Clay knew he was dwelling on irrelevant garbage
to avoid thinking about Annie's question. Finally, he answered, "Her maiden name. Clare Gannett."

"Clare Gannett? Clare Gannett? Why, she's famous,
Clay."

"She is—was—not!" he said with consternation.

"Well, not Annie Leibovitz famous, but she has a fame
of sorts here in Memphis."

*It doesn't take much to be famous in Memphis. Just be a
store that sold Elvis a pair of boxers. Or the barber who gave
him a haircut. Or the playground where he scraped his shin.*

"Annie, my mother was not a famous photographer.
For one thing, she died when she was only twenty-five—
Whoa . . . wait a minute—what are you doing?" Annie
paid for two tickets, and was pulling him determinedly
past the exhibits into another room.

"See," she said, pointing to one wall where there were
a series of photos of Elvis Presley. Casual shots . . . leaning against a car, strumming a guitar, standing in front of
the Original Heartbreak Hotel. A framed document explained that Clare Gannett was one of Memphis's pre-
mier photographers, documenting on film many of the
city's early music performers during the sixties—not just
Elvis, but many rock and blues personalities who later
went on to fame.

*Oh, great! My mother knew Elvis. First I find out my fa-
ther owned a hokey hotel named after one of Elvis's songs.
Now I find out my mother must have known the King. What
next?*

"Legend says that Elvis loved Clare Gannett—"

Clay put his face in his hands. He didn't want to hear this.

"—but she fell in love with some Yankee who came to Memphis on a business trip one day. They say the Yankee bought the hotel and next-door property where her studio was located as a wedding present for her. The studio later burned down, and Clare Gannett died in the fire. The hotel owner, your father, refused to erect anything else on that site. Isn't that romantic?"

"Annie, that is nothing but propaganda, a silly yarn spun for gullible tourists."

"Maybe. But legend says Elvis was heartbroken over losing Clare Gannett. It was after that he decided to marry Priscilla. Some people even think he wrote 'Dreams of Yesterday,' better known as 'I Can't Stop Loving You,' in her memory."

Clay turned angrily and stomped as fast as he could on one crutch out of the building. He was breathing heavily, in and out, trying to control his rage.

"Clay, what's wrong?" Annie asked softly. She came up close to him and put a hand on his sleeve.

He waited several seconds before speaking, not wanting to take out his feelings on Annie. "Annie, my mother abandoned me and my father when I was only one year old. So your telling me she had a relationship with that hip-swiveling jerk doesn't sit too well with me."

"I'm sorry, Clay. I didn't know. But maybe you're wrong about her. The legend never said that anything happened between them. In fact, she supposedly broke Elvis's heart when she married your father. Maybe—"

He leaned down to kiss her softly, the best way he could think of to halt her words. "It was a long time ago. It doesn't matter anymore."

She gazed at him with tears in her eyes. *Tears, for God's sake!* Not for a moment did she buy his unconcern.

"Hey, let's go in this place," Clay suggested cheerily, coming to a standstill in front of Forever Blue, a small jazz club. He desperately sought a change of mood. "It doesn't seem as crowded as some of the other joints."

As they entered the establishment, Clay accidentally jostled a woman standing transfixed in the doorway.

"Sorry," they both mumbled.

A short blonde in a formfitting blue dress and matching high heels was staring at the piano player as if she'd seen a ghost. Her face was taut with some strong emotion as she clenched and unclenched her hands at her midsection. Suddenly the piano player seemed to notice her. He faltered slightly, then stopped playing his rendition of "I'll Be Home for Christmas." Before anyone in the audience could fathom his intent, he jumped off the small stage and rushed after the woman who had spun on her heel and run out the door onto busy Beale Street.

Clay and Annie looked at each other and shrugged as the man rushed past them, obviously in pursuit of the mysterious woman.

"That was Michael Arnett, the owner of this club," Annie informed him. "He's a famous songwriter, too. Did you ever hear 'Only a Shadow'?"

"The Jimmy Blue hit?" Clay wasn't a fan of popular music, but he'd have to be dead not to be aware of that song and its phenomenal success.

"Yes. That was one of Michael's songs."

Michael? She calls him by his first name? "You know this guy?" Clay hated the wave of jealousy that knifed through him. He hated the possibility that he might have a milkman *and* a musician as competition. He hated the fact that the dark-haired piano man was tall, slim, and probably considered handsome by some myopic women.

"A little. Michael and I went to the same high school, but he graduated a few years ahead of me."

Okay. So maybe I overreacted a little. "It looked as if something serious was going on with that woman."

Annie nodded. "Yeah. I hope it works out."

He smiled at Annie's whimsy as he guided her in front of him into the club. At the table next to theirs, a beautiful woman with short, tousled, honey-colored hair, in a dark, conservative business suit, was talking a mile a minute to a guy in a Hawaiian shirt and baseball cap. The guy was leaning back lazily in his chair, clearly amused by her nonstop chatter. It sounded as if she was reciting the tourist directory of Memphis, and every fact and figure ever compiled.

Suddenly, the woman began belting out the lyrics to "Only a Shadow." Her date didn't appear quite so amused now. In fact, his face went white with concern. With good cause, it would seem. Within seconds, the woman pitched forward, her face almost landing in her bowl of chili, but for a last-minute rescue by her male companion.

Clay shook his head at Annie. "Nice bunch of people here in Memphis." He flinched as the woman began to sing again.

"They are nice," Annie insisted. "In fact, that man is Spencer Modine, one of Memphis's financial success stories. He made his money in California, but he returned here to start up a record company."

"Spencer Modine?" Clay rubbed his chin thoughtfully. "Hell, are you talking about the Bill Gates of Silicon Valley? The computer whiz kid who made a killing in computer software?"

"Uh-huh."

"Did you go to high school with him, too?" he grumbled.

Annie laughed. "No, I didn't."

They settled back then to order drinks and a mushroom-and-sundried-tomato pizza. A short time later, Arnett and the woman he'd pursued came back into the club. Arnett seated her near the stage, and he resumed playing. Clay moved his chair close to Annie and fiddled with the ends of her hair, nervous as a teenager on his first date.

"Annie, love," he whispered, kissing the curve of her neck. She smelled of some light floral fragrance . . . lilies of the valley, maybe. As always, there was that delicious heat ricocheting between them.

"Hmmm?" she purred, arching her neck to give him greater access.

"I don't want to go back to the farm . . . yet."

"Me neither," she said softly, turning to stare directly into his eyes.

"Will . . . will you come back to my hotel room with me?"

Annie continued to stare into his eyes, unwavering. She *had* to know what he was asking. Finally, she nodded, leaning closer to place her lips against his, softly. "I have to go back to the farm tonight, though. There's the four A.M. milking before we come back into Memphis for the Nativity scene."

He stiffened at the thought of the woman he loved demeaning herself in that ridiculous sideshow. "Annie, stay home at the farm tomorrow. Give up the Nativity scene venture. Let me help you—and your family—financially."

She immediately bristled. "No! The Fallon family doesn't accept charity."

He should have known she'd balk. But, dammit, how

was she going to reconcile accepting his money after they were married? "Whatever you say, sweetheart. It was only a suggestion," he conceded, for now.

She softened at his halfhearted apology. "I want to be with you, Clay," she whispered.

"Not half as much as I want to be with you."

The piano player had just finished up a blues song, so fast and intricate that his talent was evident. Next, in reaction to the loud requests from two ends of the club for "I'll Be Home for Christmas" and "Jingle Bell Rock," Arnett played a skillful blending of both yuletide classics. When he finished, silence reigned briefly, followed by thunderous applause.

Clay barely noticed the piano player and his girlfriend leaving the club once again. All he could think about was Annie and the fact that they were going to be together tonight. It appeared as if it would turn out all right, after all. No more celestial big toes.

He hoped.

Annie was nervous, but exhilarated, as they entered the foyer of the Original Heartbreak Hotel.

It was only ten o'clock, and the hotel lobby still buzzed with activity, its guests coming in for the evening, or just going out, in some cases. As myriad as Memphis itself, the guests ranged from sedately dressed businessmen to a group of Flying Elvi. But mostly there were tourists come to view the spectacle that was Memphis, the adopted home of Elvis . . . like those two middle-aged women over there in neon pink ELVIS LIVES sweatshirts who were eyeing Clay as if they thought he might be someone famous.

"They think I'm George," Clay informed her dryly, noticing her line of vision.

"George who?"

Clay shrugged. "Damned if I know. Straight, or Strayed, or something like that."

Annie burst out in laughter. "George Strait?"

"Yes. That's the one."

Annie hugged the big dolt. "How could anyone in the modern world not know George Strait? Clay, you are too, too precious."

He grinned at her calling him precious, then took her hand and led her around the massive Christmas tree in the center of the lobby. It was decorated with sparkling lights and priceless country-star memorabilia left by the various musicians who'd stayed in this hotel over the years. A gold-plated guitar pick from Chet Atkins. Guitar strings tied into a bow from Hank Williams. A silver star that had once adorned the dressing room of Eddie Arnold. Pearl earrings from Tammy Wynette. "Have you ever seen such a gaudy tree in all your life?"

"Clay, you need a major attitude adjustment."

"And you're the one to give it to me, aren't you, Annie, love?" he said, flicking her chin playfully. "Come on. I need to pick something up from the desk."

David and Marion Bloom, the longtime managers, nodded at Clay as he approached, and then at Annie, too. The refined couple, who resembled David Niven and Ingrid Bergman, right down to the thin mustache and the neatly coiled French twist hairdo, respectively, were probably surprised to see Annie with their boss, but they didn't betray their reactions by so much as a lifted eyebrow.

"Did an express mail package come for me today?" Clay asked.

"Yes, sir," David Bloom said, drawing a cardboard mailer out of a drawer behind the desk.

"And I have all those tax statements you asked me to

gather together when you called this afternoon," Marion Bloom added.

Clay took the mailer, but waved aside the stack of papers. "I'll examine those tomorrow."

Annie could see that the Blooms looked rather pale, their faces pinched with worry. Heck, everyone at the hotel was alarmed, from what Annie had heard when in Memphis earlier today. The possibility of imminent unemployment once the hotel closed had them all walking on tenterhooks, especially with the holidays looming. Annie would have liked to tell them that Clay would never close the hotel now that he knew what a landmark it was to Memphis, not to mention the connection with his mother. But it wasn't her place.

"We'll meet tomorrow at one with the accountant, right?" Clay asked the couple. When they nodded solemnly, he concluded, "Good night, then," and led Annie toward the elevators.

Once the doors swished shut, Annie leaned her head on Clay's shoulder and sighed. But he set her away from him and stepped to the other side of the elevator, staring at her with a rueful grimace. "If I touch you now, sweetheart, we'll be making love on the elevator floor."

She smiled.

"You little witch. You'd like that, wouldn't you?" Clay observed with a chuckle.

Soon he was inserting the key into the lock of his hotel room. Once they entered, Clay flicked on the light switch, and Annie was assaulted with a dozen different sounds, sights, and smells. A carousel—*a carousel, for heaven's sake*—was turning in one corner of the massive suite, churning out calliope music. A television in another corner clicked on automatically, playing a video of that old Elvis movie *Roustabout*. A popcorn machine began popping, and

92   Sandra Hill

a cotton candy machine began spinning its weblike confection. Hot dogs sizzled on a counter grill, where candy apples were laid out for a late-night snack. And the bed—*holy cow!*—the bed was in the form of a tunnel-of-love cart with high sides, and what looked like a vibrating mechanism on the side to simulate a water-rocking motion.

"Clay!" She laughed.

"Did you ever see anything so absurd in all your life?" A delightful pink stained his cheeks.

"Actually, it's kind of . . . uh, charming."

"Please." He begged to differ. Then, tossing his crutches aside, he leaned back against the door and pulled her into his embrace. "At last," he whispered against her mouth.

When he kissed her, openmouthed and clinging, Annie could taste his need for her. What a heart-filling ego boost to know she could affect this man so!

With clumsy haste, they pulled at each other's clothes.

"Slow down, honey," Clay urged raggedly, then immediately reversed himself. "No, hurry up, sweetheart."

"I can't wait, I can't wait, I can't wait. . . ." she cried.

Soon they were naked, he with nothing but a bandage wrapped around one ankle, she with nothing but two gold barrettes, which she quickly tossed aside.

She saw his arousal, and felt her own throb in counterpoint. Leaning forward, she pressed her lips to his chest, breathing in the clean, musky scent of his skin.

Clay gasped.

"You are so hot," she blurted out.

He grinned. "I know."

"Oh, you! I meant you throw off heat like . . . like an erotic bonfire."

Clay laughed. "So do you, Annie. So do you," he whispered, holding her face with the fingertips of both hands. He gazed at her with sheer adulation, which both humbled and exalted her. Tears filled her vision at the admiration she saw in his wonderful blue eyes.

"I love you, Clayton Jessup. I don't know how it's possible to fall in love with someone so fast and so hard, but it's the truth. I love you."

"I feel as if I've been walking through life with a huge hole in my heart, and now, suddenly, it's been filled. You make me complete, Annie. I know, that sounds so corny—"

"Shhh," she said, putting a forefinger against his lips. "It doesn't sound corny at all."

He led her to the bed then and they climbed over the ridiculously high side frames, laughing. It was an awkward exercise, with Clay's injury.

"At least there's no danger of us falling out of bed if you get too rambunctious," she teased.

In response, he swatted her on the behind, which was raised ignominiously in the air before she plopped down next to him.

Turning serious, Clay rolled onto his back and adjusted her so she lay half over him. Then he took her hands, encouraging her to explore him.

And she did.

Oh, Lord, she did.

She told him things she'd never imagined were in the far reaches of her fantasies. She used words . . . wicked words that drew a heated blush to her cheeks, and a chuckle of satisfaction from Clay.

Clay told her things, too, in a voice silky with sex. He spoke of erotic activities that made her tremble with trepidation. Or was it anticipation?

"I never expected that a man's hands could be so gentle and aggressive at the same time," she confessed.

"Who knew you'd be so passionate!" Clay said as he

performed magic feats on the many surfaces of her body. "I love the soft sounds you make when I touch you here. And here. And here."

Clay nudged her knees apart and lay over her, weight braced on his elbows. He teased her nipples with his fingers and lips and teeth and tongue—plucking, sucking, fluttering, and nipping—till Annie ached for more. It was hard to believe that the staid businessman could be such an inventive lover.

Finally, finally, finally, he penetrated her, and there was no pain, just a stretching fullness. Clay went still, his body taut with tension as he watched her.

"I love you, Annie," he whispered.

Her inner folds shifted around him in response, allowing him to grow even more, filling her even more.

"I love you, too, Clay. With all my heart."

Only then did he begin to move, long strokes that seemed to draw her very soul from her body. Then he surged back in again. Over and over, he took her breath away, then gave her new life.

She drew her knees up to give him greater access.

His heart thundered against her breast.

"Come for me, Annie," he gritted out painfully. "Let it happen, love."

But Annie fought her climax till she saw Clay rear his head back, veins taut in his neck, and let loose with a raw animal sound of pure male release as he plunged fully into her depths. Only then did Annie allow herself to spasm around him in progressively stronger reflexes till she, too, cried out with pure pleasure-pain.

Annie wept then—not from physical soreness, or emotional distress. It was the beauty and rightness of what they shared that drew her tears. There was a dampness in Clay's eyes, too.

After that, they made love again, a slow, serious exploration of each other's bodies, their likes and dislikes.

Then they made love a third time . . . a joyous, rib-tickling affair, involving mattress wave machines and carousels and sinfully sweet cotton candy.

CHAPTER SIX

It was two o'clock in the morning, and she and Clay were sitting on the floor watching *Roustabout*. She wore only Clay's dress shirt; he wore only a pair of boxers. She'd never enjoyed a movie more.

They were eating candy apples and chili dogs. He'd balked at the food choice at first, but Annie noticed that he'd then scarfed down two of both in record time, washed down with a Coke.

"We have to go back to the farm soon," she said regretfully. "We don't want to arrive when everyone is already waking up for the day. Talk about 'pink and flustery'! I'd be more like red and catatonic . . . with mortification."

"You aren't having second thoughts, are you?" Clay stood up and was taking their empty plates and glasses over to the kitchenette counter. He stopped and stared at her with concern.

"No, sweetheart, I'm not ashamed of anything we've done together. I just don't want to broadcast it to the world yet."

"Good," he said. "Because I have something for you." Clay went over to the hallway where he'd placed the express mailer that Mr. Bloom had handed to him earlier. Pulling the string zip, he took out a small box and handed it to Annie.

She raised her brows with uncertainty, then stood up

and opened the small cardboard box. Inside was a velvet box. Annie felt a roaring in her ears, and she began to weep before she even opened the tiny latch to see an old-fashioned diamond in a gold setting, surrounded by diamond chips.

"It belonged to my grandmother. I called my office this morning and had my secretary take it out of the safety-deposit box and mail it to me. If you don't like it, we can buy a new one, whatever you want." Clay was rambling on nervously while Annie continued to weep.

"It's beautiful," she sobbed.

"Will you marry me, love?"

"Of course I'll marry you," she said, and continued to sob.

"Here, let me put it on for you," Clay urged, a tearful thread in his voice, too.

It was dazzling. Not too big. Not too modern. Ideal.

"Oh, Clay, I love you so much."

"I love you, too. More than I ever thought possible."

They kissed to seal their betrothal.

Then they sealed their betrothal in another way.

"How soon before we can get married, do you think?" Clay asked much later. "I've got to get back to my office sometime soon, and I hate the thought of leaving you behind."

"I don't know. Aunt Liza will want to have a big wedding, but we can do something small, for family only."

"Is that what you want?"

"I'm not sure. I always pictured myself walking down the aisle in a white gown . . . the works. But now . . . well, I want to be married to you as soon as possible."

"We'll have a big wedding, if that's what you always wanted, Annie, love. But we'll set a new time record for arranging a big wedding. Okay?"

She nodded, unable to stop staring at the beautiful ring on her finger.

"Will you be able to come back to Princeton with me for a while? Would that be too scandalous for Aunt Liza?"

Annie laughed. "Oh, I think we could convince her that your housekeeper is chaperon enough, but I couldn't stay for more than a week. It's too much to ask Chet and the others to take on my work for much more than that."

"But, honey, at some point they'll have to pick up your slack. When you move up north, they'll have no choice but to—"

The small choked sound Annie made caught Clay midsentence.

"Annie . . . Annie, what's wrong?"

Stricken, she could only stare at him. "You think I'll move to New Jersey permanently?"

A frown creased Clay's forehead. "Of course. You didn't think I would be moving here, did you?"

"Yes," she wailed. "You didn't think I'd give up the farm, did you?"

"Yes."

They were both gaping at each other with incredulity.

"How could you think that you and I would marry and live in that farmhouse? It's too small for your family as it is."

Annie shrugged. "I guess I wasn't thinking that far. At some point, Chet will probably marry Emmy Lou, once he gets his head together. And I would imagine they'll live at the farmhouse. But we could always build a house somewhere else on our land. There's plenty of acreage."

"Annie, I'm not a farmer."

"Well, I am," she said stormily then softened her voice, putting a hand up to cup Clay's rigid jaw lovingly. "Clay, isn't there any way you could do your work from Memphis?"

"Annie, my business has been operated from the same

Manhattan office by three generations of Jessups. My family home has been in Princeton for almost a hundred years."

"You didn't answer my question."

"I am *not* moving to Memphis, and that's final." He pleaded with her to understand. "That farm of yours is a money drain, pure and simple. This afternoon I read some of the farm magazines sitting around your house. You don't have to be a rocket scientist to know that eventually you'll have to sell off some land to developers or use hormones in your cattle feed. You're about twenty years behind the times, babe."

"How dare you . . . how dare you presume to tell me how to run my farm? And you know nothing about me at all, if you think I would ever sell off even a shovelful of Fallon land."

"It's an unwise financial decision, Annie. Believe me, this is what I do for a living. This is my expertise."

"You can shove your expertise, Clay Jessup. And you can shove this, too," she said, taking off the ring and handing it back to him. The whole time tears were streaming down her face.

"Annie, don't. Oh, God, don't leave like this," he said, watching with horror as she snatched up her clothes and began to dress as quickly as possible. "Let's talk about this. You're not being rational." He began to dress as well.

"You're not coming back to the farm with me."

"I don't want you driving alone in the middle of the night."

"I'm a big girl, Clay. I've been doing it for a long time." Dressed now, she stared at him for a long moment. "Tell me one thing, Clay. Do you still intend to raze this hotel?"

"Of course. What would ever make you think otherwise?"

Annie tried, but couldn't stifle the sob that rose in her tight throat. "Call me crazy, but I thought you were developing a heart."

"You're being unfair."

"Life's unfair, Clay." She grabbed her shoulder bag and headed toward the door, anxious to be out of his sight now, before she broke down completely.

"I love you, Annie."

Her only response was to slam the door in his face.

Clay gazed at the closed door with abject misery.

How could I have made such a mess of things? How will I survive without Annie? What should I do now?

And somewhere, whether it was the television or inside his head, Clay couldn't tell for sure, Elvis gave him the answer: "I'm so lonesome I could cry . . ."

Truer words were never sung.

And Clay was pretty sure this qualified as a God's-big-toe stumble.

Two days later, on Wednesday, a despondent Clay stared out his hotel room window as Annie and her brothers dismantled their live Nativity scene for the day. Tomorrow was Christmas Eve, so it would probably be their last day on the site.

Clay had no idea if he'd ever see Annie again after that.

Oh, he'd tried to reconcile their differences, but Annie wouldn't budge.

"Are you still selling the hotel?" she'd demanded to know yesterday when he'd confronted her in the hotel café. She and her family had managed to deflect all his phone calls before that. She'd even threatened to give up their live Nativity scene yesterday, despite her family's need for money, if he didn't stop coming out and "bothering" her. "Well, answer me. Are you still selling the hotel?"

"Yes, but it has nothing to do with us, Annie. It's a business decision."

She'd made a harrumphing sound of disgust. "Would you move to Memphis?"

"Well, maybe we could live here part of the time . . . have homes in New Jersey and Tennessee." *See, I can compromise. Why can't you, Annie?* "Would you be willing to promise to never . . . uh . . . to never stick your arm up a cow's butt again?"

Annie had looked surprised at that request. Then she'd shaken her head sadly. "Clay, Clay, Clay. You just don't get it, do you? I've bred a hundred cows in my lifetime. I'll breed hundreds more before I die. If you think cow breeding is gross, you ought to see me butcher a pig. Or wring a chicken's neck, cut off its head, gut, and feather it, all in time for dinner. Believe me, cow breeding is no big deal."

It is to me. And I refuse to picture Annie with a dead chicken or cow. She's just kidding. She must be. "Don't you love me, Annie?" He'd hated the pathetic tone his voice had taken on then, but the question had needed to be asked.

"Yes, but I'm hoping I'll get over it."

No! his mind had screamed. *Don't get over it. You can't get over it. I won't. I can't.*

That had been the last conversation he'd had with the woman he loved and had lost, all in the space of three lousy days in Memphis. Then today he'd discovered a card table in the lobby with the sign HEARTBREAK HOTEL EMPLOYEE FUND. Apparently, Annie and her family had donated two hundred dollars of their hard-earned money to start a fund for hotel employees who would soon be out of work, due to him. Annie had found a way, after all, to make him, albeit indirectly, involved in the Fallon family Christmas good deed for 1998. And it didn't matter one damn bit to anyone that he'd dropped five hundred dollars in the box.

A knock on the door jarred him from his daydream. It was the elderly bellhop. "Mr. and Mrs. Bloom said to tell you the lawyers'll be here any minute. Best you come down to the office to go over some last-minute details for the sale."

The bellhop glared at him, then turned on his heel and stomped away, not even waiting for Clay to accompany him. Hell, the entire hotel staff, except for the Blooms, had put him on their freeze list. You'd think he was Simon Legree. Or Scrooge.

Minutes later, Clay was in the manager's office, doing a last read-through of the legal documents. The attorneys hadn't arrived yet, and David had gone out front to register a guest.

"Mr. Jessup, I have some things that belong to you . . . well, they belonged to your mother, but I guess that means they belong to you now."

"What?" Clay glanced up to see Marion lifting a cardboard box from a closet shelf.

"When the fire occurred at the photography studio next door all those years ago, I was on duty. I managed to save a few scraps of things from the fire," she explained nervously.

"Why didn't you send them to my father?"

"I tried to give them to him when he came to Memphis to bury your mother, but he refused to take them . . . said he wanted nothing to remind him of her. It was the grief speaking, of course."

No, it wasn't the grief speaking. That's how my father regarded my mother his entire life.

Hesitantly he opened the box. On top was an eight-by-ten photograph, brown on the edges.

"It was their wedding picture," Mrs. Bloom informed him.

Clay felt as if he'd been kicked in the gut. His father—looking much younger and more carefree than he'd ever witnessed—was dressed in a dark suit with a flower in the lapel, gazing with adoration at the woman standing at his side carrying a small bouquet of roses. Their arms were linked around each other's waists. She wore a stylish white suit with matching high heels, and she was staring at her new husband with pure, seemingly heartfelt love. They were standing on the steps in front of a church. The date on the back of the picture read *August 10, 1967.*

"How could two people who appear to have loved each other so much have fallen out of love so quickly?"

Marion gasped. "Whatever are you talking about? They never stopped loving each other."

Clay cut her off with a sharp glower. "My mother abandoned me and my father less than two years after this photo was taken."

"She never did so!" Marion snapped indignantly. "Clare came here to tie up some loose ends with her business, and to give her and your father some breathing room over their differences. But they never stopped loving each other."

He started to speak, but Marion put up a hand to halt his words. "You have to understand that there's something about the air that comes down from the Blue Ridge Mountains. It gets in a Memphian's soul. Your mother was Memphis born and bred. She had trouble adjusting to life in Princeton, and your father was a stubborn, unbending man. I think he feared the pull of this city on your mother—jealousy, in a way—and so he became dogmatic, unwilling to be flexible."

"She left my father," Clay gritted out.

Marion shook her head vigorously from side to side. "Clare wasn't giving up on your father. She had every intention of returning home. If it hadn't been for the fire . . ." Her eyes filled with tears as she spoke. She swiped at them with a tissue and pointed to an envelope in the box of miscellany.

Clay picked it up and immediately noticed the airline logo on the outside of the envelope. Inside was a thirty-year-old one-way ticket, Memphis to Newark. It was too much to digest at once. Clay stood abruptly and headed for the door.

"Mr. Jessup, where are you going? We have a meeting soon."

He waved a hand dismissively. "I'm going for a walk. I need to think."

"But what should I tell the lawyers?"

"Tell them . . . tell them . . . the deal is off . . . for now."

It was Christmas Eve, and Clay was driving a bright red Jeep Cherokee up the lane to Sweet Hollow Farm, more hopeful and frightened than he'd ever been in all his life.

Would he and Annie be able to work things out?

Would her brothers come out with shotguns in hand?

Would he fight to the death for her . . . a virtual knight in shining Jeep?

Would Annie still love him in the end?

There was a full moon out tonight, but Clay didn't need it, or the Jeep's headlights, to see. The entire barn and farmhouse were outlined with Christmas-tree lights. In the front yard was a plywood Santa and reindeer display, illuminated by floodlights. It resembled a farm version of the house in Chevy Chase's movie *National Lampoon's Christmas Vacation*. He wondered idly who had climbed up on the roofs of the house and barn to put up all those blasted lights. *Probably Annie. Or Aunt Liza. Geez!*

Clay was so nervous he could barely think straight, especially when he saw the front door open even before he emerged from the vehicle.

It was Annie.

Please, God, he prayed, *no big toes this time.*

"Clay?" Annie said, coming down the steps and walking woodenly toward him. She looked as if she'd been crying.

Who made her cry? I'll kill the person who made her cry! Oh! It was probably me.

"Where did you get the Jeep?" she asked nervously, as if that irrelevant detail were the most important thing on her mind.

"I . . . uh . . . kind of . . . uh . . . rented it." Clay's brain was stuck in first gear.

"You came back," she said then, surrendering to a sob. "I called the hotel all night and Marion said you were gone, and I thought . . . I thought you went home."

"I am home, sweetheart." Clay opened his arms to her and gathered her close. "I've done a lot of walking, and thinking, since you left me."

"I've been so miserable," she blubbered against his neck.

"Me, too, sweetheart. Me, too." He was running his hands over her back, her arms, her hair, her back again. He kissed the top of her head, her wet cheeks, her lips. He tried to show her with soul-deep kisses how much he'd missed her, and how important she was to him. He couldn't get enough of her. He was afraid to let go for fear this was all a dream.

Annie leaned back to get a better look at him. Cupping his face in her hands, she gazed at him, tears streaming down her cheeks, with such open love that Clay felt blessed.

"Annie, love, we're going to work this out. I've talked with my legal department in New York, and they see no problem with my setting up a satellite office in Memphis. Could you live with me in New Jersey part of the time, if I'm willing to live here?"

Her mouth had dropped open with surprise. "You would do that for me?"

"In a heartbeat." *It's either that, or suffer heartbreak. Easy choice!*

"How about the hotel?"

"Well, I'm not sure. I called Spencer Modine this morning. Remember, you pointed him out to me at Forever Blue."

"You called Spencer Modine? But you don't even know him."

He shrugged. "Modine certainly has the capital to finance a purchase of the hotel property, and he has the Memphis ties that would make such a landmark attractive to him. But I don't know if I'm ready to give up the hotel yet. Oh, Annie, I've learned some things this week about my mother and father that are going to take me a long time to understand."

She pressed a light kiss to his lips in understanding. "We don't have to decide all this right now."

"We?" he asked hopefully.

"We," she repeated.

"Will you marry me, Annie, love?"

"In a heartbeat," she said.

A short time later, they were heading toward the front steps, arms wrapped around each other's waists, their progress hampered by his limp and their constant stopping to kiss and murmur soft words of love.

Clay couldn't stop grinning.

"You're looking awfully self-satisfied, Mr. Jessup."

"Well, I'm a negotiator, Annie. It's part of my business as a venture capitalist. I figure I just pulled off the deal of the century. I got you, didn't I, babe?"

She laughed. "You had me anyhow, *babe*. I already talked to my brothers about taking over the farm so I could move to New Jersey. Why do you think I was calling you all night?" She tapped him playfully on the chin in one-upmanship.

"Well, you little witch, you," Clay said. But what he thought was, *Wait till you see what I bought at the mall. You haven't had the last word yet.*

Elvis was singing "Blue Christmas" on the stereo, a fire was roaring in the fireplace, the tree lights were flickering, and Clay was enjoying his first ever family Christmas Eve celebration. If his heart expanded with any more joy, it just might explode.

It was almost midnight, but already the family members were opening their Christmas gifts. Clay sat on the sofa with Annie on one side, holding his hand. Aunt Liza was on the other side, keeping an eagle eye on his hands, lest they stray.

The gifts the Fallons gave to each other were simple items, some homemade, some silly, many downright practical. Who knew that people got socks and underwear for Christmas gifts? Johnny raved over his new athletic shoes . . . the spiffiest in the store, according to Annie. Everyone received new shirts and jeans. The pearl stud earrings that Johnny had bought for Annie, probably from Wal-Mart, might have come from Cartier, for all her oohing and ahhing. And the boys exhibited just as much appreciation over cheap card games or music cassettes.

There were even gifts for Clay from the family, to his surprise and slight embarrassment. When Aunt Liza handed him a suspicious-looking small box, wrapped with Santa Claus paper, he almost choked. *She wouldn't!*

Aunt Liza *tsk*ed at him till he unwrapped it to find an audio cassette of *Elvis's Greatest Hits*.

"Whadja think I bought, you fool?" she said with a chuckle.

Chet, Roy, and Hank had pooled their money to get him a pair of low-heeled cowboy boots. Jerry Lee gave him a Wall Street joke book, and Johnny presented him with a tie imprinted with dozens of Holstein cows.

When it was Annie's turn, she made much ado over the homemade tree ornament with his name and date stenciled on the back, thus symbolizing his formal acceptance into her family. Finally, with much nervousness, she handed him what he sensed must be a special gift.

Tears filled his eyes, and he couldn't speak at first. Inside was a leather album. The words on the front, embossed with gold letters, said, THE WORKS OF GLARE GANNETT. Annie had somehow managed to gather together dozens of photographs taken by his mother. On the last page was a copy of an obituary from a Memphis newspaper, detailing her artistic talent and what she had contributed to Memphis and music history.

"Where did you get these?" he asked when his emotions were finally under control.

"I badgered the museum curator yesterday. When he heard your story, he helped me pull those photos made by your mother, and I duplicated them at a one-hour photo studio down the street."

"Thank you, love," he whispered against her hair. Then he decided it was time to reciprocate. "Can you guys help me get some gifts from the Jeep?"

There was a communal awed curse from Annie's brothers when they saw how the back of the Jeep overflowed with gaily wrapped packages, some in huge boxes.

Aunt Liza could be heard rapping on the kitchen window at that crude expletive. "I heard that, boys. You're not too old for soap, you know. That goes for you, too, Mr. Jessup."

After the boys had each made three trips, the living room was filled with his purchases. Hank closed the door with a shiver—it was turning cold outside, and snowflakes had just begun to flutter down in wonderful Christmas fashion—and he asked Clay, "Where'd you buy that spiffy red Jeep?"

"Oh, he didn't buy it," Annie explained. "It's a rental."

"That sure looked like a new car plate to me," Hank commented as he hung his coat on an old-fashioned coatrack.

"Clay?" Annie tilted her head in question to him. "Did you buy yourself a Jeep?"

"Well, no, I didn't buy a Jeep for *myself.*"

Everyone turned to stare at him then. Clay shifted uneasily, and his eyes wandered over to Hank.

There was a long, telling silence. Then Hank whooped. "Me? Me? You bought a car for me?"

"Clay Jessup! You can't go out and buy a car for someone you barely know."

"I can't?" he said. "Well, hell . . . I mean, geez, Annie, Hank distinctly said that first night I was here for dinner that if he had as much money as me, he would buy a fancy new vehicle and be the biggest chick magnet in the United States. I knew you'd be upset if I bought him a Jaguar."

"Holy cow! I wonder what I get if Hank gets a new Jeep," Johnny commented in an awestruck voice.

Annie made a low gurgling sound, which he figured was his cue to move on to the other gifts.

Chet's Adam's apple moved awkwardly as he studied Clay's gift . . . airline tickets for Chet Fallon and son, Jason, to London, dated December 26.

"At least you show *some* good sense," Aunt Liza observed. "It's about time someone pushed Chet in the right direction."

For the entire family, Clay had bought a high-tech computer system that would allow them to program in all the statistics on their milk production. Aunt Liza got a microwave, which she pooh-poohed at first, stating, "What would I do with one of those fancy contraptions?" But she was soon reading the manual, exclaiming, "Didja know you can do preserves in a microwave?" By the time Jerry Lee went ballistic over his laptop, Roy had gone speechless over the bank envelope showing a trust fund passbook covering his entire vet school tuition, and Johnny was in tears over a new entertainment system for his bedroom, complete with portable TV, CD player, and game system . . . well, by then Annie had given up on her protests.

"It's too much, Clay," she said on a sigh of frustration.

"No, it's not, Annie. Generosity is giving till it hurts . . . like you and your family do every Christmas. This is just money I spent here . . . money whose loss I won't even miss."

"But I still think you should take back—"

"Annie," Aunt Liza cautioned in a stern voice, "shut up."

They all laughed at that.

"So what did you get for Annie?" Hank wanted to know.

She gazed at the ring on her finger. "I have my gift."

But Hank ignored her. "With all the great gifts he gave

us, he must have bought you at least . . . a new barn. Ha, ha, ha!"

Annie folded her arms indignantly over her chest at the teasing, and Clay's face heated up in a too-telling fashion.

"Well, actually . . ." he admitted, handing her a gift certificate from a local contracting firm.

"You didn't!" Annie scolded.

He did. It was a purchase order for a new barn roof.

She punched him lightly in the stomach, but he didn't care. He could see the love in her eyes.

A hour later everyone had gone to bed, except him and Annie.

"I love you, Annie," he said for what must be the hundredth time that evening.

"I love you, too, Clay . . . so much that my heart feels as if it's overflowing."

"It's hard to believe that so much has happened to us in the five days since we first met."

"Maybe you were destined to come to Tennessee . . . for us to meet. Maybe there is an Elvis spirit looking over Memphis."

Clay wanted to balk at the idea, but the words wouldn't come out. "Maybe you're right. Perhaps Elvis really does live," he finally conceded. "Oh, I forgot. There's one more gift I bought for you." He reached behind the sofa and handed her the package.

"Clay, this is too much. You've already given me too much."

"Well, actually, this gift is for me." He waggled his eyebrows at her.

Hesitantly, Annie unwrapped the package, which came from a costume shop in the mall. Annie laughed when she lifted the lid. It was a Daisy Mae outfit—a white off-the-shoulder blouse, and cut off jeans that were cut off *real* high on the buttock. "You devil, you."

"So, are you going to try it on for me tonight?"

"Here?"

"Hell, no. In the hayloft."

There was an old legend that said that on Christmas Eve on a farm, the animals talk.

One thing was certain. On Christmas Eve, 1998, on Sweet Hollow Farm, the animals in the barn, under the hayloft, had a lot to talk about.

AUTHOR'S NOTE

If you believe the spirit of Elvis is still alive, you're not alone.

It's been more than twenty years since the King died, but almost six hundred Elvis fan clubs still flourish around the world. No one disputes the fact that Elvis had a profound impact on the music industry, but his magic lives on not only in his own songs, but in those of the many musicians influenced by his talent.

So, if you are one of those people who can't help singing along when an Elvis tune comes on the radio . . . or if a smile breaks out when you hear "Blue Suede Shoes" . . . or if you believe some people "live on" after death, then please look for my December 1998 release, *Love Me Tender*. In that book, there is a fake Spanish prince, a Wall Street princess . . . uh, *trader* known as "the Irish Barracuda," and a secondary character named Elmer Presley, who thinks he's Elvis reincarnated.

Maybe he is. And maybe he isn't. But one thing's for sure: the legend does go on.

NINA BANGS

Man With A Golden Bow

CHAPTER ONE

She wanted a bad man in the worst way. Bad as in hot and hard. A man able to steam up car windows with his kisses and make her dance naked in the street. A man with wicked hands who'd touch her in places that would make her scream.

Unfortunately, he wasn't here. She'd already checked under the couch. All she had was this video Carole had loaned her.

Jenny Saunders wasn't too sure about the video. She chanced another glance at the couple on the screen, then picked up her phone and called Carole.

"Carole's Baskets and Gifts. How can I—"

"Carole, about this video—"

"Jenny! You're watching the video? Is it seriously hot or what? Puts you in the mood, doesn't it? I love it when they—"

"I don't believe real people do it in those positions. Okay, maybe in New York, but not here in South Jersey."

"Listen, girlfriend, you've gotta get into a different mind-set. Anything is possible when two people are carried away by passion. Billy and I did it five times last night. That video inspired us."

"*Five* times?" She was twenty-eight years old and missing out on one of a woman's greatest experiences while her friends left her in their dust. What if she died tonight? She'd never *know*.

"Of course, maybe things'll settle down after we've been married a few more weeks. Wait just a sec." Jenny could hear Carole talking to a customer. She watched the video while she waited. Hmm. That position had possibilities. "Okay, I'm back. Look, if you're going to lose the big V, then you have to be willing to experiment."

"The big V? Virginity isn't a disease, Carole."

"Don't know about that. Anyway, it's all set with Sloan. He's on his way, and he doesn't suspect a thing. The rest is up to you. Are you wearing that little black bra I bought you?"

"Sure." She'd *never* wear that bra. There wasn't enough of it to wear. "Are you sure Sloan will show up?"

"Hey, have I ever lied to you? I can't believe you don't love that video."

"If I were a chiropractor, I'd love it." She turned her head sideways to see if she could catch any fleeting expressions of passion on the faces of the couple now in a new pretzel position. Nope. No passion. A little pain, but no passion. "I don't know about this plan, Carole. A lot could go wrong. I haven't seen Sloan in ten years. We've exchanged a few letters, a few phone calls, but that's it."

"So whose fault is it you were away the other times he came home? Sloan's my cousin. He's family. Nothing will go wrong."

"But—"

"Don't you dare back out. I will *not* let them carve 'She Died a Virgin' on your tombstone. You think too much."

"That's what I do, Carole. I'm an accountant and accountants think. And right now I think I might've made a—"

"Uh, gotta go. Another customer just walked in. Talk to you later."

Jenny stared at the phone. Just like Carole. Her friend set the trap, then ran for the hills before the tiger arrived. Not that Sloan was a tiger. He was a comfortable friend from high school, someone she'd grown up with, someone who wouldn't make her nervous. *Someone you haven't seen in ten years.*

She flicked off the TV. Carole was right. She couldn't back out. She wanted this. Jenny Saunders wouldn't spend another Saturday night alone with only her lustful thoughts for company. And no way would she come home one day to find the state putting a historical marker outside her door—The Last Living Virgin in New Jersey.

Besides, no one would ever believe it. She could talk the talk, think the thoughts, but she'd never managed to walk the walk.

It wasn't as though she hadn't tried. She'd scoped out men until her eyes crossed. Sue her for being picky, but Lenny who owned the bagel shop down on Broadway and whose date conversation centered around which cream cheese tasted best on his raisin bagels did *not* make her heart beat faster. Besides, she couldn't get physical with a guy who was as soft and doughy as his bagels.

Jenny smiled. Sloan had called after that horrific date. He was funny, comforting, and talking with Sloan was a laser light show compared to the Lennys of the world. Maybe he wasn't long-term-relationship material, but . . .

Jenny's doorbell interrupted more in-depth analysis.

She put her eye to the door's peephole, but all she could see was a giant basket. *At last.* Her Christmas basket, delivery man, and the possibility for one glorious life-fulfilling fling had arrived.

Jenny opened the door only as far as her security chain would allow. "Yes?" The basket was beautiful. Now if she could only work up the courage to look at the delivery man.

"I have a basket here for Jenny Saunders. Are you Jenny Saunders?"

She looked at him. He smiled. *Yes.* They should distribute protective glasses with that smile.

"I might be." Something was wrong though. She'd bargained on her good old high school buddy, Sloan. Someone she could feel comfortable with on her fling. Someone attractive, but not *too* attractive. Someone sexy, but not *too* sexy. Someone who wouldn't intimidate the heck out of her. This was *not* Sloan Mitello. This was intimidation with a capital "I."

"You're not the delivery man I expected. I don't open my door to strange men carrying baskets. Look what happened to Little Red Riding Hood. She ended up with a wolf in her bed." *Stupid, Saunders.* She must have bed on the brain.

"I think Little Red was the one carrying the basket, not the wolf. And it was her grandmother's bed."

"Whatever. It's the concept."

"Don't you remember me, Jenny?" His eyes gleamed with laughter and a promise that he'd be well worth remembering.

"Nope." She would swear she'd never met him. This man was tall, with broad shoulders, lean hips, muscular thighs, and shoulder-length black hair. He also had a wicked grin that suggested he was on good speaking terms with sin. She wouldn't forget someone like him.

"Sure you do. It's me. Sloan. Carole said she had baskets backed up to here." He pantomined a line on his throat.

Nice throat. She had this crazy urge to put her lips on the spot where his blood pulsed hot and strong. Jenny frowned. Crazy urges could be dangerous. As dangerous as the man standing on the other side of her door.

"Anyway, she asked me to help out by delivering a few of the local orders. So here I am with this basket from—" he glanced at the card—"a secret admirer."

"Sloan Mitello?" She narrowed her gaze. Tall and gangly Sloan Mitello? Short hair, semi-geeky? No, Sloan Mitello never looked like this man. "I don't think so."

He shifted the basket onto one hip and pulled his wallet from the back pocket of well-worn jeans that showed every muscular curve of thigh and hip. Wonderful jeans. "Okay, here's my license." He held the wallet up to the crack. "And just to make sure, how about a trip down Memory Lane?"

"Memory Lane?" *Sloan?* Absolutely, positively not. No way could she have a wild fling with this Sloan Mitello. He was too . . . too *much.*

"Your couch. Senior Week. We'd gotten bored with the people we were with, so we ended up together watching an old movie, *The Man with the Golden Gun.* You said you'd rather have a man with a golden *bow.*" He leaned closer. "Would you have opened the door if I showed up wearing nothing but a big flashy gold bow, Jenny? Would you have let me in?" His voice was dark seduction.

"Umm . . ." *Say yes, you wuss.* The woman she wanted to be wouldn't hesitate. The woman she was couldn't make up her mind.

"I *really* wanted to wear that bow, but I ran into a couple of problems."

Sure. Problems. "Sloan Mitello. I can't believe it." She was smiling. The same silly smile Sloan had always drawn from her, back when she'd allowed herself silly smiles.

"I know, I know. The bad penny." He grinned at her.

She drew in a deep breath. She'd forgotten. His body

might've changed, but he'd always had that killer smile. And once she got past the way he looked, he still sounded like her old high school buddy.

"First problem. It's cold outside. I could throw a coat over the bow and me, but what if I got in an accident on the way over? How would I explain to the cops why I'm just wearing a bow?" His grin widened. "I've changed, Jenny. Time was when I wouldn't have given a damn what anyone thought."

"Changed? You?" One of the things that had separated them. He'd been a brilliant free spirit, a never-has-to-crack-a-book kind of guy.

She'd had to work after school to help her family make ends meet after Dad's latest money-making scheme crashed. And she *hadn't* been brilliant. She'd had to study long into the night. She hadn't had time to think about . . .

Okay, so she'd thought about him, but she knew too much about the Sloans of the world to risk more than friendship with him. Besides, in high school it had been hard to imagine making love with someone who, in third grade, had given her a dead spider neatly nestled in a Godiva chocolate box he'd found.

"Next problem. How do I get the sucker to stay right *here*?" He backed away from the door so she could see exactly where *here* was. "Hey, I'd have to cover up the gift part so it'd be a surprise. Know what I mean?"

The visual had her gulping in another lifesaving supply of oxygen. Okay, no more of the virgin-who-would-be-bad routine. She'd wanted a hot and hard man, so here he was. Now what was she going to do with him?

"Besides, you have a nosy neighbor downstairs. She'd be punching out 911 before I even got up the stairs." He moved close to the door again until only one vivid green eye was visible. "I'm cold out here, Jenny. Let me in."

Said the wolf. Jenny unhooked the chain, then opened the door.

He swept into her tiny living room bringing cold air and memories.

"So you're back in town?" *Well, duh?*

"Yep. I have some unfinished business."

All motion and energy, he looked out of place next to her calm ivory furniture.

Placing the basket on her coffee table, he swung in a circle, glancing briefly at her furniture, at her few tasteful bought-to-fit-with-the-decor pictures, at her neat and perfect *everything.* And judged. She knew what he'd say before he said it, because despite the years they'd been apart, she remembered Sloan.

He turned back to her, his long dark hair sliding across the shoulders of his short leather jacket. "You need some red in here, Flame."

Flame. Some dusty corner of her memory smiled at the almost forgotten nickname. He'd said if he had hair her shade of red, he'd grow it down to his butt. Looked like he was working on the butt thing while her hair was a short smooth cap.

"I don't need red. The decorator said this living room was me." She didn't *need* Sloan back in her life either— all the colors of the rainbow wrapped in shades of intense emotion.

But she *wanted* him. Give her a few days to adjust to the new Sloan and he'd be a perfect fit for her brief-encounter-of-the-sexual-kind. For the first time in her life she'd walk the walk.

His glance slid across her hair, lingered. "You've got red whether you want it or not, Jenny. Make the most of it."

He moved close. Close enough for her to smell the promise of snow on his open jacket, the scent of warm

male on his black T-shirt, to watch the swell of chest
muscles as he took a deep breath.

Close enough for all of *her* breath to leave her in a startled whoosh as he ran callused fingers over her hair, then
continued until he touched the spot where her pulse beat
a tom-tom response.

"You need long hair, Jenny. Long ribbons of fire rippling down your back, over your shoulders, down to . . ."

His husky murmur died away as his fingers traced a
path down the vee of skin exposed by her blouse, paused
where the vee ended, seemed bent on traveling to new
and unexplored places.

She was sweating even though she knew darn well
she'd set her thermostat at a perfect seventy-two degrees.
But her body's thermostat was measuring a different heat-
wave right now. One with long dark hair, hot green eyes,
and a hard, beard-shadowed jaw.

The Sloan Mitello she'd known had never messed with
her personal heat indicator. What was he doing? She
stepped back, then sank onto her decorator-approved
couch. Hard. Her bottom didn't even make a dent in it.

Hard. There was nothing soft about the new and improved Sloan Mitello.

Mental picture. Position four on Carole's tape. Jenny
draped over her ivory couch, Sloan's dark hair trailing between her thighs. His lips . . . Jenny smiled. *Bring on the
chiropractors.* A new woman was about to be born.

"Thanks for delivering the basket, Sloan." Time to get
back to the mundane so she could regroup and plan her
strategy. She wasn't used to impulsive. She'd spent her
whole life thinking things through carefully, weighing all
the angles, making informed decisions.

"Mind if I catch the end of the Flyers' game before I
leave?" He turned to search for her remote.

"Sure, go ahead." *Think. What to say? Wow, I was just dreaming about Mr. Hard-and-Hot, then I open the door and there you are.* She might be the queen of flip, but her lips wouldn't form the words. Perhaps something a little more subtle.

He located the remote and reached for it. "It's a week until Christmas and Carole's business is booming. I'd barely gotten in the door when she handed me some baskets and told me to deliver them. Couldn't believe the coincidence when I saw your name on one of the baskets."

"Right. Coincidence." *How about orchestrated with all the finesse of a bulldozer.*

"How's life been treating you, Jenny?"

"Life's been good." She frowned as he turned on the TV. "My accounting business is growing and I—" *Ohmigod!* She'd forgotten about the video. She'd turned off the TV, but not her VCR.

Too late. She was toast. Her life flashed before her eyes, but Sloan didn't notice. He was gazing raptly at the screen.

The silence stretched on . . . and on . . . and on.

"Uh, you can catch the end of that game if you hurry."

He didn't look at her. "Nice camera angle there."

"I don't believe real people do those things."

He finally looked at her. His gaze trailed over her body like Little Red's wolf planning his day's menu. "Believe it." His eyes lit with laughter. "Want to try?" He hit the stop button.

As the baddest virgin in Jersey, she should've swiveled her hips, winked at him, and murmured, "Thought you'd never ask."

Instead, she resorted to babbling, a skill she'd honed to an art form. "A friend gave me that tape. It's not mine. I was just sorta glancing at it when you came."

Silence.

"Look, I don't need to watch tapes. I know about things like that." *Say something before I gag on my own foot.*

"Really?" He looked intrigued.

"Sure. First there's the come-on." *Let me do your tax returns, and I'll find so many loopholes and write-offs Uncle Sam will be paying you for the next twenty years.*

"Then there's foreplay." *Come to my office and we'll do the paperwork. Bring your receipts.*

"Finally, there's the climax." *My refund check came! I love you.*

"Sounds impressive." He rose to put the remote on top of the TV.

Numbers were her game. What was the probability of another man having buns exactly like Sloan's? Firm. *Male.* One in ten thousand, one in a million? Interesting research question.

"It figures you'd end up as an accountant."

"What? What figures?" Suppose he *had* shown up with just a gold bow? He'd need a way to keep it from sliding off. Of course she hadn't gotten a look at his . . . If *that* was big enough, nothing would slide off.

"It figures you'd work with numbers."

"What's wrong with numbers?" She wondered if they sold stick-on bows with a Post-it backing. Something that wouldn't be an owie when you pulled it off. She thought about pulling it off and licked her lips.

"They're safe. Always the same."

"I prefer reliable. Reliable's important." A ribbon thong had possibilities too. She could picture the gold ribbon snaking down between those amazing buns, separating, delineating.

"What about exciting, fun. Isn't fun important, too?"

"Exciting and fun can't be counted on. If I add a column of figures, there's only one right answer. Exciting

and fun can have an infinity of answers. I wouldn't know
which was the *right* answer. How would I know which way
to go?"

Go? Where would the ribbon go next? Hmm. It would
slide between those yummy thighs and come out . . .

"It's hot in here. Does it feel hot to you? Feels hot to
me." She bounced off the couch and reached the thermostat in record time. Without looking, she flicked it down
to what she hoped was Arctic Zone level.

Turning back toward him, she met his gaze across the
room. "What were we talking about?"

"Haven't a clue." His grin touched her, swept away the
ten years he'd been gone along with the strangeness that
had frozen her brain cells.

Relaxing into the remembered familiarity, she walked
back to the couch and sat down. "I'm surprised you
thought of that gold bow thing."

Abandoning the remote, he moved to the couch and
sat down beside her. She fought to retain her old-friends-
meeting-again attitude. But he didn't feel like an old
friend. She wasn't sure what he felt like, but it definitely
wasn't an old friend.

"I have a great memory, Jenny." He edged closer.

"Right. Great memory. Gee, I wonder what's in my basket?" Reaching out, she lifted the basket from her coffee
table and plunked it down between them. Not exactly
the Great Wall of China, but it'd do in a pinch.

*Hello? You're supposed to be encouraging up-close and
cozy.* But she needed some time. Her decision to have a
fling had been a cerebral decision. She was a cerebral person. The man sitting next to her appealed to a completely different body area, and she hadn't had enough
time to make the move from penthouse to basement.

The laughter glittering in his green eyes mocked her

puny effort. "Are you telling me you don't remember the movie?"

She removed the red cellophane wrapping from around the basket. Concentrated on the satisfying crinkling sound. "Nope. I don't remember a thing."

"That's because you'd chugged four beers."

"I *never* drank four beers." She carefully removed the first item from the basket. Lavender bubble bath.

"Sure you did. You were fun that night." A line formed between his eyes as he studied the bubble bath. "Looks like your secret admirer's in touch with his feminine side."

She stopped to stare at him. "*How* much fun?"

His grin widened. "Not *that* much fun. Anyway, it was close to Christmas, and you said you'd rather have a man with a golden bow any old time."

"I remember. Vaguely. Doesn't sound like me, though." She lifted out the next item. Peppermint foot balm.

"Exactly. That's why you were so much fun." He peered at the foot balm. "Wow. A clue. Know any men with a foot fetish?"

She paused in the midst of pulling out a soothing vanilla candle. "I was fun because I wasn't me? Correct me if I'm wrong, but that sounded like an insult."

He shrugged, and for the first time looked a little uncomfortable. "Hey, everyone's more fun when they lose a few inhibitions." He took the candle from her. "You know, if you drip candle wax on a man's bare chest—"

"You'll set his chest hair on fire?" *Now* she was getting mad. "I guess you were never more fun then, because you didn't have any inhibitions to lose."

"Yeah. Hot wax would burn like hell. Warm chocolate syrup might be fun, though. Have any in the kitchen?" He reached across the barrier of the basket and tugged at a piece of her hair. She jerked her head away and smoothed the hair back into place.

"Getting a little ticked off, are we?" He didn't try to hide his laughter.

"Never." She yanked a bag of potpourri from the basket and slapped it down on the couch with such force the cellophane split. Unidentified dried vegetation drifted around her on a sea of flowery scent strong enough to clog her nasal passages. "I never get upset."

"What the hell is that?" She'd finally found something to put him in full retreat. He slid to the end of the couch and eyed the bits of leaves with suspicion.

"Flower Garden of Desire." Lord, what a mess. She'd have to drag out the vac after he left.

His bark of laughter startled her.

"You're kidding. No man in his right mind would give that kind of junk to a woman."

She narrowed her gaze. "A sensitive man would."

"Who is this secret admirer?"

"I don't know. If I knew, then he wouldn't be a secret admirer anymore, would he?" Uh-oh, time for a shift in topic. "So what've you been doing with your life lately, Sloan? Last I heard, you were working for some electronics company. And before that it was public relations. I've lost track of the others."

He shrugged. "Oh, this and that."

A dreamer. Sloan Mitello has been a dreamer in high school, would always be a dreamer. Just like her dad.

"Anything permanent?" Dreamers might be great men, but they made lousy providers. Always moving onto the next big dream, then when that failed, moving onto another, then another.

"Sorta."

"So let's hear about it." Dreamers dragged their families

along for the ride, getting up hopes that the next venture would be the big one. It never was. She knew. Been there, done that.

"I have a business, Jenny." He edged closer again.

"Where?" Maybe she'd misjudged him.

"On the internet."

Not substantial enough. A business should be something you could touch, go to each morning at nine o'clock.

She gave herself a mental head-slap. *He doesn't have to own a Fortune 500 company to be great in bed.* "What's the name of your business?"

He glanced at his watch. "Sorry, I didn't realize how late it was. I have two more baskets to deliver. Look, I'll get back to you."

Oh-no. She couldn't let him go yet. They hadn't worked out a fling arrangement. If she wasn't such a wimp, they'd be in her bed by this time. But she was a wimp, and she couldn't abandon completely the habits of a lifetime. She had to work up to things slowly.

Okay, relax. Carole said he was staying till after Christmas. You can just order another basket. Lucky she was on vacation from work till after Christmas. She'd have plenty of time to orchestrate this fling.

Her panic eased. But before he left, she wanted to know something. "What's the name of your business?"

He'd risen and was already at the door. Opening it, he glanced back and smiled. "Desiresfulfilled dot com." Then he quietly closed the door behind him.

Jenny sat amid the clutter of the basket she'd ordered for herself. Desiresfulfilled dot com? Sounded like a porn site to her.

CHAPTER TWO

Sloan shifted the candy-cane shaped basket onto one hip so he'd have his other hand free to ring Jenny's bell. Her secret admirer had struck it lucky this time. When Sloan had seen the garbage the guy had ordered for this second basket, he'd dumped it and filled it with really great stuff. He hoped Carole never found out.

What kind of guy would send a woman something called Flower Garden of Desire? A loser, that's who. He didn't deserve Jenny.

Jenny. He closed his eyes, remembering every expression in those big blue eyes, the slide of her hair over his fingers, the scent of warm woman. Yep, Jenny Saunders had changed.

He'd been interested in high school, but he'd seen past her smart mouth and known she wasn't ready. Besides, he'd had worlds to conquer. He'd gotten a scholarship to Berkeley and headed for California. Between study and work, he'd been too busy or too broke to make many trips home. And when he had, Jenny had been away. But things were different now.

Even though he hadn't seen much of Haddonfield in ten years, Carole had kept him in touch. She'd told him every time one of Jenny's boyfriends bombed. Sloan smiled.

He glanced down at the basket balanced on his hip. He

never did baskets. Now if you had a desire to own a castle for a day or to go diving for the Loch Ness Monster, Sloan Mitello was your man. But this once . . .

This basket was a winner. He'd slaved over a hot stove making Jenny's favorite cream-cheese-and-olive sandwiches. Okay, so the stove had been stone cold, but anything he did in the kitchen that had more than two steps—take out of fridge, then nuke in microwave—was hard labor.

He rang the bell. He had time on his hands, and the holidays were for fun. Besides, someone had to save her from this secret admirer jerk.

He shifted the basket. She was probably checking him out through the peephole now, trying to decide if she'd pretend she wasn't home. *Come on, Jenny, open the door.*

A minute later, he huffed out on a puff of impatience, and started to turn from the door. Probably better to walk away now. Besides, why give some loser credit for those cream-cheese-and-olive sandwiches?

She opened the door.

He didn't question his spurt of gladness. "Secret admirer basket number two. Special delivery."

"This late? I thought it'd be . . ." She cast him a startled glance, then bit her lip.

"Thought it'd be what?"

"Nothing." Her leopard-print robe stopped at mid-thigh, and her red hair was tousled. She gazed at him with sleepy uncertainty. He eyed the leopard print. Maybe there really was a wildcat in there somewhere. Hey, a guy could hope.

Her bottom lip was full, moist, and he drew in his breath on the sudden desire to taste that lip, trace it with his tongue, explore the sweetness of her mouth. Body parts responsible for signaling approval applauded wildly.

"Don't you believe in calling, Sloan? It's eight o'clock at night."

Jenny's words said one thing, but her glance said another. Her gaze slid past him, never quite making eye contact. Nervous? Why?

"I'm glad to see you, too." He walked in without her invitation. "I'm the king of impulse. One of my endearing qualities." He set the basket in the exact middle of her couch so she wouldn't have to build a barricade between them.

He sat down beside the basket. "Come look at your basket."

"Mine?"

"Sure. Says right here, from your secret admirer. Hope he had better taste this time." Wow, would you look at those legs? Long, smooth, forever. He watched her walk to the couch and sit down.

"Look, it's eight o'clock, and I was in bed."

His mental video fast forwarded. *Her bed.* A tangle of white sheets. She'd have white sheets because Jenny was a white-sheet sorta woman. A life-was-real, life-was-earnest kind. But she'd look great on those white sheets, her nightgown riding up those incredible thighs to . . . He hit the stop button. *Whoa tiger.* "In bed? You were in bed at eight o'clock? No one's in bed at eight o'clock."

She shrugged. "I'm a morning person. I like to get a head start on my work."

"Break the rules for once, Jenny. The night is young. Open your basket. I want to see."

She sighed. "You're not going to go away, are you?" No matter what her mouth said, her eyes said "stay."

"Not a chance. Let's see what's in the basket."

She sat down on the other side of the basket. Her robe hiked up another few inches. He didn't notice, but his body did. His body passed on the information.

He watched her gingerly pull a gold box from the basket. "Godiva Chocolates? Chocolate is bad for you."

"Godiva is good for you. Trust me." This wasn't the Jenny he'd known. The Jenny he'd known could be bribed with chocolate to do any number of things, like research papers . . .

He tried to ignore other, more interesting possibilities. What kind of woman thought Godiva wasn't good for her? Godiva was desire, sex, and orgasm wrapped in one gold foil package.

Then he remembered. Third grade. The spider. He grinned. "Relax, Flame. No spider this time. Besides, you broke my young heart. That spider was my most prized possession, and you rejected it. Loudly."

She returned his grin as she reached into the basket and lifted out his bag of sandwiches. "Cream-cheese-and-olive sandwiches? Ohmigod, real cream-cheese-and-olive sandwiches!"

"This guy must know you pretty well."

"I guess he does." Her voice was husky as she looked up from the sandwiches.

This was *not* feeling too great. It didn't make sense. He was mad at this secret admirer jerk who *hadn't* sent the basket that was making Jenny all emotional. Go figure.

"What else is in here?" She rooted around and pulled out his homemade ticket with the word "fun" scrawled across the top. Frowning, she read it. "A ticket to the West Street Holiday Light Show?"

"Wow. Imagine that. The guy has good taste after all. Remember? That's the neighborhood where everyone decorates their houses with lights and makes the electric company happy for a whole year. We went there at Christmas during senior year."

She shook her head. "I don't have time for that kind of thing anymore."

He stood. "Get dressed. Let's go."

"No." She bit her lip. "We could just stay here and . . . talk."

"No?" Some women *really* had a tough time having fun. "Here this guy spent time making the ticket and you won't even use it."

"It was a waste of his time." She stood, probably signaling he'd used up his allotted ten minutes of her life.

"It was only a waste of time if you don't use it." Sloan wondered about her nightgown. He pictured short and sheer, clinging to full breasts, flat stomach, and curving hips. He'd always pegged Jenny as a pj type of woman.

She picked up a piece of chocolate and absently unwrapped it. "If I go with you now, I'll be tired in the morning."

Exasperation made him want to storm out of her apartment, but something held him in place. Maybe it was the past, the memory of them watching an old movie together, having fun together.

Cut the sentimental crap, Mitello. Admit it. She's a beautiful woman, and you want her. Simple.

He stood. She backed away. He moved forward. She backed away. Finally, her back against what he assumed was her bedroom door, she held the chocolate between them like a small talisman.

His body tightened with his need to reach around her and open that door, to back her across her bedroom, to fall with her onto those white sheets. "Take a bite, Jenny." Anywhere would be okay. Well, almost anywhere. Love bites were an accepted precursor to . . .

"What?" Her eyes were wide, her lips slightly parted. He leaned toward those lips, pulled by a force stronger than gravity.

"Take a bite of the chocolate, Flame. It'll put you in the mood." Suspicion flickered in her gaze, but he caught a flash of excitement too.

"The mood for what?" He didn't mistake her breathless tone as she raised the chocolate to her mouth and bit off half of it.

A chocolate smear on her lower lip became a holy grail. "For having fun. What else?"

He braced his hands against the wall on either side of her head to help him withstand the pull of her lips.

No good. He was a goner. Lowering his head, he kissed her.

What was it about the taste of chocolate on a woman's lips, on *her* lips? The sweetness drew him. He ran his tongue lightly across her lower lip, savoring the promise, and when she parted her lips slightly, he didn't hesitate to taste more deeply.

Lost in the kiss, he drew her closer, and felt her still clutching the piece of chocolate between them, the soft pressure of her breasts, the hard pressure of his growing enthusiasm.

And knew he had to let her go. He sensed her hesitancy, her confusion. Knowing where he wanted this kiss to lead, Sloan darn well needed Jenny clear-headed and willing when it happened. Drawing back, he grinned. Okay, maybe not so clear-headed.

Jenny stared at the slightly flattened piece of chocolate she still held, then set it down. Not even Godiva could compare with that kiss.

Now. She could have her fling tonight. He was interested. He'd gone to the trouble of filling her basket. *He'd kissed her.* He'd invited her to look at Christmas lights with him. *He'd kissed her.*

All she'd have to do was open her bedroom door and invite him in. *No.* It was too soon. She always planned things carefully, allowing for all eventualities. She hadn't planned for tonight. He wasn't supposed to deliver the basket until tomorrow.

You are such a coward, Saunders. She'd been backpedaling since the moment he'd walked in, but she needed a little more time. After all, she hadn't seen him in ten years. He took a little getting used to.

Noticing the chocolate smudge on his shirt, she rubbed at it with her finger, felt his sudden intake of breath at her touch, and smiled. "Sorry about your shirt."

She wouldn't mention the kiss. *But she'd think about it.* It was the joy of a windfall profit, the excitement of tax time. Hmm. Both great things, but they didn't quite compare to *The Kiss.*

"So will you go with me to the light show?"

His voice still held the huskiness she imagined it would have just after waking, or just after making incredible love. *With her.*

Don't blow it now. "I'll . . . change." Reaching behind her, she opened the door, slipped into her bedroom, and slammed the door shut. *Making incredible love with her.* The thought took her breath away.

Ten years ago, had it occurred to her? Sure, but she'd been smart enough to realize Sloan Mitello was a dreamer, and she didn't want any kind of emotional involvement with a dreamer. But a fling? A fling didn't need a lot of emotional involvement.

Pulling on her jeans, she let her thoughts drift back to his kiss. It was . . . the tartness of just-squeezed lemonade, the sweetness of saltwater taffy.

Both things that were bad for her. Lemonade gave her heartburn, and saltwater taffy was pure sugar. She avoided them.

But what could it hurt to go out with an old friend? Besides, she needed time to plan every step of her fling. She ignored the jeering cluck clucks from her personal truth monitor.

"I don't know, Sloan. Looks like an awful lot of work, putting up all those lights." She snuggled against the warmth of Sloan's side as they stopped to admire another house covered with thousands of fairy lights. "And the electric bill will probably settle the national debt." Sloan's arm across her shoulders was nice, but she would *not* miss it when her fling was over. And her truth monitor was *not* at this very minute writing up a lying ticket.

She felt his frustrated exhalation. "Just enjoy it, Jenny, then walk away. You don't have to pay the bill."

Glancing up at him, she wondered. Someone had to pay for all the flash and beauty. And what if you couldn't walk away? "I pulled up your website last night. Fulfilling people's dreams must be a pretty tall order."

"Desires, Jenny. I fulfill people's desires."

"Same thing."

"Uh-uh. Dreams are what you have when you sleep. They're soft and blurred around the edges. Desires are grounded in reality. They're hard and passionate. Challenging."

"But how reliable are they? What if one month people decide they don't want any desires fulfilled? Who pays your bills?" She could feel his growing frustration, sensed a pending explosion.

"I pay my bills."

"But suppose you wanted to get a loan. No loan officer

I know would pay out a penny to someone who made desires come true. Besides, if you make people's desires
come true, then they don't have them anymore. They're
worse off than before. Sounds cruel to me." Any minute
now he'd blow. She could feel his tension in the clench-
ing of his hand on her shoulder, knew she was purposely
goading him, and hadn't a clue why.

Her truth monitor pulled out a fresh pack of tickets
and began writing up a bald-faced-lie citation. Fine.
She'd liked his kiss, realized it was driven by frustration,
and wanted to experience it again.

Besides, she'd finally figured out what his kiss was. It
was . . . *summer*. Warm sand, blazing heat, crashing waves
that took your breath away, and a dangerous undertow
that would knock you off your feet if you weren't careful.
Yep, definitely summer.

Of course, summer was bad for her too. Scratchy sand
on neon-red sunburn. Waves and undertow that conspired
to drown her. Guess she'd have to avoid summer . . . after
her fling.

"People never run out of desires, Flame. I bet even you
have some."

"Even me? That was meant as an insult, but you know
something, it wasn't. Dreams, desires, whatever, are hope-
builders. They're not for me." She'd been about ten when
she vowed never to follow any of life's yellow brick roads.

He'd stopped to gaze at a huge house that would've put
Buckingham Palace to shame. Cost? Probably in the ob-
scene range, with the same number of twinkling lights.
She felt like shielding her eyes from the glare. "Now I
know why my lights have been flickering. This place is
one giant power drain."

Sloan shrugged. "So the guy likes Christmas. What can I
say?" He turned to face her, his powerful body silhouetted

against the massive light display, his dark hair whipping in a sudden gust of cold wind.

And for a moment, she allowed herself a desire. Sloan bending over her as she lay on her white sheets, his long hair falling forward, strong tanned arms braced on either side of her as he moved closer and . . .

She smiled. That was one desire she intended to come true, as soon as she had everything planned with no chance of anything unexpected happening.

"Christmas is driven by merchandising. It's just an excuse to spend money." She gazed past him at the house. "This? This serves no purpose."

"This serves *my* purpose. I had this house built, Jenny. Ever wonder why I never invited friends over to visit when we were kids? Mom and I lived in a small apartment. Had to turn sideways to get around the one bedroom. I slept on the couch. And we never had Christmas lights. Most of the time we didn't even have a tree. No money." He allowed her to hear the edge in his voice.

His? She'd never guessed about his life. Carole had never said anything. "You're joking. Dreams don't buy this kind of place. Dreams don't buy much of anything."

Sloan dropped his arm from her shoulder, and she mourned the loss. "What do you have against dreams, Flame? The truth."

He wanted truth? She'd give him truth. "Dad is a dreamer. He filled my childhood with dreams. Next Christmas he'd get me a horse. After this deal came though we'd move into a nice house. And I believed him because he was my daddy and he'd promised. Until I got old enough to realize Dad's deals never came through, and I was never going to get that horse. We lived in dumps with barely enough to eat most of the time until we moved to Haddonfield and Mom got a pretty good job."

"There're worse things than not getting a horse."

"Sure." Like not believing in promises anymore. "Do you know how many Christmases I stood at my window waiting for that dumb horse?"

"So you signed off on all dreams?"

"Right." She narrowed her gaze on his house. "Of course, getting your desire might not be all that sensational."

"Hey, insult me, but leave my house alone."

She sighed. "Sorry. It just seems like an awful big place for one person to be rattling around in . . ." Uh-oh. Maybe he had plans to fill it with a wife who could fulfill all his desires.

He grinned. "Nope. Just me for now."

"Oh." Now there was a well-rounded response. "I guess I sound like the Scrooge of dreams, but you know, I really think dreaming is an addiction. After a while, the dream itself became Dad's fulfillment." She looked away. "I even wonder if dreaming might be hereditary. There're times when I want . . ."

"Want what, Jenny?" His voice. Warm, *tempting.*

"Nothing." She looked back at him. "Nothing at all."

"Hmm." He didn't sound convinced.

She glanced at the fairy-trail of twinkling lights, and knew there was nothing left to say. Nothing left to share. They didn't have a darn thing in common. *Except that incredible kiss and the fling she intended to have with him.*

His huff of resignation formed a small cloud in the frigid air. He put his arm around her and turned her to face him.

She noticed a few stray snowflakes drifting around him, and when one settled on his lips, she reached up and touched it with her fingertip, felt it melt beneath her body heat, felt the softness of his lip.

Before she could withdraw her finger, he clasped it and drew it into his mouth. With hooded gaze, he watched her. The moist heat of his mouth threatened to turn her whole body liquid, like spring's first hot assault on winter's last snowman.

She could feel the rhythmic stroke of his palm up and down her back, her nipples' sudden sensitivity. And when, for a moment, he pulled her against him, the hard thrust of his body between her thighs assured her he felt the same.

He released her finger, and she backed away from him, her breaths coming in quick gasps that had nothing to do with exertion. *This is what you wanted.*

His hard face creased into a smile that would've convinced Little Red Riding Hood and all her extended family to climb into bed with him.

He drew his bottom lip between his teeth, and she wanted him to kiss her so badly she felt the ache all the way to . . . She clenched her thighs to hold the ache in.

"It's funny. We come from the same kind of background, but you settled into a nose-to-the-grindstone job and I—"

"Settled into a life of drifting." Oops. Maybe she'd been a little too blunt.

Placing his arm across her shoulders, he forced her to face his house. "You know, sweetheart, you've given me a reason to stop my no-account drifting for at least a week. I'm going to be the guy who brings Christmas back to you."

He leaned close. "Ever lived inside someone else's dream, Flame?"

CHAPTER THREE

"Why would I want to do that? Living inside your dream could be real scary." Amazing. She was shivering in the cold, but the place where his arm rested was toasty warm. "Besides, I thought you said they were desires."

"For the experience. If you don't have any dreams of your own, you might enjoy living someone else's second-hand." Lifting his arm from her shoulders, he reached beneath the collar of her coat and gently massaged the base of her neck. "And you're not ready for desires yet. Dreams become desires."

If he thought that would relax her, he was mistaken. Neck nerves screamed "He's touching me!" then galloped off to spread the news to her brain. Her brain was a notorious gossip. Details would be all over the neighborhood in seconds.

"One week till Christmas, Flame. Live my dream with me. Why not? It might be the only one you ever have."

He'd moved close, and his warm breath fanned her neck; his husky murmur fanned her imagination. This was it. Her moment of truth. She swallowed hard. Okay, maybe she could put if off for a few more moments. "I guess you really must be settling down, Sloan. When're you moving into your house permanently?"

He looked as though her question had surprised him.

"Soon. I came here this week to make sure everything's ready. Then I'm flying to California to—"

She couldn't stand it anymore. "Exactly *what* are you offering?" If she was jumping out of a plane without a parachute, so be it. But she had to know.

He shrugged, then smiled. His smile was the promise of all things dark and delicious. "Whatever you *want* me to be offering, Flame."

That was pretty clear. "Okay, let's get this deal straight. I live in your energy-efficient castle for a week, enjoy your dream, however misguided, then go home. End of experience."

"Bare bones? I guess that's it."

"But what will I *do* for a whole week?" *Besides have hot sex with you as soon as I get up the nerve to suggest it.*

He exhaled sharply. "Right. You need a job description. How about decorator? I need some feminine input for the color schemes in a few of the rooms." His lips curved up in a take-me-to-bed smile. "Do a good job and you might even get a visit from Santa."

"Bribery? Sounds like bribery to me, Mitello." She'd *really* rather do this in the familiarity of her own apartment, but Mrs. Clark downstairs would be whacking her ceiling with a broom handle at the first sound of a banging headboard.

Besides, after this week is over, do you want to go to bed each night with the image of Sloan's body beside you, the remembered warmth of his hand on your breast, the scent of him clinging to your dreams, the sound of his breathing haunting the silence of dark nights?

This was supposed to be a fling. Short, sweet, and over. She didn't want to climb into bed with his memory every night. It would be better if she stayed at his house.

He shrugged. "It's all about incentive, Flame. What do you have to lose? You might even learn something about desires. For example, mine paid for this house." He pulled her against his side again as another cold blast swirled around them.

For a moment, she allowed the flex of his hip to distract her. "What do I have to lose?" *My virginity.* A hoped-for outcome. "Nothing, I guess."

"Afraid, Flame?" His words were soft, almost lost in the whistling wind. "Afraid you might like it too much here? Afraid that deep down where the real Jenny Saunders lives there's a dreamer? Someone whose dreams could turn to desires?"

"Of course not." She *wasn't* like her father. She'd never be like her father. *But are you sure?* "I don't have anything to prove to you."

"When was the last time you had fun? I bet you haven't done anything just for the hell of it since the mud puddle."

She smiled. She'd forgotten all about the mud puddle. A warm June afternoon after a heavy shower. It was still Senior Week, and everyone was still crazy. A walk in the woods where they'd found this big muddy spot. She'd caught him off balance and pushed him in. He'd stripped down to his shorts, then he'd taunted her. "Afraid of getting dirty?" His tactics hadn't changed much.

She hadn't stripped off her shorts or top, but she couldn't resist his dare. They'd laughed and rolled in that mud until she couldn't laugh anymore. If she closed her eyes she could almost breathe the heavy humid air, feel the slickness of his skin beneath her fingers. *His skin.* Strange she'd remember that.

"Well?" He sounded a little anxious.

Good. She wasn't finished thinking about that mud.

*Admit it. The thought of rolling around in slippery mud now
with Sloan Mitello is . . . dangerous ground. Literally.*

"You gonna walk away from it?"

She smiled. *Not until I can tell Carole I did it six times in
one night.* "Okay, but you might live to regret this." She
cast a speculative glance at all his lights. "Make sure you
show me where your ciruit breakers are."

He hugged her close. "Will do."

Her moment of bravado oozed out all over the sidewalk. She'd agreed. She was committed. By the time she
walked away from Sloan's house, she'd be a woman of the
experience that worried her.

They'd gone back to Jenny's apartment, gathered her
things together, and were now climbing the stairs to her
room in his house. And Sloan still wasn't sure what this
was all about.

Sure it was physical, but physical didn't have to be in
his house. Physical could be anywhere.

Question. Why had he fed her that hokey line about
bringing Christmas back to her? He didn't want to be *involved*. So now he was trucking up the stairs of his house
loaded down with her stuff. *That* sure seemed involved to
him. Didn't make sense.

At least she wouldn't be getting anymore secret admirer's baskets for at least a week. He smiled as he opened
her door.

"*This* is my room?"

Sloan nodded. He'd looked forward to her expression
of horror. Jenny didn't disappoint.

"Santa's behind is sticking out of the fireplace. I can't
believe you got *all* twelve days of Christmas in one room. I
hope that's an artificial partridge. Why is Rudolph standing on the mantle? I can't sleep with twinkle lights around

my bed and a tree next to me. I *never* liked camping out."
She twirled in a circle looking for new complaints.

"Oxygen."

"What?" She focused her outraged gaze on him.

"The tree will supply oxygen so you'll be able to breathe
between complaints."

"Look, this was your idea." Her gaze was now focused
on the top of the tree. "This whole house is frenetic.
Don't you yearn for one spot that isn't overflowing with
holiday spirit?"

He shrugged. "Not really. I have a whole childhood of
holiday spirit to catch up on."

She still stared at the tree top. "Well guess what? This
room is going to be your calm spot in a sea of celebration,
because first thing in the morning I'm going to ban all
holiday spirit from this room."

His muttered "Scrooge" didn't break her concentration
on the top of his tree.

"You know, that's a really unusual ornament."

He glanced at the top of the tree in time to see a small
whiskered face emerge from the branches. He breathed
out a sigh of growing impatience. "That's Toby." Reaching up, he snatched the tiny white kitten off the tree.
"Sorry. I'll try to keep him out."

Sloan shifted his gaze away from Toby in time to catch
Jenny's transformation.

Her expression softened, her lips tilting up in a smile
that turned his insides to mush. Why couldn't she look
at *him* with that expression? Okay, maybe not that exact
expression. He'd like a little more lust in it, a little more
I-want-you-naked-in-bed-with-me.

"He's cute. Yours?" Her tone suggested surprise.

"Yeah. I came across this box of abandoned kittens yesterday, so . . ."

"You took him in."

He would've rescued a thousand kittens to have her look at him with exactly the expression she had now.

"That was sweet, Sloan." She moved to his side and reached out to stroke the kitten.

Her stroke didn't end with Toby, but continued up his arm until her fingers reached his hair. She smelled of cold air and warm woman.

Sloan couldn't help himself. Placing Toby on her bed, he reached out and traced the line of her jaw. Smooth. Determined. *Clenched.* He was making her nervous. But he couldn't help himself. Even if he sent her screaming into the night, he had to taste her one more time tonight. That was his immediate desire, and he rarely left desires unfulfilled, especially his own.

Transferring his hand to the back of her neck, he pulled her to him. As she turned her head against his shirt, he could hear her mumbling something about adjustment time and ahead of schedule. Made no sense to him.

He fingered the short strands of hair at the base of her neck. What a waste. He longed to run his fingers through silken flame, but he'd have to make do with something else tonight.

Gently, he kissed the soft skin beneath her ear, then ran his tongue the length of her neck to where the pale silk of her blouse stopped him. It would take no effort to lift the edge of the blouse and continue his journey. His body was already making travel arrangements, and his bags were packed. He shifted to relieve the pressure.

Her soft sigh moved against his chest, warming him from the inside out. He gently turned her face up to him and kissed her forehead, then the end of her nose, then . . .

Then he moved away from her.

She wasn't ready. Her cheeks were flushed and her eyes bright, but he sensed her inner trembling, her tenseness. She hadn't been ready in high school either, and he'd walked away from her. Not this time. He'd give her some space and his own personal brand of attention, and by the end of the week . . . He smiled. She'd be ready.

"I guess I'd better unpack, then get some sleep. It's been a long day." She bent down and unplugged the twinkling lights. "Talk about sugarplums dancing . . ." Absently, she pulled her blouse away from where it clung to her breasts. "I guess you have things to do, so you can leave."

The outline of her breasts, which no amount of blouse adjusting could hide, didn't say "leave." The flick of her tongue across those luscious lips didn't say "leave." *Nothing* about her said "leave."

"Right. Leave." *Relax.* But he wasn't in relax mode. He had to get out of here before he did something that would definitely prove *his* readiness. "Sleep tight, Jenny."

As he shooed Toby out, then shut the door behind him, he got a final glimpse of her bemused expression. Was there a little bit of regret in her gaze? A little bit of sexual frustration in her clenched fists? He hoped so.

Because his whole body was vibrating with sexual readiness, with heat and want and *denial*. Incredible. No matter how often he reminded his body that this was Jenny, his old *pal*, his body ignored him. Its chant of "Sex, sex" was getting to be a real pain. Literally.

Sloan Mitello wasn't into pain. He was into fulfilling desires, his own as well as other people's. Even though Jenny wouldn't believe him, he had quite a few unfulfilled desires. Now might be the time to check off one of them. A minor one, granted, but one with tantalizing possibilities.

Sloan walked to the back door, flung it open, and

stepped outside. He glanced at the ten-foot high wood fence surrounding his property, then strode along the path that wound between now-bare oaks and maples to the cleared area with the frozen pond.

He should be freezing, but his body's memory of Jenny was heated need. Snowflakes fell faster as he looked up at the night sky. He grinned. Showtime.

Methodically, he stripped off his clothes, then stood naked as the freezing crystals touched his body then melted, running in rivulets over his chest, his stomach, his thighs. Bracing his legs, he inhaled raggedly as needle-sharp pricks of coldness settled on the part of him that needed it most.

He pictured Jenny here beside him, her smooth body bare and gleaming in the snow's false light. She'd laugh and raise her arms to the drifting flakes. He'd watch the lift and thrust of her breasts, the flakes settling on each nipple, her nipples hardening. He'd reach for her, but she'd dance away as she reminded him, "Not ready, Mitello." Damn!

Closing his eyes, he wondered why the flakes didn't hiss as they touched him, forming a cloud of hot steam. Opening his eyes, he held out his hand to catch the flakes, then smoothed the coolness over his body. Flinging his head back, he felt the snow touch him everywhere like tiny fingertips.

Exhaling sharply, he glanced down. Nothing short of an ice bath would affect his body's hot-and-hard mind-set.

The slam of a closing window shifted his attention.

Jenny.

He turned the thought over in his mind, enjoyed the possibilities. Hmm. Maybe she wouldn't dream of sugarplums tonight. A man could hope.

Gathering up his clothes, he carried them back to the house. No use putting them on when he was going straight to his shower. His *warm* shower, then to his hot dreams.

Just before going inside, he glanced up at Jenny's window. Dark. He smiled.

CHAPTER FOUR

Jenny crept from the window. She'd opened the darned thing to cool off her hot thoughts of Sloan. But after what she'd seen, she might never have a cool thought again.

When she was sure he'd gone inside, she plugged in the twinkle lights. She didn't want the bright light of a bedside lamp to draw his attention if he went outside again. Mesmerized, she watched the blinking little lights do an uncoordinated dance around her bed.

Sloan had changed her concept of "snowman" forever. In the shifting shadows cast by the lights, she could still see him standing naked in the falling snow, his head thrown back, hair a dark halo framing a face etched with need. For *her*. His hard body gleaming against a white background. Aroused. For *her*.

For the first time since this new Sloan rang her doorbell, she felt confident. She could do this. She *wanted* to do this.

With renewed determination, she picked up the phone to call Carole. She needed to let her friend know where to reach her.

While Carole's phone rang, she sat down on the bed facing away from the door and window, but that did little to erase Sloan's image from her mind. Finally, Carole answered her phone with a sleepy hello.

"Sorry, Carole. I didn't realize how late it was."

"Jenny?" Carole's voice lost its sleepiness. "So what happened? Did it work?"

"The basket was perfect, and I'm staying with Sloan this week. He's interested and I'm ready. If everything goes as planned, I'll have my fling by the end of the week. Then I can go home and get on with my life." A breath of cool air played across the back of her neck. She mustn't have closed the window tightly.

"This could lead to greater things, girlfriend. Maybe you and Sloan can work on a longer relationship."

"Not likely." Jenny smiled. Since her marriage, Carole had turned from confirmed single-forever-and-proud-of-it to dedicated matchmaker. "Sloan's a great guy, but he's fling material, not a long-term relationship kind of man."

"You don't know that for sure."

"Sloan's a dreamer, just like Dad. He might be successful right now, but a dreamer's world can collapse at any moment." *She knew.* "No, I'll have my fling with Sloan, then down the road a while I might meet a nice stable guy with a dependable nine-to-five job and I'll marry him."

"Boring, Jenny. Really boring."

She didn't want to get in an argument with Carole when she had plans to make. "Anyway, I'm ready for my fling. Talk to you after it happens." She hung up before Carole could mount another defense of Sloan.

"To paraphrase an old Hanes commercial, you're not ready until *I* say you're ready."

Ohmigod. She turned slowly. Sloan leaned casually against the frame of the open door. "Why didn't the door squeak? Every door should squeak."

"That's quite an opinion you have of me, Flame."

He wore only a towel wrapped around his waist, and despite her horror, Jenny's gaze was drawn to the muscular length of him. Obviously her optic nerves were *not* in sync with her brain.

He dropped several towels on a chair near the door. "Thought you might need these."

"I'm sorry you heard that, Sloan. Do you want me to leave?" She didn't *want* to leave, not when she was so close.

He raised an eyebrow. "Did I say that? Besides, where else will you find such a convenient *fling*?"

Jenny winced. He was right. She'd never find someone this right again. "So where do we go from here?"

He shrugged away from the doorframe. "When I feel you're ready, I'll give you your 'fling.'"

"So you're saying you'll call the shots?" She didn't like it, but she'd have to agree if she wanted to stay.

"Pretty much." He smiled. Not a nice smile. "One thing I need to know. Where'd you get your opinion of me?"

She drew in a deep breath. He deserved the truth. "I went to school with you, remember? You always had some wild scheme that never panned out. And as far as I can see, you've drifted from one thing to another since you graduated. This house is great, but it could be gone tomorrow." *So could you.* She'd never give her heart to someone she couldn't depend on. "I know you, Sloan Mitello."

For the first time, she glimpsed anger in his eyes. "You don't have a clue who I am, who I *really* am. You're too busy with your preconceptions to find out." He turned from her. "See you tomorrow, Flame." He was gone.

Jenny lay down and closed her eyes. What a mess. But things would look better after a good night's sleep.

She fell asleep on her side, one hand clenched between her thighs. Protection or invitation? Her last thought left things open to discussion.

The decorations were falling off the tree. She refused to open her eyes when the first one bounced off her chest, then crawled to the side of her neck and curled up against her. Even when the second one landed on her head, then tangled itself in her hair, she didn't open her eyes. It was the third one, the one that landed on her feet, then bit her big toe, that did it.

She forced her lids open. Three pairs of big eyes in little fuzzy faces peered at her. None was Toby. One was orange, one was gray, the last was calico. If the old tale of each color standing for a different daddy was true, then mama cat had been a very busy lady. No virginity issues there. "Go away and leave me alone, fuzzies."

"I'm afraid that won't be possible, madam."

"What?" She bounced to a sitting position and came face to face with the Ghost-of-Christmas-Best-Forgotten.

"Mr. Mitello called this morning and employed me to take care of you during your stay here. I've cooked breakfast. Eat it." His nose gave new meaning to patrician, and his eyes were almost crossed from looking down it at her.

"I don't eat breakfast, and who're you?" She hugged her jammies tightly to her and slipped a tentative toe to the floor.

"You do now, and I'm Ridley." He was a caricature of all the uppercrust servants that ever lived. Or died, in Ridley's case.

She glanced at the tray he'd set down on her bedside table. Ugh. Oatmeal. "I don't like oatmeal."

"You will drink the orange juice and eat some of the oatmeal before you set one tootsie out of this bedroom." He glared at her. "Madam."

"Now just a minute . . . Ridley. I don't have to—"

"Mr. Mitello won't be pleased to learn I made something

you don't like. He might even fire me. I have twelve grandchildren." He paused to let the number sink in. "All expecting gifts for Christmas."

"Oh." Emotional blackmail. She was a sucker for it. No matter how she felt about her own dreams, she didn't have the heart to stomp on Ridley's. "Well, maybe just a bite."

She was on her fifth spoonful of sticky oatmeal, trying for six, when Sloan appeared. He filled the doorway, bringing with him the scent of snow and woodsmoke, and the memory of what they'd said to each other last night.

Dressed in white T-shirt and worn jeans, he was every woman's fantasy of a bad man who'd make it good for her.

And he would be *her* fling. He'd promised. When she was ready. Of course, she was ready now. She was sure of it.

"How's it taste, Flame?"

"It'll be delicious." Position ten on Carole's video. She could hardly wait.

"Ridley, make sure you cook oatmeal every morning for Jenny." Sloan smiled, his gaze cool and knowing.

"I live to cook, sir." Ridley cast Jenny an innocent glance, picked up her abandoned tray, then made a dignified exit.

Sloan walked over to Jenny's bed and sat beside her. After depositing the three kittens on the floor, he cast her an amused glance. "So . . . you love oatmeal, do you?"

When would he mention her fling? "I hate oatmeal. I was eating for Ridley's twelve grandchildren."

"Ridley doesn't have any children, *or* grandchildren." He glanced at the kittens, who were making a determined effort to scale the comforter.

She couldn't see his expression. Should she apologize for what she'd said last night? *When would he mention her fling?* "He lied to me? I can't believe he lied to me. Why did you hire someone who lies like that?"

He finally looked at her, and the wicked slant of his grin made her almost believe in the possibility of dreams. *Almost.*

"He told me he had to support his old and sickly parents."

"And?" She noted that his gaze had shifted to the top button of her pajamas.

"His parents died thirty years ago."

"And you still hired him?" Why were they talking about Ridley, and when would he mention last night?

"What can I say, his references were great." His gaze slid over her. "A person might lie to me, but if they have good references I could be persuaded to give them a second chance."

Come on, Sloan, get to the point. Jenny frowned. "Employers probably gave him good references so they wouldn't have to eat any more of his oatmeal." She cast him a suspicious glance. "He said you hired him to take care of me. Why?"

He loved it. The way she pushed out her lower lip when she frowned. The way she'd tried to be kind to Ridley. The way she thought she'd have her fling and walk away from him. "Since you don't have any dreams of your own, I thought I'd fulfill a few you *would* have if you believed—"

"Okay, okay." She put her hands over her ears. "Here's a dream you can fulfill. Get Ridley to order take-out for dinner."

"Done." He gently pulled her hands from her ears. "So, you think you're ready to have sex with a stranger."

"No." She averted her gaze, staring at the twinkling lights by her bed. "I mean, yes. You're not a stranger."

"Sure I am. It's been ten years, Flame. Do you know all the places I've been, all the things I've done? Or do you only know what Carole told you, what I told you the few times we communicated? Maybe you should run back to Lenny and his bagels. He'd be a lot safer."

"No." Her gaze never wavered from the lights. "Does Brinks deliver your electricity bill payment?"

"Let me worry about the electricity bill. Are you ready to do it right now?" Those pj's had to go. Since he'd done the naked-in-the-snow desire last night, he needed something new to replace it. How about a Jenny-hot-and-naked-in-my-bed desire? No, that wasn't new.

"Pretty blunt, aren't you, Sloan?" She finally looked at him.

"And you weren't? Could've fooled me."

"Okay, I'm sorry for some of the things I said, and I shouldn't have plotted behind your back. So consider yourself apologized to." She cast him a disgruntled look. "This is hard for me. You could be a little more subtle."

"Well hell, afraid I'm not a subtle kind of guy. If I'm going to be part of your fling, maybe you should tell me what kind of man I'm supposed to pretend to be." He probably shouldn't have given her that opening. He didn't like the glitter in her eyes.

"You have to be sensitive. I'm into sensitive." Her gaze turned thoughtful. "I like poetry. Maybe you could send me poems."

Cripes. She wanted a man who sent her poems? He'd never gotten past the "Mary Had a Little Lamb" stage in poetry. He'd thought a lot about Mary. *Without* her lamb.

"And you have to be a good dancer. I'd definitely want that."

Great. Some of the women he'd danced with had ended up needing foot surgery.

Her expression brightened. "Oh, and I'd like you to be thin and ascetic-looking with big soulful brown eyes."

Hmmph. A dead-ringer for the old hound dog he'd rescued when he was a kid. Sloan could starve himself for months and never qualify as thin and ascetic-looking. "Sounds like I'm a real fun guy."

"Yeah, and we could listen to chamber music on cold winter nights." She pursed her lips. "Do you like chamber music?"

"Depends on whose chamber we're doing it in." So he was a rhythmically and musically challenged, insensitive, over-muscled jerk. He'd deal with it. "Of course, as Mr. Perfect I won't have any dreams."

She didn't even blink. "None."

"Right." He watched her climb from bed, walk to the closet, then pull some clothes out. "Look, I have a few things to do. I won't be tied up long. Hope you won't be bored."

She shook her head and smiled, the first natural smile he'd seen this morning. "I have to check my e-mail, then I'm going to do a little redecorating here." She cast him an impish grin. "You did say you wanted some help with color schemes, didn't you?"

"Redecorate away." He rescued the kittens, who were stranded halfway up their own personal Mt. Everest, then turned and made his escape.

Jenny watched him close the door behind him. Why had she fed him that nonsense about what she'd want him to be? *Because you didn't have the guts to tell him he's perfect just like he is.* Wow, was she into self-honesty or what?

Fine. Three seconds of painful introspection were enough for one morning. She gazed around the room. Beautiful but busy. Sort of took after its owner.

She'd have to create her own island of serenity in this

room if she expected to survive the week. Besides, calming down the bedroom would take all her concentration. Wouldn't give her time to draw mental pictures. Like his bare legs tangled with hers on the bed, his bare body covering hers.

Passion led to dreams of more passion, and she had a suspicion that Sloan Mitello's lovemaking wouldn't be like a library book that you could renew if you weren't done with it.

Jenny glanced around the room. She'd worked her buns off, but it was worth it. Much better. She felt calmer already. She gazed at her laptop. No interesting e-mail.

She was about to shut everything down, but then she decided to take just one peek at Sloan's site. What damage could just one peek do?

Fascinated, she stared at the empty box on her screen. *Let us fulfill your desire.* No discussion of money, of contracts, just type in your desire. Made it sound so easy.

Of course, she wouldn't get sucked into something like that. Only a fool would believe you could make dreams come true so easily. Her fingers moved on the keys.

Surprised, she realized she'd typed something. "I remember the mud puddle." She felt a little embarrassed, and she hadn't a clue why. There was no reason to be embarrassed. Defiantly, she hit enter. She hadn't really voiced a desire, she'd just reminded him of old times. "So what's the big deal?"

There was no one to answer her question.

Leaving her room, she spent time scoping out the rest of the house. Wow. She'd never realized there were that many holiday decorations in the world.

And why did he need an indoor garden room complete

with mini-pond and waterfall? Sloan wasn't a sit-by-the-pond-and-ponder-life's-secrets kind of guy.

What did she expect? The Sloan she'd known ten years ago had been an ordinary guy. . . . Okay, so Sloan had never been quite *ordinary*. But this Sloan was larger than life, so she shouldn't be surprised when his house was over the top.

Where was he, anyway? Maybe she'd go back to her room and read for a while, get her mind off of where and when *it* would happen.

Deep in her book, she was startled by a knock. Dragging herself from the chair where she'd curled up, she pulled open the door.

"Hi, Flame. I thought you might . . ." He glanced into the room. "Sonovagun." Striding past her, he stopped and stared. "Who needs the Grinch when you have Jenny Saunders, Terminator-of-Holiday-Cheer?"

Maybe she'd gone too far. This might call for some soothing. A neck rub? It'd always worked on Mom when Dad had come home with a new scheme for making a million. Besides, she needed to get used to touching him in an impersonal way before . . . *Just do it.*

"Sit down, Sloan." She pushed him to a sitting position on her bed, then knelt behind him. Placing her hands on both sides of his neck, she gently massaged. Tight, very tight. And those were *her* muscles. His were even tighter.

"Relax and feel the calmness, the peace of this room," she murmured against his neck. "I didn't really change that much. The comforter is reversible. The ivory is much more calming than red and green. And I got rid of the tree and lights and Santa and—"

"Right. No big change." He moaned as she massaged

down his back to the base of his spine. "Damn that feels good."

No joking. Her hands were doing some serious shaking as she stroked his body, felt the bunch of muscles beneath her fingers. "I can feel you relaxing already."

"Sure. Relaxing." His breathing didn't sound relaxed. "I'm so relaxed, I think I'll lie down."

She moved out of his way as he lay down on his back. What to do?

He watched her out of half-closed eyes. He smiled. "Keep going. I can feel those muscles tightening again. All this white stiffens me right up."

She huffed. "All that white snow didn't stiffen you up last night," She considered her statement. "Okay, maybe it stiffened you a little." *Foot-in-mouth disease strikes again.*

His smile broadened, grew wicked. "What're you afraid of, Flame? I thought you said you were ready."

"I *am* ready." And Little Red Riding Hood thought *she* had problems with wolves in beds. But he'd given her the opening she'd been hoping for, permission to work her wiles on him.

Fine, so she didn't have any wiles, but she could learn. She straddled his hips. His growing interest in her relaxation technique was obvious, and she slid back and forth over it to make sure she was right.

Yep. Very interested. She must be working harder than she'd thought because she was gasping for air.

He closed his eyes, and his grin vanished.

Reaching under his shirt, she worked her fingers over his stomach, his chest, then paused when she reached his nipples. Gee, couldn't forget his nipples. Had to relax them too. Rolling them between thumb and forefinger, she clenched her thighs at his groan of pleasure.

She didn't know how much more relaxation she could

stand before she ripped his jeans off and planted herself on top of his—

"Dinner is served, sir."

No, no, no! She collapsed onto Sloan's heaving chest and completely agreed with his grunted four-letter appraisal of the situation.

She started to climb off, but he held her in place. "Get out, Ridley."

"As you say, sir."

She twisted her head so she could see Ridley. A Ridley who was the picture of expressionless calm. A Ridley who had a dirt smudge on his nose. She took courage from this small sign of human weakness.

Ridley backed from the room. "I'll see you in the morning, sir. And madam, your oatmeal will be ready at precisely eight o'clock." He closed the door on her reaction.

Arrgh. "If that man tries to con me into one more bowl of oatmeal, I'll—"

"Shh." Sloan put a finger to her lips, effectively silencing her.

Amazing, but any part of him touching her resulted in a complete loss of rational thought patterns. Now, what had she been saying?

"Guess the oatmeal killed the mood, huh?" He allowed her to climb off him, then stood.

She couldn't quite meet his gaze. "Umm . . ." Think. She knew thousands of words. So why couldn't she remember even one?

"Hope you like hoagies." He pulled down his shirt, then strode to the bedroom door.

"Hoagies?" Good. One word was better than none.

"Yeah. I had Ridley order them from Mario's. I told him to put everything on them. That okay?"

"Sure." Whoopie! She'd remembered another one.

"Then guess what, Flame?" He grabbed her hand and pulled her out the door.

Oh, no. She'd forgotten about the mud puddle. *Please don't let him say anything about the mud puddle.*

"After we eat, you're going with me to make someone's desire come true."

Thank you, God.

CHAPTER FIVE

"Ready to go, Flame?"

"Mmm." She closed her eyes as she savored the last bite of her hoagie. Not much on earth could compete with one of Mario's hoagies. The salami, the cheese, the peppers, the—

"Here's your coat." Sloan stood behind her chair.

"Hmm." She felt sort of guilty. Sloan had wolfed down his dinner, then gone off to change while her taste buds had wallowed in unrepentant gluttony.

"We can walk to Mary Kelly's place. Great exercise."

She swallowed, then narrowed her gaze as she turned to confront him. "Are you suggesting that . . ."

Her voice trailed off for lack of oxygen. *Santa Claus.* He was dressed as Santa. A very sexy Santa, pillow-enhanced stomach and all. If he crawled down her chimney she wouldn't be waiting with just milk and cookies. "Why are you dressed—"

"I'll explain while we're walking." He bundled her into her coat, then carefully buttoned her up. One button at a time.

His knuckles grazed between her breasts. Lingered. She felt the pressure as though there was no flesh, no bone separating her heart from his touch. Her heart's pounding seemed to grow with each second his warm hand remained against her.

And when his fingers slid down to the button over her stomach, she almost gasped with relief. For a moment she'd thought she'd have to put her hand over her heart to keep it in.

Her stomach wasn't much better though. He slid his fingers under her blouse and laid his palm flat against her skin. She knew the sensation, had felt it this summer when her roller coaster car had hovered for what seemed like eternity above an endless drop. It was excitement, frightened anticipation, the need to scramble from the car before the plunge, the knowledge there was no escape. And as his fingers glided lower, scraping the top of her jeans, sliding between skin and cloth, she felt the earth drop from beneath her.

"I . . . I can finish that." Her fingers fumbled at the last few buttons, while he moved away from her.

"Right." His voice was rough as he strode to the door and yanked it open, letting in a blast of frigid air.

He didn't look to see if she followed, and she had to trot to catch up with his long strides. "What's Mary Kelly's desire, and why're you bringing me along?"

He kept distance between them, not glancing her way. "Mary can tell you her desire. And I brought you along to show you that desires *do* come true. Maybe not exactly when we want them, but more like when we *need* them, when it's *right* for them."

He laughed and shook his head. "Doesn't make a hell of a lot of sense, does it?"

She cast him a cautious glance. "Not exactly." She had to know something. "Did you make your desires come true at the right time? Wouldn't it have been better if you'd had all this when you were a kid?"

He finally looked at her. "Maybe, maybe not. If I'd had

all this when I was young, I might not have worked so hard, fought my way up to being a success. My desires were my incentive. What's your incentive, Jenny?"

She tugged the collar of her coat higher around her ears. "I don't need an incentive."

"Wow, what a woman. No dreams, no incentives. Self-motivated to the core." His glance mocked her. "But wait, there's a crack in your armor. Your dream about having a fling with some man."

Only with you, no one else. The truth leaped out and bit her before she could run. She wanted to squirm away from it, deny it, but it held on and tightened its grip. "You're good at twisting words, Sloan."

He ignored her comment. "What about happy, Flame? Are you happy with your life?"

"Sure, I'm happy. What's not to be happy about?" Her words came out in little white puffs of defiance.

"Hey." He held up his hand. "Just asking."

Strange, he was still fuming over the plan she'd cooked up with Carole and her assumption he was a doing-what-feels-good kind of guy. Sure, he wasn't into long-term relationships. And sure, any man would jump at the chance to have a fling with Jenny. So what was he so ticked off about? Damned if he knew.

But no matter how angry he was, he still wanted her to be happy in her life, not just in his bed. And it seemed to be getting more important by the minute. Why? The personal happiness of a woman had never driven his past relationships.

He cast her a sideways glance as she stomped along beside him. Didn't look like she was thinking happy thoughts right now.

Exhaling a breath of resignation, Sloan reached out

and clasped her hand. He was rewarded when she turned to him with a brilliant smile. She certainly had no trouble making *him* happy.

He kept her hand warm in his all the way to Mary's house. "Okay, go up, knock on her door, then when she answers, tell her you're Santa's helper, and he's on his way down."

She blinked. "Santa's *helper*? Down? Down where?"

He leaned over and kissed her on the nose. "Down the chimney. See you in a few minutes."

Sloan turned and strode toward the back of the house, where a ladder awaited him. He hoped to God Mary had had them build that chimney wide enough.

Jenny didn't give herself a chance to stand and ponder. Climbing the steps to the big old Victorian house, she rang the bell. No matter how crazy this whole thing seemed, she had to admit it was more fun than sitting in front of her computer looking for tax loopholes that Smith Inc. could crawl through.

The small gray-haired woman who opened the door was everyone's image of a grandmother. She offered Jenny a kind smile. "Yes, dear?"

Jenny waited expectantly for her next words which would obviously be, "Have a cookie." Nope. No cookie offer.

Okay, she could do this. Jenny opened her mouth and forced the ridiculous words past lips that hadn't uttered a ridiculous word in years. *Until Sloan Mitello rang your bell.* "Umm. I'm Santa's helper, and he's on his way down."

The small woman actually clapped her hands, and Jenny muttered a mental *Oh boy*.

The woman reached out, grasped Jenny's hand, and dragged her into the house. "Come in, come in, dear. I'm Mary Kelly and this is so exciting."

Jenny allowed herself to be led into a large living room that looked like it had been lifted from a Currier and Ives print. Large overstuffed chairs, doilies, knickknacks, a gigantic tree decorated with what must be hundreds of balls, and a huge fireplace that was blessedly, at least for Sloan's sake, unlit.

Now, how to phrase her question in a diplomatic way. "And what is Santa bringing you tonight?"

Mary laughed. "Oh, he's not bringing me anything tonight. I'm just going to sit on his knee and tell him what I want."

Jenny forgot about diplomacy. "Sit on his *knee?*"

Mary's smile widened. "Let me guess. Santa got you from the Santa's-Helpers-for-Hire temp service, and he hasn't had time to fill you in."

Jenny was past words. She nodded and cast a nervous glance at the chimney. If the scrabbling sounds on the roof were any indication, Santa was about to make a dramatic appearance. And not a minute too soon.

Mary laid a comforting hand on Jenny's arm. Jenny noted the boulder-sized diamond in Mary's ring and did some readjusting on her grandmother image. No flour-covered hands fresh from baking Christmas treats for the grandkiddies here.

"I'm not crazy, dear. Sit down, sit down." She pointed to the nearest chair. Jenny sank into the soft cushion and wondered if Mary would be interested in a trade for a designer couch. "I come from a family that didn't believe in filling children's heads with useless dreams. When my friends were standing in line at Wanamaker's to see Santa, I was being told there was no such person, and you only got in life what you worked for."

She sat down on the chair's arm and peered at the chimney where grunts and muttered curses echoed.

Jenny bit her lip to keep from grinning. No ho-ho-ho's. Maybe Santa shouldn't have chowed down on that last hoagie.

Mary sighed and glanced back at Jenny. "My parents were good people, but they didn't understand that everyone needs dreams, even if they're just small ones." Standing, Mary moved to the fireplace, knelt down, then peered up the chimney. Satisfied that Santa didn't need rescuing yet, she came back to Jenny's chair.

"By the time I was old enough to do what I wanted, I was also too old to sit on Santa's knee. Clients wouldn't have much confidence in me if they saw me sitting on Santa's knee in some mall." She patted Jenny's hand. "Their trust is so fragile."

Jenny was getting more and more concerned. *Come on, Sloan.* "What do you do?"

"I'm a corporate lawyer." Mary straightened the doily on the chair's arm.

Corporate lawyer?

Mary smiled. "My colleagues call me The Shark. A silly title, don't you think?"

Jenny gulped. "Right. Silly." Luckily, she was saved from having to make further comment as Santa's feet, legs, hips, and buns slid from the chimney. Then stopped.

"Where's the rest of Santa?" Mary sounded aggrieved. Half a Santa would probably be grounds for a breach of contract suit.

Jenny jumped to her feet and hurried to the chimney.

"Ho, ho, ho! Santa's stuck. Santa's helper needs to give Santa some help *now*." Santa did *not* sound amused.

Jenny felt she would explode with the effort to hold back her laughter.

"I had that chimney built specifically for Santa. Obviously the company didn't get the dimensions right. I'll talk to their lawyers tomorrow."

Somehow, Jenny felt sorry for the chimney builders. But she didn't have time to worry about anything right now except getting Sloan out of that chimney.

Wrapping her arms around his hips, she pulled. Nothing. Well, almost nothing.

Her cheek was pressed against his buns. Firm buns. Muscular buns. She could feel them clench. *A woman of experience would rub her cheek against them, maybe even indulge in some appreciative purring.* All she could manage was a rise in heat at the point of contact.

"Jenny?" His voice was husky, almost strangled. She hoped the sides of the chimney weren't pressing on any vital organs.

"What?" *A woman of experience would place her lips on one mouthwatering bun and slide her tongue across the rounded contour.* Too bad. There would be no Santa bun for Jenny. On the up side, she wouldn't have to worry about getting rid of the cotton taste.

"How're you doing, dear?" Mary's voice sounded anxious.

"Fine. Just fine." Snuggling her face against his bun, she gave another ineffectual yank. Darn, bun-lust had made her weak.

"Jenny!" Sloan's voice sounded desperate.

"Hmm?"

"I can't come out like this."

"Why not?" She was having a real hard time concentrating. She'd refocus. In a minute. *A woman of experience might gently nip his bun.* She considered it.

"Dammit, Jenny, move your hands up."

She blinked. What did her hands have to do with anything? But obediently, she slid her fingers up to his groin.

She widened her eyes at the same time she reluctantly dropped her hands from him. Wow. That certainly refocused her. She knew the many things an experienced woman would do with *that*. After all, she'd seen Carole's tape.

"Jenny, get Mary to pull me out." His words came in gasping breaths as though he'd just finished a race. "By the legs."

"Sure." She hadn't *wanted* to let go. She'd wanted to fill her hands with him, fill *her* with him.

She sure hoped Sloan decided she was ready soon. Not only was she ready, she was overripe and on the verge of falling off the vine.

"I . . . I can't budge him, Mary. You try."

Mary nodded. Taking Jenny's place, she wrapped her arms around Sloan's legs and yanked. He popped from the chimney like a champagne cork.

Keeping his back to them, he dusted himself off, then grabbed a pillow from a nearby chair. "Ho, ho, ho! Come sit on Santa's knee, Mary, and tell him what you want for Christmas."

Dropping into a chair, he plopped the pillow onto his lap, then patted his knee. Mary sat on his knee, then waited expectantly.

"Have you been a good little girl, Mary Kelly?" Sloan's breathing had returned to normal.

"Oh, yes." Mary frowned. "Except for maybe that hostile takeover, but that's not important."

"Well, tell Santa what you want him to bring."

Mary's eyes took on a predatory gleam. "I want a new Lexus. Black. I want a condo in Atlantic City near the casinos and with a water view. I want stock in Dell, Microsoft, and Amazon. Oh, and I need someone good to organize my home." She blinked. "I'm not being greedy am I, Santa?"

"Santa thinks you *deserve* those things. I'll be making

my list and checking it twice, Mary, and I'd just bet you'll have a very merry Christmas."

A *Lexus*? Jenny wondered how *she* could get on Santa's list.

Mary cast Jenny a sly glance. "Santa, there's someone else waiting to sit on your lap. I want her to go next."

"Me?" Jenny glanced behind her. Yep, no one else around. "I don't want anything for Christmas."

"Of course you do, dear." Mary's gaze sharpened. "This is part of my dream. I want someone else waiting to talk to Santa."

"Part of your dream, huh?" Jenny glanced at Sloan, who was frantically shaking his head. "Since you put it that way . . ."

Mary slipped off of Santa's knee, and Jenny sidled over to stand in front of him. No time like the present to start on this experience thing. If she was going to do it, she might as well do it right.

Jenny tried to control her smile. It wasn't her regular one. She could tell from the way her lips felt that it was a cat smile. If a cat could smile.

She drew her tongue slowly over her bottom lip and watched Sloan's eyes widen, then narrow. While he was busy interpreting the meanings of her cat smile and lip licking, she whipped the pillow from his lap and planted herself firmly in its place.

"Oh, my. Look at the time." Mary bustled toward the doorway. "I have to make a business call. Don't do anything important without me."

Jenny didn't even notice when Mary left. She was too involved with wiggling her bottom deeper into Santa's lap.

"That might not be the safest position, Flame." Sloan's low growl signaled the end of his Santa persona. "Could lead to a growing problem."

"It already is." Jenny couldn't control the breathless sound of her voice.

"Maybe we need to examine our option."

"Option? Singular? Maybe we need to enlarge our choices." She couldn't stop herself from sliding her bottom across his lap.

"I already have." He moved beneath her, the thrust of his hips strong. "And if you don't stop rubbing that tempting bottom against me, I'll exercise my option right now and disgrace the Santa image forever."

She opened her eyes wide. "And would that be your Option Claus?"

He buried his face against her neck and groaned. "That was awful, Jenny."

She breathed out, the sexual tension broken for the moment. "I guess I need to tell you what I want for Christmas."

"Hey, Santa's my name and gifts are my game. Let's hear it."

Okay, she wouldn't be greedy. She'd only ask for a few things. Nothing big or expensive. She *did* need a new couch.

"I want . . . a horse and some chocolate syrup."

CHAPTER SIX

Sloan was attuned to her every breath, every movement as they walked back to his house. She probably regretted her impulsive wishes already, but it was too late. Much too late.

The snow muffled their steps, but nothing could muffle the pounding of his heart, the surge of blood gathering in one strategic area, the desire that built with every white puff of breath he breathed into the cold air.

First things first. Reaching out, he took her hand into his. He felt the slight tremble of her fingers.

He said nothing, allowing the warmth to creep back into her hand, allowing the trembling to still. She had to sense the need that churned in him, that urged him to lay her down in the snowy bank beside that old maple tree and make love to her until the snow turned to steam.

"So, do you do those things often, Sloan?"

She wiggled her fingers in his hand, and he tightened his grasp. *No escape, Flame.*

"I *never* do those things. My assistants take care of the warm fuzzies. But Mary's a friend and lives close by, so I made an exception. I just do the interesting stuff." *Ask me what the interesting stuff is.*

She didn't ask. "Those were some pretty big promises you made to Mary. Won't she be disappointed on Christmas morning?"

He smiled. "Mary has four ex-husbands. All CEO's of major companies. You want to talk about power behind the throne? Let's just say each of them will ante up to keep Mary happy."

"How'd you meet Mary?"

"Through one of her ex-husbands. Even shiftless wanderers make friends once in a while."

She cast him a sharp glance. "You'll never forget what I said, will you?"

He smiled. "Not unless you give me a reason to."

She seemed lost in thought as they approached his house. He admired the blaze of light. His neighbors' puny efforts at tasteful holiday decorations paled in comparison.

"You know, I bet your house gives the airport fits."

He exhaled sharply. "Okay, I'll bite."

She slanted him a teasing grin. "How many planes have tried to land in your backyard because they thought they'd spotted the runway lights?"

He abandoned her hand and slid his arm around her waist, pulling her close. "What can I say? I'm a man of large appetites. I like bright lights, big houses, and warm women."

She molded herself closer to his side, and he tightened his grip. Funny how perspectives changed over the years. In high school, she'd been a pal. A little too serious most of the time. A little too disapproving of him.

Now? She'd never be just a pal to him again, not with the sizzle and spark that leaped between them. He was busy deciding how to explore all that sizzle and spark when he looked up to see Ridley waiting at the door. Not a good sign.

"Thought you were gone for the night, Ridley."

"Someone has to maintain your site, sir." He carefully

pulled a white handkerchief from his pocket and wiped a smudge of dirt from his face.

Jenny looked puzzled. "I didn't know you helped Sloan with his website, Ridley."

"I was *not* speaking of a website, madam." Dismissing Jenny, he turned back to Sloan. "I haven't the foggiest idea what you have in mind, sir, but making frequent trips to add water to it will, of course, count as overtime."

"Right. Overtime."

"You water Sloan's plants for him?"

"Hardly, madam." Ridley lifted his chin into the air and moved past Jenny.

Sloan watched Ridley climb into his car, then turned back to answer Jenny's obvious next question.

"What was he talking about, Sloan?"

Sloan rubbed the back of his neck to relieve the tension. "Who knows."

"You're lying. You always rubbed the back of your neck when you were lying."

Sloan dropped his hand. "Let's go in the garden room entrance."

"Why? What was Ridley talking about? What're you trying to hide? And why're we going in this entrance?"

Sloan turned his back to her barrage of questions as he unlocked the door, then turned around to face her.

"Why'd Ridley have dirt on his face? I don't—"

Wordlessly, he scooped her up in his arms, kicked open the door, stepped into the darkened room, kicked the door shut, then dropped her into his ornamental-pond-turned-mud-puddle.

Ignoring her shriek of outrage, he flipped on the dim lights hidden behind foliage. The many mirrors captured the scene of Jenny scrambling to her feet like some angry she-devil rising from a prehistoric swamp. At least he'd stopped her questions.

"You . . ." Words eluded Jenny. There weren't any that could describe her fury, her thirst for vengeance, her . . . *excitement.*

Sloan grinned at her, his smile a flash of wickedness in the almost-dark room. "Hey, I'm just granting your desire."

"I did *not* desire to be sitting in a mud puddle—"

"You typed it into my desire box."

"—with all my clothes on." She lowered her gaze to the area of his personal desire box.

"Then take them off, Flame. Take them all off."

His husky suggestion wrapped around her. *I want a bad man in the worst way.* Why not now?

Tonight, she'd get rid of her inhibitions along with her clothes.

Never breaking eye contact with the green glitter of his heated gaze, she stripped off her muddy coat and dropped it over the ornamental rocks beside the pond. "There's something more I forgot to type in the box."

"There's always room for more." His whisper promised that he was the king of more.

"A mud puddle's no fun alone." She couldn't believe she was about to venture into the dangerous area of *fun*, which had an infinity of answers.

She turned her back to him and quickly unbuttoned her blouse. Okay, no stress here. She'd just modify his take-them-all-off statement. She'd get down to bra and panties, then they'd roll around and laugh just like the other time. *Then* she'd be ready. Her truth monitor's cluck clucks were *really* getting on her nerves.

She watched him in the mirror. His gaze never left her as he stripped off his Santa suit . . . and everything else. He'd always been an all-or-nothing guy.

The room's glow highlighted his body in shades of gold and shadow, stole away the boy she'd known in high school and replaced him with a hard, dangerous stranger.

He stepped into the mud, moving toward her with the measured tread of a predator, sure of his prey.

She took a deep, steadying breath. *Can the melodrama, there's nothing hard and dangerous about him.* She glanced in the mirror. Okay, nothing *dangerous*.

Closing her eyes, she anticipated the moment he'd touch her, wondered if she'd feel anything different this time.

"Don't move." His voice was soft beside her ear. His breath, warm against her neck.

His fingers slid across her shoulders, down her arms, as he removed her blouse. When she felt his fingers move to the clasp of her bra, she could only shake her head.

"Whatever you want, Flame." His attention shifted. "It's your memory." Within seconds he'd removed her jeans.

Turning her to face him, he ran the tip of his finger down the front of her panties, paused between her legs. "Whenever you're ready." His whisper was hot need, and she clenched her legs against the urge to shout *yes*.

Too fast. Everything was moving too fast.

He was a dreamer. *I want him.* Okay, maybe he wasn't really a dreamer. After all, he had this place. *I want him.* He was totally right brained. Look at what he did for a living. Look at what he'd done to this house. *I want him.* Fine, so between his right brain and her left brain they'd have one whole brain between them. Good enough for one night of fun. After all, this was just a fling.

She wasn't sure. She didn't know. Biting her lower lip, she indulged in some mental hand-wringing.

"Shh." He slid his finger up over her stomach, between her breasts, and touched her lips.

"I didn't say anything." Should she close her lips around his finger, signaling that the fun could begin? Or should she bite him, thereby ending fun thoughts as he rushed to his local emergency room for rabies shots?

"Sure you did. I bet people blocks away could hear the battle between your brain and your baser instincts. Watch out. Baser instincts fight dirty."

While she was busy mulling that thought over, he slipped to his knees. All mulling came to a sudden halt as Sloan's hand glided up her bare leg.

"What do you remember most about the first time, Flame?" His hand continued up her thigh, and he fingered the lace at the edge of her panties.

Her legs wobbly, she sank to her knees in front of him. The mud felt cool against her heated flesh. "Mosquitos. Lots of mosquitos."

"Liar." Laughing, he pulled her down into the mud with him.

She squealed as he rolled her beneath him. Squealed? Clients would desert her in droves if they heard her. Squealing was not an accepted accountant noise.

She blinked up at Sloan. The truth? She didn't give a damn what her clients thought. She was having fun.

Suddenly, her laughter died. The mood shifted as he straddled her hips and studied her through eyes that gleamed beneath half-lowered lids. "I just remembered something."

"Uh-oh." She shifted her hips along with her attention to his most striking point of interest. *So close*. She could reach out and slide her fingers along his length, cup him in her palm—

"I remember writing a message on you."

She wanted to laugh, to restore the feeling of light-hearted fun. Nothing came out. "*On* me?"

"Yep." Slowly, he slid the mud over her stomach, and her stomach muscles clenched in anticipation. He allowed his splayed hand to rest there until his heat seeped into her, warming her. "Seemed like the right thing to do at the time."

"Sort of like when guys leave messages inside hearts on tree trunks? That kind of thing?" Her breathing quickened, her need to touch him, to clasp him in her hand, almost unbearable.

"I guess so." Dragging out the torture, he ran his fingers between her breasts, leaving a trail of mud and frustration.

Touch me everywhere. Now. "It must be a guy thing, like when bears leave claw marks on trees to mark their territory."

"Could be." Lingeringly, he molded each breast with his hand, then rubbed the pad of his thumb across each nipple.

Like a puppet whose strings were all attached to a master puppeteer, her hips arched at the bare-wire sizzle of his touch.

She had to share. Reaching out, she drew her fingernail the length of his erection.

He shuddered, then stilled. "Not a good idea, Flame. If you touch me like that, I could get serious real fast."

She smiled up at him, then purposely licked the dryness from her bottom lip. "How serious?"

He shook his head, and the slide of tangled hair across bare shoulders gleaming with mud strengthened the image of primitive male power. "Always the number person. On a scale of one to ten, I'm at about six."

"Hmm. Lots of room for serious growth then." Giving in to temptation, she clasped him. "But not here." She swallowed to clear the huskiness that had crept into her voice, the feeling that she couldn't get enough air.

"You'd be surprised." His response was muffled as he leaned forward and covered her mouth with his.

His lips were hot, hungry. He slid his tongue across her closed lips, and she opened to him. Deepening the kiss, he explored her, and she knew he could taste all her desires, the ones she'd dreamed and the ones she hadn't even thought of yet.

She was working hard on those unimagined dreams when he pushed away from her. As the clamor of her pounding heart and the harsh rasp of her breathing eased, she heard the voices of carolers in the street.

Sloan grinned. "Sorry. When it happens, I don't want to be lying in mud listening to 'Rudolph the Red Nosed Reindeer.'"

She nodded, the only movement she was capable of now.

"So don't you want to know what I wrote on you?"

She nodded again, fascinated by the rapid rise and fall of his gleaming chest. He'd been as much into the moment as she had.

Closing her eyes, she concentrated on the track of his fingertip between her breasts.

I. He'd traced the word "I." Made sense. What other word would fit in that narrow space? She kinda yearned for a longer word, though. One with maybe seven letters. He could start at one nipple, put the fourth letter right in the middle, then end up at her other nipple. Her nipples ached with the need for their very own letters.

He moved lower. Jenny frowned. Not a word, but a shape. She concentrated on the slide of his finger over her slick skin, tried to ignore the trail of goose bumps decorating his artwork.

A *heart*. He'd drawn a large heart. Okay, no reason to

hyperventilate here. It didn't mean a thing. There were lots of messages out there with the same lead-in. I—heart drawing—cats, I—heart drawing—baseball. Millions of possibilities.

The only drawing space left was her lower abdomen. She wished she hadn't eaten that last Mario's hoagie. He had enough space down there to fill in the whole Phillies' roster, including the hot dog vendors.

She felt him edge her panties lower on her hips. Lordy, he couldn't need more room unless he intended filling in the amount of his last electricity bill.

He started on the last word. Strange, he was beginning in the middle of her stomach. Must be a short word.

She stopped breathing completely as he traced a long line down below her panty's edge, beneath the silky material still covering unexplored territory, then touched the spot that dragged a groan of pure sensation from her.

Jenny didn't care what word he was spelling, all she wanted was his finger to remain there, to rub that spot until tears trailed down her cheeks, until she screamed with raw pleasure.

Opening her eyes, she stared at his bent head with unfocused gaze, then reached out and grasped a handful of his tangled hair in a grip she hoped would anchor her to Earth.

Suddenly, his finger was gone. She mourned its loss with every disappointed cell in her body.

Slowly, she realized he was finishing the letter. Y. The "o" and "u" that followed were an anticlimax . . . until the meaning of the message hit her.

He lifted his head and gazed at her. She couldn't read anything in his expression, his eyes.

It had been a kid thing, something they would've laughed over ten years ago.

But now? She broke his gaze, glanced at the mirror behind him, noted dispassionately the image of his bare body crouched over hers—muscular, mature.

They weren't kids anymore, and somehow the message didn't seem like something to laugh at.

CHAPTER SEVEN

He'd managed to surprise himself, and that didn't happen often to Sloan. Why had he remembered that stupid heart after all these years? It hadn't meant anything.

Then why the basket thing? Why was it so important that she live with you in this house? Why're you so hot and hard you'd take her even if a dozen Rudolphs were singing outside your window? Figure that out, hotshot.

"It doesn't mean anything, you know." Jenny's voice echoed his thoughts.

And made him mad. "It *could* mean something. How do you know it doesn't mean anything?"

She lay in the mud, her body slick, her hair sticking out in every direction, a smudge of dirt on her nose, and an uncertain smile on her lips. She was beautiful.

"I don't know." She shrugged, and her breasts lifted, hot-wiring his adrenaline. "But it could mean a lot of different things, like I admire you, or I get a kick out of you."

"I get a kick out of you?" He cast her his best you've-gotta-be-kidding look.

Her lips curved into a slow, deliberate smile. "What're we arguing about, Sloan?"

He drew in a deep breath. "Darned if I know. Want to share a cold shower?"

Her smile widened. "I don't think so, but wouldn't a roll in the snow be quicker?"

Sloan knew his gaze was heat and hunger. He didn't give a damn. "You watched me last night."

"Yes." She ran her tongue across her lower lip. "We could do it together. Now. I'm ready, and the carolers are gone."

The very thought of Jenny standing naked in the snow, her nipples hard from the cold, waiting for the warmth of his mouth . . .

"You're not ready."

"I can't believe you. Who're you to say I'm not ready? Are you waiting for Santa to leave a gift-wrapped announcement under your tree proclaiming that Jenny Saunders is ready?"

"I'll know when it's right." *When you come to me. With no questions, no reservations.* In what millennium would that happen? He didn't think he could wait that long. And why did it matter anyway?

She sighed. "Are we reversing roles here? Remember, I'm the careful one and you're the impulsive one."

"We're back to me being impulsive again, aren't—"

"Wait, wait." She met his gaze. "At first I thought impulsive was all bad, but look at me . . ."

He looked at her. At her lips swollen from his kiss, at her full breasts barely covered by her flimsy bra, at the curve of her stomach and hip. His eyes lingered on the small piece of silky cloth still guarding her femininity, and he wondered why the path of his gaze didn't burst into instant flame. "Okay. Looked at you."

"I said 'look,' Sloan, not burn and pillage."

"That wasn't burning and pillaging." He didn't smile. "You'll know when I'm burning and pillaging."

Her expression indicated a growing interest in the pillaging part. "Anyway, I've just done my best imitation of a mud wrestler. Can't get more impulsive than that. And you know something?" She reached up and touched each of his nipples with the tip of her finger. "I loved it."

"If you're looking for my power button, it's down on my surge protector." He couldn't control the huskiness of his voice anymore than the explosion mode of his surge protector. If he didn't disconnect fast, his whole system would crash.

He rose and moved away from Jenny. "So you're admitting that in some situations, impulsive actions can be good things."

"Yes." She slowly rose to her feet.

He should've helped her, but if he touched her again tonight, it'd be all over. And he had plans. Big plans that didn't include another roll in the mud. He was the king of desire fulfillment, and Jenny still had a few unfullfilled desires, even if she didn't realize it yet.

"Hey, it's a start. So where did you first get the idea that I was impulsive?"

He thought she wouldn't answer. She slogged out of the mud and sat on the bench beside the pond. He sat down beside her, making sure no part of him touched any part of her.

She sighed. "I don't know. A bunch of things. You always had these wild dreams in high school. You were going to contact aliens one day on your computer."

"Done that a few times."

She didn't smile.

"Lots of kids have wild dreams in high school. It's part of growing up." *Like drawing stupid hearts on women's stomachs.*

"Then you show up at my door sounding like you did ten years ago, telling my you'd been doing this-and-that. Didn't sound too stable to me. And you have to admit, this internet business sounds a little bizarre."

She reached out and traced an aimless pattern on his bare thigh. He didn't move away, but he didn't react either.

"Great believer in giving a guy the benefit of the doubt, aren't you, Flame?" He didn't care if he sounded cold.

She withdrew her hand from his thigh. "I did give you the benefit of the doubt. I'm here, aren't I?"

"You're here for your fling. Character flaws don't matter much when you're only scheduling a one-nighter."

"Low, Mitello." She stood, still managing to look composed. "If you're finished with your mud slinging, figuratively speaking of course, then I'll go up to my room and take a shower."

There was nothing composed about the seductive sway of her bottom. Made him almost forget about being mad. Almost.

Jenny awoke to a discreet tap on her door and a surrealistic memory of the night before. She forced one eye open, then glanced at the clock. Yep, Ridley. Right on schedule with another bowl of yummy oatmeal.

Mumbling her hope that the IRS would audit him for the rest of his irritating life, she covered her head with her pillow.

Translating the mumble as permission to enter, he opened the door, strode to her bedside table, then plunked her breakfast where she could smell the tempting odor of congealing oatmeal.

Jenny yanked the pillow from her head and glared at Ridley. "I won't eat that oatmeal, and you can't make me." Lord, she sounded about six years old.

Ridley sniffed his disdain. "Madam left muddy footprints all the way through the house. I had to wipe up every one of them before I made madam's breakfast."

He was good. Very good. He'd sharpened guilt into a

deadly weapon. Hating herself for doing it, she hiked the
sheet up to her neck, sat up, then picked up her spoon
and forced down a little of the cereal. "There. I ate some.
Satisfied?"

Ridley cast her a contemptuous glance. "There were
many, many footprints."

She sighed. "So I have to eat many, many spoonfuls."

He lowered his chin a fraction in acknowledgment.
"Then of course, you'll want to enjoy your present."

"Present? What present?" She scanned the room, and
there by the fireplace she saw *it*.

"Ohmigod, it's my *horse*. Sloan got me my horse!" All
her childhood Christmas disappointments faded into the
past as she gazed at the life-size carousel horse gleaming
white and beautiful in the morning light. "If you don't
want to see a naked woman, Ridley, you'd better run, because I'm naked and I'm getting out of this bed right now
to look at my horse."

Ridley didn't hang around. "As you wish, madam." He
hurried from the room with none of his usual dignity.

Jenny grinned. Her very own horse and a win over Ridley. Life was good. She wondered if Sloan would be surprised when he found out she'd thrown away her pj's.
And he *would* find out.

Scrambling from her bed, she didn't even take time to
fling on her robe as she rushed over to her horse. She slid
her fingers along its smooth neck, touched the gold trim
on its saddle and bridle, admired its upflung head and tail
flowing in an imaginary breeze. "You're beautiful, sweetheart."

"I agree."

Sloan's low comment didn't even surprise her. She'd
expected . . . no *wanted* him to show up. She didn't turn
around.

"Thank you for the horse and . . . for sharing your dreams. Sometimes you don't realize there's anything missing from your life until your life changes." That was the closest she could come to telling Sloan how she felt. She hoped it was enough.

"Sounds like you did some thinking last night." He'd moved up behind her, and she could feel the scrape of his terry robe, the knot at his waist digging into her back.

"Heavy duty." She reached behind her and undid the knot, felt his robe fall open.

"Me too." She heard him shrug from his robe; then he molded his bare body to hers. "I realized all the shiny new things in the world can't wipe out old memories, good or bad. And some memories are worth saving, worth building on."

"Uh-huh." That's all the verbal response she could manage. What would he do? She shivered in anticipation.

"You know, this sorta reminds me of Godiva." He ran his nails lightly up the back of her thighs, then bent to kiss the sensitive skin behind her ear. "The lady, not the chocolate."

She grabbed the horse's saddle to steady herself. "Sure. Lady Godiva."

"She had a lot more hair though. Covered up a lot of great stuff."

He slid his fingers across her bottom and she swallowed a gasp.

"Like these. Nothing should cover these." He spread his palms over each cheek, then squeezed gently.

She clenched her thighs in response and took a firmer grip on that saddle.

"I just remembered something, Flame. Even ten years ago when I was pretending that we were just friends—"

She couldn't let that pass. "We *were* just friends."

"Maybe, maybe not. But even ten years ago I loved watching you leave a room. You'd wiggle that sweet behind—"

Outraged, she could feel her cheeks heating. Both sets. "I *never* wiggled my behind."

"Sure you did. Men notice that kind of thing. You were a champion wiggler."

"I . . ." What could you say to that kind of revelation?

"Shh." He turned her to face him, then lowered his head and kissed her.

Kissed her hard and long, his tongue tasting every part of her mouth, forcing her to meet his thrust, to meet his desire with her own.

Wrapping her arms around him, she slid her hands over the tense muscles of his shoulders, down the smooth expanse of his back, then grasped his buttocks, pulling him firmly against her. The heavy ache grew in direct proportion to his pressure as he slowly rotated his hips, teasing, tempting.

Suddenly, he picked her up. *Yes! Bed here we come.*

But she should've known. Bed was conventional, and this was the man who'd dumped her in the mud last night. Instead, he lowered his head and flicked her nipple with his tongue. Then before she could get attached to the idea of his mouth on her breasts, he lifted her onto her horse.

"You know, I think I'm supposed to have one leg on each side of the horse, Sloan." With her breaths coming in short pants, she was amazed she could string that many words together.

"Not for what I have in mind, Flame."

He rolled each of her nipples between his thumb and forefinger, then trailed kisses down over her stomach.

Grabbing the horse's mane and the back of the saddle,

she tried to steady herself, and wondered why she just
didn't slide off the other side like the glob of quivering
Jell-O she was sure she'd become. Cherry Jell-O. She'd
always liked cherries.

"Relax, Jenny, and enjoy the ride."

His low murmur did *not* relax her, and when he ran his
tongue along the inside of her thigh she allowed a moan
to escape.

To think that she'd had Sloan's mouth, Sloan's body at
her fingertips ten years ago, and all she'd done was sit like
a lump in front of the TV watching *The Man with the
Golden Gun*.

She'd had her very own golden man and hadn't recognized him.

Suddenly, she realized that while she'd been busy with
past regrets, her body was very much in the moment and
taking care of its own needs.

She'd spread her legs to give him easier access to all of
her. She wanted his mouth, his hands on every inch . . .

He pushed her legs further apart, then put his mouth
on her.

His tongue touched her, stroked her, slid inside her,
and she felt tears trailing down her face.

Abandoning her grasp on the horse, she clasped his
shoulders, tried to pull him closer when closer wasn't possible.

"No, no, no!" *Yes, yes, yes!* Her chant picked up the
rhythm of the spasms shaking her, and when the explosion came she celebrated it with a final scream of "No!"

She collapsed from the horse like the boneless rag doll
she'd had when she was four years old. Sloan held her
tightly until she stopped shaking, until *he* stopped shaking.

"Sloan, what about you? You didn't . . ."

"Shh." He kissed her eyelids. "My time will come. But not here, not now."

"Saving yourself for the right woman?" She'd meant the comment to be funny, but instead was shocked by a stab of pure jealousy. Jealous? Possessive? *Her*?

"Definitely." He grinned. "What's with the 'No' bit?"

Jealous. She frowned, considering this new unattractive facet of her personality. And beyond the jealousy, something even more sinister lurked. Violence. She wanted to blacken both eyes of Sloan Mitello's "right woman."

"Jenny?"

She blinked. "Sorry. Why'd I scream 'no'?" She cast Sloan a wicked-vixen smile. "Guess I'm just a contrary woman."

Sloan slipped into his robe, then headed for the door. "I like a contrary woman. Adds spice to a man's life." He threw her a lingering glance over his shoulder as he opened the door. "And I like my spices hot. Really hot." He shut the door behind him.

Jenny turned back to her intrepid white steed. "Who was that masked man?"

CHAPTER EIGHT

She'd been so wrong. About Sloan, about herself. *Christmas Eve*. Such a short time to make a lifetime of discoveries.

Over the past week, Sloan had slowly opened up about his ten years away from Haddonfield. She'd put together the pieces of his moves to various jobs, each gaining him experience in an area he'd need when he started his own company. She saw behind his words to the research he'd done on the burgeoning internet and its possibilities for someone who used it wisely.

When had Sloan gained so much depth? Maybe he'd always had it, but she had never looked beneath his surface charm, her own prejudices.

When had she started to let go of her past, stopped thinking in terms of absolutes like all dreamers are losers, and wish fullfilment is a cruel hoax? She didn't have to look past the moment Sloan Mitello walked back into her life.

The ultimate irony? Maybe her revelation had come too late. After the horse, he'd laughed and teased, but hadn't touched her again. And dammit, she wanted, no *needed* him to touch—

"Madam hasn't touched her oatmeal. It's difficult cooking breakfast along with the many other duties Mr. Mitello requires." Ridley managed to mold the sharp angles of his face into a expression of long-suffering, over-worked servitude. "And when one's cooking isn't appreciated . . ." He shrugged, allowing her to guess at the depth of his disappointment.

"Uh-uh." Jenny shook her head and grinned at him. "Won't work this time." Up early after a restless night of dreaming about Sloan, she was dressed and ready for Ridley.

"Tomorrow's my last day here. Have any plans, Ridley?" *I sure don't.* Somehow this week had managed to become her life's entire time line. She couldn't conceive of a before or after.

"One manages." Ridley tried for pitiful and failed.

"You know, there's a lonely widow down the street who's looking for a strong man to organize her home. I bet she'd appreciate a man like you." *Forgive me, Mary.*

Ridley brightened. "Does she enjoy a hot bowl of oat-meal?"

"Yep. In fact, she said she really hated cold cereal." God would get her for that one.

Ridley looked happy, or as happy as he would ever get. "It sounds like the perfect situation."

Jenny handed him the address and phone number she'd written on a scrap of paper. "Here. I bet she'll be so impressed she'll want you to start immediately. It'll be hard coping without you for my final day, but your future is more important than a few piddling hours of discomfort on my part."

Ridley grinned. A sincere grin that surprised Jenny with its charm. "You'll make a bloody good liar someday, Madam. I assume you'll give me an excellent reference."

Jenny grinned back. "Right." Maybe she was actually doing Mary a favor. "How do you feel about playing Santa?"

Ridley frowned. "Santa?"

"Never mind." She pointed to the oatmeal. "Why don't you take that back to the kitchen? Give it to the kittens."

"They won't eat it." He turned and left the room carrying the dreaded oatmeal.

"Smart cats." Now to call Mary before Ridley did.

Jenny watched evening fall as snowflakes drifted past her window. Sighing, she returned her attention to her computer, but numbers seemed to have lost their charm for the moment.

Tomorrow. She'd pack her things, then go back to her off-white world. How could she walk away from Sloan?

Jenny stared at the numbers on her screen, then hit a few keys.

Better, but *scarier.* "Let us fulfill your desire. Sounds easy, doesn't it, horse?" She'd have to give her horse a name, but she'd do that when she got back to her apartment. She smiled at the thought of the fanciful animal in her blah apartment. It wouldn't be blah for long though. Changes were a-comin'.

Okay, she'd thought about her work, her horse, and her apartment. Anything else she could think of to put off the inevitable? Nope. She'd thought of everything.

She stared at the screen. What if he didn't respond? What if he wasn't interested? But he'd *promised* her a fling. Problem. She'd upped her expectations. A fling wouldn't be nearly enough now.

But what if he took back his promise? She'd never faced rejection before. *You never chanced anything before.*

Jenny took a deep breath. Somehow she knew this would be the most important chance she'd ever take. She typed.

I want a bad man in the worst way. A bad man with a golden bow.

She'd done it. She wouldn't worry about it anymore. He probably wouldn't even check his messages until after Christmas. She'd just go back to her work on the Chandler account.

Several hours later, she gave up. She'd probably be hearing from Chandler's lawyers if she didn't fix this mess. Later. She couldn't concentrate now.

He hadn't come.

Well, what're you going to do about it? Sit at your window and feel sorry for yourself like you did when you didn't get a horse? "No way. Wishes come true for those who make them come true. Right, horse?" Horse had no opinion on the matter.

Damned if she'd cower in her room, then spend the rest of her life wondering what might've been. Time to give destiny a kick in the behind. Turning off the computer, she stood and headed for the door before she could think of consequences, things like embarrassment and humiliation. *Heartbreak.*

As she was about to fling open the door, she spotted the piece of paper stuck beneath it. Probably nothing but a good-bye note from Ridley along with his recipe for making the perfect oatmeal. Still, her fingers trembled as she picked it up.

A bad man is waiting for you.

For absolutely no good reason, a tear slid down her cheek. Okay, she could change into something sexy or she could just go as she was. As-she-was won. She didn't want to waste one minute of her time with Sloan. Looking down at her bare feet, she shrugged. One less thing to take off.

Drawing in a deep breath of courage, she hurried down the hall. She paused outside Sloan's room to peer at the note taped to his door. *Bad man waits within. All desires fulfilled.*

Smiling, she remembered. He'd be wearing the gold bow. She pictured the exact placement of that bow and how much fun it'd be to take off. *Hey, have to cover up the gift part so it'll be a surprise.* She was still smiling as she opened the door.

Only a dim glow from the fireplace lit the room. The furniture was dark wood, dominated by a massive four-poster bed and the man stretched magnificently nude on it.

Sloan lay on his side, shadows thrown by the flickering flames playing over his long muscled back and strong buttocks as he gazed out the darkened window. "What do you want, Jenny?"

"I . . . I have a desire." She focused on the tangle of midnight hair that spread across one bare shoulder, and like a dark curtain, hid his expression, his emotions from her.

"Not a dream?"

"No." It was too deep, too strong. A hunger she felt she'd never satisfy. "This is a desire."

"Tell me what you want."

What *she* wanted? Didn't he want a part of it? And why didn't he turn over to speak with her? "I want to touch you, all of you, the way you touched me." *No, I want more, much more.*

"And?"

"I want you deep inside me, filling me." *Completing me.*

"Come here, Flame."

As she walked toward him, she felt overwhelmed by

the bed. Its rich wood gleaming in the firelight, it whispered of countless lovers who'd lain there, secrets it would never reveal. Ageless, it beckoned her.

The raw sexuality of the man lying atop the rumpled burgundy sheets made her catch her breath. Somehow, with the night, the bed, the man, everything had changed.

Sloan had reached out to her, drawn her into his life. Now he waited, silent, and she didn't know what to do. Okay, so she *did* know what to do, but the strangeness intimidated her.

"Touch me."

Well, that was pretty specific. "Turn over."

"Uh-uh." She could hear the laughter in his voice mixed with something darker. "It won't be a surprise if I turn over."

A surprise? She knew where the bow would be. "Too bad. I guess you won't be able to undress me. But I'll undress myself and tell you what's happening. You won't miss a thing."

"You'll pay, Flame."

She certainly hoped so. "Unbuttoning my blouse now. First button, second button—"

"Faster." He sounded as though his words were forced through gritted teeth.

"There, all done. Now I'm slipping the blouse off and dropping it on the floor." Even though the room was warm, she shivered at the touch of air on her bare skin.

"Describe your bra."

"My bra? It's black, and it has lace across the top. It's sort of cut low so it just covers . . ."

"Your nipples?"

"Yes." Her voice had turned hoarse. His words were almost like a touch—warm, intimate.

"Take the bra off."

"Like to give orders, don't you?" Did it matter? Reaching behind her, she unhooked the bra and let it fall. "It's gone."

"Touch your breasts, Jenny. Hold them in your palms, feel the warmth of flesh against flesh, then slide your thumbs across your nipples." His voice was low, urgent. "Imagine it's my hands cupping you. What do you feel, Flame?"

She didn't have to do this. He couldn't see what she was doing. But she *wanted* to. Closing her eyes, she lifted the weight of her breasts, imagined offering them to him. When she touched her nipples, imagined his lips closing hot and moist around each one, she moaned softly.

"God, you're killing me, Jenny."

She gloried in his torture. Another unattractive trait to add to her growing number. "Why don't you turn over, Sloan?"

"I can't." His voice was that of a man on the rack.

"Oh, well." Her voice might sound controlled, but she was glad he couldn't see her shaking fingers as she undid the snap of her jeans and slid them off. She should describe this, but she was having difficulty breathing, let alone talking.

"Talk to me, Jenny. I know you've taken off your jeans. I could hear you. What color are your panties?"

"Why're you so sure I'm wearing any?"

Once again, she sensed his amusement. "You're a follow-the-rules kinda woman. And the rules say you wear panties. So what color are they?"

"Black." She felt as mutinous as she sounded. He had her pegged as Ms. Predictable, but Sloan Mitello was about to get a surprise.

"Black. I like a woman in black." His voice was husky, approving. "Take them off."

She slid the panties off without comment. In a defiant gesture, she reached up and hung them on the top of the bedpost nearest her. She liked the effect. Sort of like raising the skull and crossbones flag on a pirate ship.

The excitement building in her was new, exhilarating, *freeing*. Jenny Saunders would take no prisoners tonight.

CHAPTER NINE

Kneeling on the bed, she gazed down at Sloan. What more could a woman want under her tree, under *her* on Christmas morning? *What more could a woman want for a lifetime?*

The thought touched her and felt right. But whether it was for a lifetime or just one magic night, she'd take what she could of Sloan Mitello. "Roll onto your stomach, Sloan."

"Someone else likes to give orders, but hey, it's your desire." He sounded intrigued. "This'll crush the bow."

"All in a good cause." She straddled his hips, almost groaning at the pleasure of having his body between her legs.

More. She needed him touching the ache that had started the moment she'd seen him stretched out on the bed.

Scooting up until she was over his buttocks, she spread her thighs wide so that his flesh touched hers. Then closing her eyes, she slid back and forth, back and forth. The building heat had nothing to do with friction.

He moved beneath her, lifting his hips to increase the pressure. She could hear his heavy breathing matching her own.

Harder. She leaned forward to increase the contact, her nipples sliding over his sweat-dampened skin, and as her body begged to feel more of him, she raked her nails the length of his back, then followed the path of her nails with her tongue. She'd never thought of herself as a cat, but she was seeing some disturbing similarities. So who gave a meow anyway? Not her.

Her jungle-kitty act must've woken the sleeping tiger in Sloan, because with a hoarse growl, he turned over.

Scrambling into a kneeling position, she finally took a good long look at him. *All* of him. She swallowed hard, not sure if her voice would work. "The bow."

"Told you you'd crush it." His eyes gleamed in the firelight, giving away nothing.

"It's . . ."

"It's covering my gift to you."

"It'd take a mighty big bow to cover all your gifts to me." She felt tears filling her eyes. Darn it, she wouldn't cry.

"Sure, but this bow is gift-specific." His voice lowered to a murmur. "It'll only cover the most important gift."

"It's over . . ." She reached out with trembling fingers and gently lifted the shiny gold bow from over his heart.

Jenny couldn't say a word. Tenderly, she kissed the spot where the bow had rested, then moved to his nipple. Sliding her tongue across the nipple, she gently nipped it.

His groan was all she could hope for. "Stop. Forgot something important."

"No." Not *now*. "Please don't stop me."

"Uh-uh. Can't go on without this." He picked something up from beside him, then handed it to her.

"Hershey's chocolate syrup?" A childhood quote came to mind. "Yes, Virginia, there is a Santa Claus." He was tall, muscular, and crying out to be served with chocolate.

She clasped the plastic container, but there was something strange . . . "This feels warm. How did you . . . ?"

"I heated it by the fireplace"—his gaze seared the

length of her body—"and thought of you. Naked. I wouldn't need a fireplace to heat it now." He slid his fingers over his arousal.

She felt the heat from his body, steamy with the scent of sex, and a want so powerful she imagined smoke rising from it.

"Use it, Flame."

He hadn't been too specific about how she should use it, but he'd soon find out she had a lot of ideas.

She concentrated on opening the top, ignoring Sloan's impatience. Good things were worth waiting for. He'd taught her that this week. "I've always had a passion for chocolate syrup. The smooth texture, the rich taste, the way it makes me feel good. That's why from now on I'll put it over everything I love."

She forced herself not to react to his sharp intake of breath. "I'll put it on my Cocoa Puffs every morning."

"You eat Cocoa Puffs?" His voice was nine parts sexual frustration and one part horror.

"All the time." She carefully dripped chocolate dots around his right nipple, then plopped one huge dot on top. She'd always thought she didn't have any creativity, but she kind of liked the pattern.

Too bad she was going to destroy it. Leaning over, she scooped up every dot with the tip of her tongue, except for the big one. She had plans for that.

Sloan sucked in his breath with every touch of her tongue, and she gloried in her power to give him pleasure.

He smoothed his hand over her hair with fingers that shook, and for once she wished her hair was long and flowing. Long enough to spread across his chest, glide over his flesh, and allow one more part of her to touch him.

Maybe she'd let it grow long. She'd think about it later.

Closing her lips over his nipple, she swirled her tongue over it, then sucked the last taste of sweet chocolate from it.

He tightened his grip on her hair and forced her lips away from his nipple. "God, woman." That's all he seemed able to say.

"We were talking about chocolate syrup, right?" She skimmed her finger down over his stomach and enjoyed the ripple of his muscles. "I'll put it on my pizza, too."

His bark of laughter loosened sexual tension strung tighter than her monthly budget. Good. She wanted him to last a long time. But how long could *she* last?

"Bet you like anchovies on your pizza."

She widened her eyes. "Doesn't everyone?"

"That's disgusting, Jenny."

He didn't think it was disgusting a minute later when she poured a trail of chocolate over his stomach in the shape of a pepperoni pizza. *With* anchovies. She ate the whole pizza. Except for one anchovy that got stuck in his belly-button.

She was working hard with the tip of her tongue to scoop out that anchovy when Sloan reached out and stilled her.

"Leave it. I can't stand much more." His voice was hoarse with growing loss of control.

She smiled her wicked-cat smile. "If you want to go through life with an anchovy in your navel, who am I to stop you?"

"Where were we? Oh, yes. Chocolate syrup. I'll put it on spaghetti with Italian sausage and meatballs." She winced. That was too much even for her.

"Getting a little obvious, aren't you, Flame?"

Jenny glanced at her eventual destination. Obvious didn't begin to describe it. She slid her tongue across dry lips. She couldn't wait much longer. But she also couldn't let Sloan get away with thinking she had no imagination.

"Me? Obvious? I was just making conversation. I don't intend to do anything with it." Her nose would begin growing any second now.

"You'd better do something with it, and soon." His threat hung between them.

"Oh, I forgot. I'll put warm chocolate syrup on ice-cream cones." She scooted lower.

"Doesn't that make the ice cream melt?"

"Always." This would be her creative masterpiece.

She made twin swirls with a question mark in the middle of each swirl, then moved onto his main attraction. It was hard to make a dust devil design when your hand was shaking, but she managed it. At the very top of the dust devil she drew a big star, symbolic of her fulfilled desires. The star was a little lopsided, but an artist was allowed creative license.

"You're killing me." Sloan's voice was a tortured groan.

Me too. She slid her tongue across the swirls, leaving the question marks for last.

He bucked beneath her as she answered each question, and she could hear his harsh rasping breaths over her pounding heart.

The dust devil called for her tip-of-the-tongue technique. Around and around and around. She felt dizzy by the time she reached the star, and his hips were lifting rhythmically, brushing her nipples with each lift until they were so sensitized she felt she would scream.

The star. The heck with technique. She closed her lips over him, slid along his length, then worked her way up and down until she'd almost finished—

She didn't get to finish. There was still a little speck of chocolate left when Sloan heaved beneath her. Before she could gather her scattered thoughts, he'd pulled her beneath him.

He loomed over her. His long tangled hair trailed across her breasts, and she closed her eyes to savor the sensation of the dark strands sliding over her nipples. She was definitely going to let her hair grow.

"I wanted this to be long and slow, Flame. I wanted you to enjoy your entire desire, but God, I'm only human."

She opened her eyes and blinked at him.

"I'm going to fast-forward to the end." His face was dark shadows and tense angles. He smiled, a savage pirate smile. "We can rewind it later, then play it again. Slow and sweet."

Sounded good to her. She'd think of new ways to—

She did no more thinking as he lowered his head and captured her mouth in a kiss that took her breath away along with any still-functioning brain cells. He tasted of glowing firelight and dark nights. *Urgency.*

When he abandoned her mouth and kissed a trail over her throat to her breasts, she tangled her fingers in his hair, as though she could transfer her need through the dark strands.

It must have worked, because he slid his tongue around each breast, then drew a nipple into his mouth. She cried out at the touch of his tongue on what felt like bare nerves. And when she felt she'd shatter with what his tongue and teeth were doing, he transferred his attention to the other nipple.

She couldn't stand it one more second.

"*Now*. I want you now. And *yes* I'm ready."

"I don't want to rush this too much." She could hear the smile in his voice.

"*Now*, Mitello, or you . . . are . . . a . . . dead . . . man."

"You're homicidal. I like that in a woman."

Her breaths were coming in heaving gasps as he pushed her legs apart. Only her senses spoke to her now: her wet readiness, an aching need to feel him inside her, the heat of his body, the scent of hot male desire.

He rose above her, and she closed her eyes so she could concentrate on *feeling*.

"I love you, Jenny Saunders." She almost didn't hear his whispered message as he pushed into her.

She felt his tension, his attempt to go slowly. No. She didn't want slow and careful. She wanted hard and fast.

Raising her hips, she wrapped her legs around him, clasped his buttocks with her hands, and pulled him to her hard. She knew her nails were digging into him, but she couldn't stop herself. She wanted him now. *Now*.

His body tensed and she felt the tightening of his buttocks just before he plunged so deeply into her that she knew *no one* would ever fill her this way again. Her brief pain was only a blip on the radar screen of her senses.

Again and again he thrust into her, a raw primitive rhythm that built until she felt, she felt . . .

When it happened, it wasn't pretty sparkling fireworks, it wasn't a heavenly choir singing. It was a massive explosion, and she didn't even have the power to scream as it shook her.

An explosion. There was no other way to describe it. Bits and pieces of her would be drifting to earth for days.

Her eyes landed first, so she opened them. Her voice was around somewhere if she could only find it. She probably wouldn't catch her breath for days. Heaven only knew where the rest of her was.

Sloan pulled her into his embrace until she'd stopped shaking. "I think we burned up during reentry, Flame."

She could only nod.

"I'd like to make love for the rest of the night." His eyes lit with anticipation.

Jenny gazed at him. "Six times. We have to do it six times."

"I have a confession to make." He stretched, feeling relaxed for the first time since he'd rung Jenny Saunders's doorbell.

"Confess away. No, let me guess. Those aliens you always wanted to contact switched bodies with you and you're really a native of the planet Zork. Kinky."

"Close. I know how attached you are to this house, but it isn't really mine."

She blinked at him. "What?"

"I built this house for Mom. I tried to tell you at the beginning, but you distracted me. This is Mom's desire. The biggest, fanciest house money can buy, filled with Christmas cheer to make up for all the bad years. We'll have to fly to California today to bring her home." He lowered his gaze in mock sadness. "Guess we'll have to make do with something smaller. Won't have all these great decorations either." He brightened. "But next year I'll buy all the lights you want. Can't have Christmas without lots of lights."

"I love you, Sloan Mitello."

Sloan slanted her a wicked grin. "Sure you're not saying that because we made love six times?"

She looked puzzled. "But won't we do that *every* night?"

"You'll kill me, woman. I'm glad I don't have to explain to anyone why I have fingernail marks on my butt." After last night, he didn't care where he had nail marks. "And I didn't know you were a—"

"Virgin?"

He nodded. "I knew you wanted a fling, but I didn't think it'd be your first time." His voice lowered. "You made me feel very special, Flame."

"You'll *always* be special to me, Sloan." She lay on her side, her fingers idly sliding across his still-damp chest. "I've figured out why no one I dated ever suited me. I guess, subconsciously, I was comparing them to you and they always came up short. Now I know I'm a never-settle-for-less kind of woman."

"We're like fine wine, Jenny. It was there in high school, but we needed aging before we were ready to pop our corks."

"Makes sense to me." Her fingers slid to his stomach while her gaze turned thoughtful. "Desires are addictive. I feel another one coming on."

"Great. That's my job, let's hear it."

She leaned close and whispered in his ear. "I've decided to wear something special for our wedding."

"Okay, I'm open to suggestion." He looked puzzled. "Fancy white gown? Lots of glitzy stuff?"

"Something a lot more cost effective." She nibbled on his ear. "Something classic that never goes out of style."

"You'd better tell me right now, because you're not the only one working on a desire."

"A big shiny gold bow."

DARA JOY

Santa Reads Romance

CHAPTER ONE

Writers. They were the bane of his existence.

Unfortunately, they were his bread and butter too.

C. Hunter Douglas slammed the heel of his hand against the steering wheel of the rental car. *What came into their strange little minds that caused them to react so . . . so . . .*

They had to be from another planet. Probably plants of an alien race, put here to slowly drive the sane mad.

He peered through the windshield into the darkness.

A snow squall had sprung up out of nowhere, adding to his rising irritation. The Weather Channel had conveniently left this piece of information out of its travel report this morning. He should have realized. Maine. Christmas week.

It was a trip only a sailor returning home from war or a desperate publisher would attempt to make.

His hand slammed on the wheel again.

One million dollars.

Of his money.

And no manuscript.

Normally he was not a violent man, but the idea of grabbing the oh-so-talented Rex Stevens by the throat and slowly squeezing the air from his self-indulgent lungs held great appeal. He'd show the horror writer something really scary. A pissed-off publisher.

What was he going to do?

Publicity and marketing had been set in motion, a book tour ready and waiting, appearances on talk shows, tie-ins . . . Shit, the whole thing was going to fall apart!

He had counted on this. Placed all of his dwindling profit-margin eggs in Rex's basket of frightening words. His uncle had made some terrible financial decisions; Hunter had been called in to clean up.

Everything would have been nice and tidy if the "writer"—he grimaced at the word—had delivered as contracted!

When the manuscript had still not arrived three weeks after the deadline, an uncomfortable, nauseous feeling had settled in the pit of his stomach.

It was a feeling he recognized.

Hunter called it his "imminent author sickness."

He had called the man and his agent several times, leaving message after message. The agent was in the hospital for his ulcers (Hunter bet he knew why), and Rex had not returned his calls.

So Hunter had flown up to Maine.

He would've flown to Timbuktu to get his hands on that manuscript.

Only when he arrived on Rex's doorstep in this godforsaken rural town, the housekeeper had cheerfully informed him that Mr. Rex was not there.

Mr. Rex was in Sri Lanka.

At an *ashram*.

In search of himself.

Hunter's left eye twitched. *Writers*.

CHAPTER TWO

May threw another log on the fire.

She watched the sparks fly up the chimney as if it were the most interesting sight she had ever seen. Unfortunately, the amazing spectacle was over in less than a minute.

She sighed, wondering what else could suddenly capture her attention. Surely something?

Come to me.

Her green eyes began to cloud over at the subliminal suggestion.

You must come to me . . .

Her shoulders scrunched up as she tried to fight off the insistent voice.

Get your butt over here!

The damn laptop was trying to get her attention again. It was the voice of conscience and reason. It was the voice of a deadline fast approaching. It would not leave her alone!

May desperately scanned the room, searching for an important task that needed to be done immediately. Perhaps the ceilings needed vacuuming? Never mind that they weren't her ceilings—anything was better than staring at that empty screen.

This was the stupidest idea she had ever had.

And she had had some whoppers.

When her neighbor Billy had told her about his cabin

in Maine, May had practically begged him to let her use it for a few weeks. It seemed the ideal hideaway where she would write, diet, and reflect.

The perfect solution.

She could remove herself from the temptations of everyday life, finish her book, and maybe lose a few pounds at the same time.

Most importantly, she would not be surrounded by well-meaning family and friends who smothered her in sympathy invites at Christmas. The holiday that never failed to remind her: a) she was alone; b) she was alone and; c) *she was alone.*

It was supposed to be "the great escape." After all, she would be working; she had the perfect excuse to turn down all the invitations.

Everything would be accomplished in one swell foop.

Only it hadn't quite worked out that way.

Even though Billy had warned her that the cabin was remote, secluded, and had little in the way of conveniences, she had somehow ignored all that, her inner sights focusing on a new and improved May. A May armed with a *completed* novel.

After two days here, she was beginning to question the wisdom of the plan.

The one-room cabin with kitchenette was starting to get on her nerves.

Whatever had possessed her to come here equipped with only a laptop, a sack full of frozen diet dinners, a giant box of Cheerios, and ten pounds of Braeburn apples? What kind of diet was that?

Thankfully, she couldn't bear the thought of giving up coffee cream, so she at least had a small carton of Half-and-Half to stare at and dole out like liquid platinum.

Well, enough suffering! Tomorrow she was going to

drive into the little village she had passed on her way to the cabin and lay in some writer's survival supplies. Lots of Chippy Nicks, Chocomongos, and Jelly Wellys. Her stomach growled agreement with the fine idea.

Seeking security of another kind, her sights went to the overflowing carton in the corner near the fireplace. At least she'd had sense enough to bring her favorite romance novels. She sighed contentedly at the lovely sight. Food she could live without. Creature comforts she could live without. Romance novels, however, were a different story.

Come to think of it, this cabin was the perfect setting for a romance book.

Her imagination took flight. Yes . . . remote cabin, two strangers thrown together by chance . . .

She giggled to herself. How often had she read that particular story line? Too many times. It was the *plot du jour.* Although she had loved so many of those stories. . . .

A few snowflakes fell softly against the windowpane.

Her brow furrowed. She hadn't heard anything about snow this morning on the radio. Probably just a small snow shower.

Shrugging, she threw another log on the fire and avidly watched the sparks fly up the chimney.

That's another minute down.

CHAPTER THREE

Perhaps if his mind hadn't been wandering along the lines of throttling his favorite author, he would've noticed the man sooner.

He had just turned down the main street of the town. The snow had picked up in the last fifteen minutes, although visibility wasn't that bad. He should've seen him.

Even though it was just past eight in the evening, the streets were deserted. It seemed as though one moment it was clear sailing, and the next a surprised visage materialized in front of his windshield, followed by a sickening thump.

Christ! He had hit somebody!

Hunter slammed on the brakes, sweat breaking out across his forehead. The car skidded to a stop, but Hunter was already out the door while the car was still rocking.

A red lump lay unmoving in the gutter. He ran to the huddled shape, falling to his knees in the shallow snow. Hunter had never been so scared in his life.

The man was dressed in a Santa suit.

Next to him, lying on the pavement, was a large sack full of presents. If possible, Hunter felt even worse. He had run over Santa Claus! Not even a disgruntled publisher would intentionally do that.

"Talk to me!" Gently he placed his hand on the man's

shoulder. "I didn't even see you there, pop, I swear it! Hey, buddy, say something, please! Are you hurt bad?"

Leaning over, he worked his palm under the man's shirt to feel for a heartbeat. Something wet licked his hand.

"Jesus!" Hunter fell back in the snow. What the hell was that?

A piteous groan came from under the prone figure. It did not sound human.

Hunter blanched. He had read too many of Rex's books lately—they always seemed to involve horrific happenings in the backwoods of Maine . . .

"Don't just sit there gawking at me, boyo! Help me up!"

The acerbic words penetrated Hunter's fog-brain. He let out a sigh of relief. At least the man was conscious and speaking.

"You okay, mister? Maybe you shouldn't move."

"And how am I supposed to be gettin' up if I don't move? C'mon now, help ol' Santa up. Benny's not happy."

Against his better judgment, Hunter crawled toward the man, helping him to sit up. A wave of cheap gin assailed his nostrils.

Uh-huh. The picture was getting clearer. The old coot had probably fallen into the path of his car in a drunken stupor. Idly Hunter wondered what Benny was supposed to be a euphemism for. As if he needed to know.

"Santa" sat up, swaying slightly, his eyes round and bleary. He shook his head several times, slapped the back of his head twice, and hiccupped.

Hunter viewed him askance. "Are—are you sure you're okay, old-timer?"

"Fit as a fiddle. It's Benny took the brunt of it, poor little fellow."

Hunter winced. Yeah, the old coot had probably landed

right on his . . . well, he'd never heard it called a *benny* before. "Ah, yah, must've hurt like hell. Sorry."

The man looked at him reproachfully. "And him being such a tiny little thing."

Hunter stared at him. He blinked. What could he say to that? He rubbed his forehead. "Hey, you know, cold weather and all . . ."

Santa raised one bushy eyebrow and, shaking his head, muttered under his breath. It sounded suspiciously like "twit."

The old coot seemed okay. Drunk as a skunk, but okay. Impatiently, Hunter looked at his watch. He had a flight leaving from Bangor in a little over three hours and this was one flight he did not want to miss. The sooner he exited this horror-hotel the better; so far the trip had been one long nightmare.

Besides, the chances of him getting another flight out tonight during Christmas week were probably five trillion to one. Conservatively speaking.

"Well, if you're sure you're all right . . ."

"I told ya, lad, I'm fine."

Nodding, Hunter turned and started to walk back to his car, missing the old man's surprised look. He had just reached the driver's door when an ear-splitting yell pierced the night, shattering Hunter's eardrums.

"Me leg! I can't move me leg!"

Hunter raced back to him, face pale. "You are hurt! Don't worry, I have a cell phone in the car. I'll go call an ambulance. Stay put—I'll be right back—"

"I ain't getting into no meat wagon!" the voice wailed indignantly.

"But you—"

"You'll take me then, won't ya, sonny?" Santa looked at him slyly.

Hunter sighed. He was being sucker-punched and there wasn't a damn thing he could do about it. "All right."

The old coot grinned. "Put your hands out so I can give ya Benny."

Hunter's eyes widened. He stepped back. Three steps.

"Now, there's nothing to be afraid of. Benny's real friendly. I'm sure you're going to be very fond of him—"

"The hell you say!" Hunter took another step back.

Santa clicked his tongue and rolled his eyes heavenward as if asking for divine interference. Reaching into his voluminous velvet shirt, he extracted a small reddish-brown bundle of fur with floppy ears. A blue bow was tied around its neck.

A puppy. Benny was a puppy. I've been living in New York too long, Hunter concluded. He tentatively reached down and took the little guy from the man.

The puppy immediately licked his hand. Then, wagging his wispy tail, he looked up at Hunter with big brown eyes.

Cute little tyke. Unconsciously, he petted the dog's head. "Nice puppy," he murmured distractedly. He had never been around dogs much. "What kind of dog is this?"

"That there's a genuine long-haired dachshund. Don't see too many of them dogs about. Kinda special, they are. Benny's being relocated."

"Relocated?"

"His old family didn't treat him none too well, poor mite. And him being the fine dog he is."

Hunter stroked the soft little head. "Too bad. How old is he?"

"About a year old."

Hunter was surprised. "I thought he was just a puppy."

"He is; always will be. That's the magic of some dogs," he confided before hiccupping drunkenly.

Hunter looked at him askance. "Ah, yah. Do you need a hand up?"

"Probably. But ya need to take me bag first." He nodded to the sack lying near him on the snowy pavement.

Hunter quirked his brow. "Let me guess, gifts to be dispensed?"

"Right ya are, boyo. I was headed to the children's home before ya ran me down like some no-account slug in the gutter." He speared him with a pointed look from beneath bushy brows.

"Now wait just a minute, old-timer, you—"

"The bag, sonny."

Letting out a hiss of disgust, Hunter retrieved the huge sack of wrapped gifts, throwing it onto the back seat of his car. Then he helped the old coot into the front seat, almost passing out from the alcohol fumes.

He wondered if it would affect him like secondary smoke in the closed confines of the automobile.

The way his day had been going? Absolutely.

He could see it now. He would get pulled over by the Maine police and get arrested for secondary drunk driving, and while he was hauled away, he would babble pitiful phrases about million-dollar advances and an *ashram* in Sri Lanka.

Hunter decided he definitely needed a vacation.

"You'll just have to do it, boyo!"

"Santa" lay on the hospital bed, propped up by three pillows and surrounded by four pretty nurses. Never mind that the ER doctor could find nothing wrong with the old coot. For a man supposedly in pain, he seemed remarkably comfortable. And smug.

Go figure, but the young women couldn't do too much

for the guy. Even his white beard looked as if it had the snarls combed out of it.

Hunter's brow furrowed. Odd how the man had seemed to sober up as soon as they entered the emergency room. Even the noxious alcohol fumes had mysteriously disappeared.

In response, the corner of Hunter's mouth lifted in a semblance of a sarcastic grin. "I don't think so, pop. I got a plane to catch."

A screech of utter despair filled the room. "Aw, the children! How will they get their gifts? *The chi-i-l-l-dren!*"

The pitiful wail of anguish bounced off the green walls, causing the four nurses to cross their arms over their ample chests in unison and level looks of utter disdain at Hunter.

He felt like a first-class heel.

He tried to explain. "Look, I have to get back to New—"

Santa stopped in mid-wail to pin him to the spot. "Ya can still make yer plane! Won't take but fifteen minutes! Ya told me on the drive ain't no family waitin' home for ya anyway. Think of the children . . ."

"Well, I . . ." Hunter could feel himself caving in. How could he refuse? And live with himself. Just because he was alone and didn't have anyone to share Christmas with was no reason to be a Grinch. As long as he still made his plane, that is.

The old codger knew the instant he had won. He pointed to the red velvet suit draped over the chair next to the bed.

This was where C. Hunter Douglas drew the line. "Absolutely not, pop."

A petite red-haired nurse joined in. "Oh, but you can't deliver the gifts to those poor children not dressed as Santa! That would be even worse than no gifts at all."

Santa nodded vehemently in agreement.

Dammit. He might as well just do it and get it over with. Maybe then he could get out of this godforsaken town! Anything was better than those five sets of dog-eyes staring at him. Make that six including Benny, who had started up a soulful whine in chorus.

He stormed over to the chair and grabbed the velvet suit.

"What about your beard?" the red-headed nurse asked.

"What about it?" he snapped.

"Well, you don't have one! The hat will cover your hair, but the beard . . . I've got it!" She snapped her fingers. "I'll make you one from some cotton batting and surgical thread."

"Good idea, Rudy." Santa praised the nurse's ingenuity.

She smiled broadly. "I'll be right back."

"I can hardly wait," Hunter muttered under his breath.

Hunter started to put the mangy outfit on over his Armani suit, came to his senses, and headed for the cubicle bathroom. When he exited all in red, his business suit was draped carefully over his arm.

"I never realized how fine I look in that suit." The old-timer on the bed grinned wickedly at him. He was really enjoying this.

Hunter narrowed his silver eyes. The daunting effect was somewhat spoiled when the pom-pom at the end of the hat smacked into his nose.

"Here we go!" Nurse Rudy raced back into the room with a fluffy wad of cotton attached to a string. "Bend down and I'll tie it on for you."

Hunter knelt his tall frame so she could tie it behind his ears. She began stuffing his wavy dark brown hair under the rim of the hat. "Can't let the kids see this. You know, I have some scissors in my pocket; I could trim it off . . ."

"No!" Hunter abruptly stood.

Walking over to a small square mirror on the wall, he peered at his new high-powered image. "I look like a cross between a sheep's butt and a horse's behind."

The nurses giggled.

Santa stroked his beard. "I will admit ya don't carry it off with quite the same flair I do."

Hunter faced him. "You can have the job back any time, pop."

The man's eyes twinkled. "Right ya are, sonny! Now, here's the directions to the place; I wrote them down for ya." He handed him a heavily scrawled piece of paper.

Hunter scanned it. "Are you sure this is close by; it seems—"

"Country roads. Don't worry about that none, just follow those directions exactly and ya won't have no problem."

Hunter stuffed the note in his pocket. Then he hoisted the heavy sack over his broad shoulder. "Well, see ya later, Santa. It's been . . . interesting."

"Wait a minute!" Hunter turned around. The codger held the puppy out to him. "Ya forgot Benny."

Hunter sighed resignedly, putting out his hand for the dog.

"He don't like the cold much!" Santa yelled after him.

Hunter waved acknowledgment without turning around.

Before he left the hospital he scooted the dog safely inside his shirt.

CHAPTER FOUR

Turkeyfoote Road.

Where in the hell was Turkeyfoote Road?

It seemed as if he'd been driving for hours, although his watch claimed it was only about thirty minutes.

He had left the outskirts of the village twenty minutes ago. The snowfall had picked up considerably; his wipers were just keeping up with it. If he didn't find the turn-off soon, he was going to turn back, drop off the gifts and Benny. The small dog was still nestled next to his chest, refusing to leave the warmth of his shirt.

At this pace, he might miss his plane. And he still had to drive to Bangor. These dark country roads were—

A small wooden sign staked to the ground seesawed in the wind to his left. It was placed next to—not a road exactly, more a trail.

On the front of the wooden sign someone had drawn in red paint what one might assume was a turkey foot.

It was a good enough indication for him.

He swung the car to the left and followed the narrow rutted pathway. After ten minutes of bouncing and sliding on the dirt track, he wondered what had possessed him to take that turn.

The snow was falling fast and furious now.

He had just decided to turn back when he rounded a bend and spotted some lights in the distance. About 300 yards up the road a house sat on a hill. It was too dark and snowy to see much of its shape, but Hunter had no doubt that it was the children's home. He had followed the directions exactly.

Unfortunately, at that point the road became steeper and rougher. In this snow, without four-wheel drive, he didn't think he'd be able to drive much further. The surface was slick and pitted with ice.

Deciding it was best to walk the remaining distance—he wasn't going to take any chances of getting stuck here—he stopped the car, grabbed the sack from the back seat, tucked Benny's head back in his shirt, and headed up to the house.

CHAPTER FIVE

The lights flickered and went out.

May peered out the window. The storm was really picking up. Earlier she had tried to tune in a local radio station on her Walkman but all she got was static. Reception hadn't been the best these past few days, and she supposed with this snow . . .

The firelight cast eerie shadows on the walls.

She swallowed. This was creepy. She had never done anything like this before. *Why, oh why, had she come here by herself?*

The wind howled outside. An eerie sonata.

Billy had told her there was a generator in the cellar, but she didn't have the foggiest idea how to use it. And even if she could use it, there was no way she was going down in that dirt cellar by herself in the dark! It was a *Tales from the Crypt* waiting to happen.

She would just scrunch close to the fireplace all night and hope she didn't freeze. It seemed to be doing a fairly good job of keeping the room warm. And she had plenty of firewood.

Tomorrow she was going to go back home.

May had had all she could stand of the little hideaway.

She wanted TV, phone, CD-Rom, and home delivery.

This was the last time she would . . . She leaned closer to the window. *Was something moving out there?*

A fuzzy blur of staggered movement seemed to weave its way through the snow. May gulped. *Something was out there.*

Oh, God.

Her rapid breath fogged up the glass. Quickly she wiped the pane with a circular motion of her palm. She did not want to lose sight of it!

Squinting, she tried to get a better view through the heavily falling snow.

It was big, whatever it was.

It—it seemed to have a . . . huge *hump* on its back!

Oh, God. A thin film of sweat dotted her brow.

As the figure got closer, she could discern the shape of a man. This was not necessarily comforting.

May stood on tiptoe to watch his progress through the storm, taking solace from the fact that he seemed to be having considerable trouble negotiating the pathway to the cabin. He kept slipping and sliding on the icy walkway.

When he got close enough so that the firelight from the window illuminated him better, May put her hand to her throat in utter terror. It was all she could do not to scream out loud. *He was wearing a Santa suit!*

There was no doubt in her mind now that he was a homicidal maniac. There had been a very popular slasher movie where the killer had done the exact same thing. What better way to sucker in your victims than dressing as kindly old Santa?

May thought she was going to be sick.

He was making his way to the front porch now. She could hear the heavy fall of his uncoordinated feet dragging across the wooden planks.

Thinking quickly, she grabbed a hefty piece of firewood and stood behind the door. Her best chance would be in taking him unawares. She knew this because she was an author who was very good at plotting.

Carefully she inched over and unlocked the door.

And waited like a spider.

CHAPTER SIX

Hunter hefted the sack on his shoulder and went to knock on the door. He had been surprised at how small the house—no, cabin—was when it came into better view. How many children could live here? It seemed kind of primitive . . .

The door creaked slowly open.

Placing the sack down on the porch, Hunter gingerly stepped forward. "Hello?" No answer. He crossed the threshold. "Anybody here? I'm deliver—"

Something whacked him hard on the back of the head.

Hunter went down like a ton of bricks.

He was thinking he was the biggest fool of all time just before the world went black.

CHAPTER SEVEN

Got him! May slammed the door shut. No sense letting out the warm air.

She ran into the kitchenette looking for the ball of twine she had spotted when she first arrived and was putting away her groceries. Grabbing it off the nail on the inside of the sink cabinet, she raced back into the main room, hoping the maniac hadn't come to yet.

There he was! Lying on his stomach just where she had left him—looking like a beached red whale.

May made short work of tying his hands behind his back. Then she wrapped the twine around his feet, which surprisingly were not clad in black Santa boots, but in rather expensive-looking brown leather shoes. His socks were soaked through, but she didn't feel the least sympathy for him or his wet feet.

May had him trussed up like a Christmas turkey in no time flat.

Now that he wasn't going anywhere without her approval, she felt confident enough to roll the scoundrel over.

She first noted that his dark lashes (which were rather long for a man) framed cheeks that looked rather pale even through his tan-colored skin. He appeared younger than she originally thought. At first glance in that suit, she had taken him for a man in his fifties. Now she saw that he was probably only in his early to mid thirties.

Which made him all the more dangerous.

Removing his stocking hat, she was surprised at the mass of luxuriant wavy brown hair that fell over her hands. It wasn't to his shoulders, but close to it, falling a few inches shorter in a tapered cut.

She hadn't seen his entire face yet, but so far he was exceedingly nice-looking. May shook her head in disgust. *Now, why would a man who looked like this have to resort to being a fiend?*

Maybe he was a moron.

That really had a tendency to turn women off.

His fake beard was slightly askew. Carefully she removed the fuzzy beard, frowning as it fell apart in her hands. It looked like he had just taken some cotton balls and threaded them through a string! What a pervert!

Her mouth parted slightly as she caught her first glimpse of his completely unmasked face.

It held to the original promise, revealing a strong chin—which no doubt indicated a pugnacious streak—a classically straight nose neither too large nor too small, and well-shaped lips. The bottom lip, she noted absently, was slightly fuller than the top; the indentation below it hinting at a sensual . . . no, she wouldn't even think it.

He looked . . . familiar somehow.

Now that his whole face was visible, May noted that his tan skin did have a palish cast to it.

Maybe she had whacked him a bit too hard?

Not that she'd had a choice! Still . . . she couldn't stand to see any living thing suffer; even if the living thing was a maniac.

Gingerly she placed her palms on either side of his face, lifting his head a few inches off the floor.

His skin was a bit clammy, too, but he seemed to be breathing fine.

The man gave a slight moan and his lashes fluttered. Slowly his eyes opened, trying to focus on her.

May caught sight of those silver eyes and instantly recognized him.

"*You!*" She dropped his head like a hot potato.

It hit the wooden floor with a clunk.

The man's startled groan was cut off as he passed out again.

Oh, great! She had just beaned and trussed up C. Hunter Douglas, wunderkind and vice-president of Fortuna Books! Should do wonders for her career.

What on earth was he doing here?

Obviously, he had come to see her, but why? May bit her lip. Wait a minute . . . her first book had done remarkably well. There was a rumor going around that Fortuna was looking into starting up a romance line. That's it! Somehow he had found out she was here, probably from her agent, and had come up here to woo her away from her present publisher.

Well, it wouldn't work!

She was very happy where she was. Besides, this was rather *nervy* of him, intruding into her solitude. During Christmas. Publishers!

He would have to stay here until the morning (especially since he was out cold on her floor), but come morning he could just pick himself up and leave!

In the meantime, May thought it best to untie him.

She rolled him over, unwrapped his hands, then flipped him back. It wasn't easy—the man seemed to be six feet plus of solid muscle. Apparently, wrestling writers to the ground like heifers from a shoot on a regular basis did wonders for toning the body.

Better check his breathing. She grimaced, reaching inside his shirt to place her palm over his heart.

Something licked her fingers. May screamed.

"Ahhh!" She fell backward on the floor.

A small furry head poked out of the red velvet, tongue lolling.

A puppy! Her face lit up with a huge grin at the sight of the silly-looking thing. Until she realized that Mr. Douglas had probably counted on such a reaction from her. The nerve! Using a sweet animal to get under her defenses.

Now that she knew his game, she would be totally immune.

The small dog wiggled out from his host's garment, shaking his body in an attempt to smooth out his fur. The action only caused the silky strands to fly in every direction with static electricity. He looked at her and grinned.

Awww . . . May melted completely.

"C'mere, boy!" The dog trotted over to her with a frisky step. "Aren't you the sweetest wittle fellow?" She rubbed the soft face, and his small, wispy tail thumped on the floor.

He was the cutest little wiener dog! She was a goner; already she was speaking baby-talk to him. When a person did that with an animal, the animal knew he had you. Didn't matter if it was a cat or a dog, they all gave you that same smug look which said quite clearly, "personal sucker."

"Let me check on your owner and then I'll see about you." Leaning over Douglas again, she placed her hand over his chest, feeling the steady thump thump thump of his heart.

Then she opened his eyelids to check his pupils. They were slightly dilated, but he didn't seem too bad off.

In any case, she had no telephone to call for help. There was a radio in the cellar, but she hadn't had any reason to use it before this and doubted she could find and work it in the dark. Besides, the electricity was out.

She figured Douglas would sleep the night through and wake up in the morning with a gargantuan headache and a temper to match.

The best she could do was keep an eye on him throughout the night.

CHAPTER EIGHT

May was really starting to get worried.

She had sat on the bed watching the publisher all night. The temperature in the cabin had soon plummeted with the heaters not working.

She had put on her heavy coat and, knowing it had to be freezing on the floor, had rolled him in the bed quilt.

It had not been an easy task.

She practically had to sweep him around the whole floor like a human rolling pin before she could get him situated on the quilt properly.

After that, the dog had sat up near the foot of her bed, and with his stubby paws waving madly, begged her to pick him up. As soon as she did, he dived under her coat for warmth and had not come out since.

Of course, the up side was that he was also acting as a small hot water bottle for her.

Her gaze went worriedly to the windows. It had been snowing steadily all night; in fact, it was a downright blizzard. The wind had picked up at around midnight, shaking the rafters and lending a weird howling sound to the scene.

Even though Douglas couldn't exactly be considered company, especially since he was still out cold, May was almost glad for his bizarre intrusion. At least she wasn't alone in this storm. Not that she would ever admit that she was even remotely pleased with the man's intrusion.

Around dawn, he finally regained consciousness with a loud, protesting groan.

Sitting up, he rubbed the back of his head, silver eyes narrowing slightly when he came across the goose egg on the back of his head.

She must have made a slight sound, because his head snapped up.

The action caused him to wince. He watched her for a few moments silently. When he spoke, his words reflected his anger.

"If this is some type of kidnapping scheme, you can tell your accomplice with the white beard it won't work. I plan on—"

May cut him off. "*Kidnapping scheme?* You've got to be kidding! *You* came here, Mr. Douglas. Completely uninvited, I might add. And you can just forget your little ploy to win me over!"

Hunter squinted his eyes, fighting down a wave of nausea from his throbbing head. "What the hell are you talking about?"

"Don't you remember me, Mr. Douglas? You came here to see me." He examined her face. A little too long. Her black hair was a snarled mass around her shoulders.

"Honey, I'm sure I would remember someone who looked like you."

She made a face at him.

"If you're not trying to kidnap me, why did you hit me on the head? And where are the kids?"

He wasn't making any sense. Uh-oh. Maybe she *had* conked him too hard. "Kids?" she asked tentatively.

"Yeah, the kids. I brought them their Christmas gifts just like your friend asked."

"I don't think so. You came here to see me."

He stopped rubbing the back of his head to stare at her,

disbelieving. None of this made any sense. Which meant he was either concussed or he was dealing with a . . . He didn't want to think of the possibility. "I did?"

She nodded. The bump on his head was probably making him foggy. "I'm a writer," she proudly informed him.

Hunter closed his eyes and groaned. Better he was concussed. He had to be cursed. He was certainly in the wrong place.

"Look, I don't know how this happened but I ran over Santa Claus last night and—"

May snorted. "Did you skin him before or after you 'bagged' him?" She let her gaze travel insultingly up and down his body, letting him know her opinion of his attire.

Hunter tried to explain. "He made me deliver some gifts for him to the children, so I had to—"

She held up her hand. "Please. Don't embarrass yourself further."

He opened his mouth to respond; she cut him off.

"The point is, Mr. Douglas, you've wasted your time. I'm perfectly happy with my present publisher. I'm really sorry about the bump on your head, but what did you expect? Sneaking up on a writer in the Maine woods was not very smart. I can't imagine you've had much success with the technique."

He stared at her dumbfounded. "Do you actually believe I—"

"After all, this is my retreat, my *ashram* . . . " She stopped speaking because his eyes had suddenly thinned into two silver slits.

"What did you say?" His voice had gone dangerously soft.

"Um, never mind." May ran her fingers through her tangled hair.

"Who the hell *are* you?"

"You know—" she began.

"Humor me."

"May Forrester. Well, that's the name you would know me by."

The name did not register. "Sorry," he said with a shrug.

Hunter threw off the quilt, attempting to stand. The room swirled around him, and he grabbed at the bedpost to steady himself.

"Hey, go easy!" May reached over to steady him. "You've had quite a bang on your head."

He opened one eye and glared at her. "Just what did you hit me with?"

May swallowed guiltily. Not that she believed his fumbling explanation. For what other reason would he be here? "A piece of firewood," she admitted quietly.

"Mmm. Pine or oak?"

"Oak," she mumbled.

He rubbed his throbbing temples. "I thought so."

"Look, I'll go make us some coffee. Maybe that will help your headache. It's not as if we can go anywhere." She gestured to the windows.

He looked at her, then let his gaze travel to the windows. Snow was blowing against the glass. He crossed the room in three strides to see what was going on out there.

The view was not encouraging. It was a real "nor'easter." Already drifts were over four feet high and rising.

He turned back to her, an expression akin to horror on his handsome face. "Are you telling me I'm snowbound in a cabin with a . . . a . . . *writer?*"

Like she was a leper or something! May crossed her arms. "As if you didn't plan this! You knew very well what you were doing. I'm not happy about it, but since I'm stuck with you for the time being, I suppose I'll have to make the best of it." With that she turned and headed for the small kitchenette.

It was starting already. He had no idea what she was talking about. And why should he? She was one of *those.* There was no sense trying to reason with her; this he knew from experience. A *writer.* His left eye twitched.

He suddenly remembered something. *Where was the dog?*

Had he somehow dropped him on the porch before she whacked him? *Oh, no.* The little fella never would have made it through the storm last night. "Benny!"

Sick to his stomach, Hunter ran to the front door, only to stop short when she called over her shoulder, "If you mean this adorable puppy here, he's all right. In fact, he's still burrowed under my coat. But I warn you, he won't help your cause."

Hunter let out a sigh of relief. If anything had happened to the little guy . . .

He shivered, suddenly realizing how cold it was in here. Now that he was up and walking, every part of his body fairly screamed in soreness. Strange, but he felt as though he had been rolled across a rough floor all night, then left to stiffen on it.

"Why is it so cold in here?" he called out in the direction of the kitchenette.

"Electricity went out last night. The cabin's heated by electric baseboard, and even when it is working it's none too hot in here. How do you like your coffee?"

"Black." He walked over to the firewood piled by the fireplace. "Is this all the firewood you have?" There was concern in his voice.

"No, there's plenty of cut wood in the cellar."

"I hope it's enough so we don't freeze to death."

May ignored the "we." "There is a generator down

there, but I haven't had a chance to look at it yet." She walked into the room and handed him a mug of coffee. He sipped the brew gratefully, letting the steam hit his face.

"I'll have a look at it when I finish my coffee. Phone out, too?"

"There is no phone."

He stared at her incredulously. "You came out here by yourself, a woman alone, to a secluded place that has no access to a telephone? What if there was an emergency?"

The formulaic expression he wore was one she was becoming familiar with; it said, "writer = alien species."

"I never thought of that—I just wanted some solitude." She gave him a pointed look. "So I could write. I told you, this was to be my *ashram*."

He shuddered, holding up his palm. "Please, not before breakfast."

What was that supposed to mean? May wasn't sure she liked C. Hunter Douglas.

"I have a cell phone in my car. It'll need a charge, but it should be fine."

"And how do you propose to get this cell phone? Have you looked outside lately?"

"As soon as it stops snowing, I'll make my way to the car."

May calmly took a sip of coffee. Typical New York businessman! Ignoring the small matter of four-foot drifts, hurricane-strength winds, and white-out conditions. If she didn't know better, she would have taken him for an agent.

"And where exactly is this car of yours parked?" she asked calmly.

He rubbed his ear. "About three hundred yards down the road."

"Uh-huh." She took another sip of coffee. "I have news

for you, Attila, I managed to get a station on my Walk-man last night for all of fifteen minutes, but I did hear words to the effect of 'storm of the century,' ninety-mile-per-hour winds, and something in the range of three and a half feet of snow."

Hunter was surprised. "This wasn't predicted."

"They never are. Apparently this baby went out to sea, picked up a ton of moisture, and headed back inland. The weathermen were going bonkers, from what I heard."

He ran his hand distractedly through his hair. "Dammit! I need to get out of here today. I have to get to Sri Lanka!"

May eyed him strangely. "Uh-huh. Are you sure you're feeling all right? How many fingers do I have up?" May wasn't holding any fingers up.

"Don't be cute. Since it seems we're both stuck here for the time being, how are we set for supplies?"

There was that "we" business again. "There's plenty to eat. More than enough for two." For the amount of time *he* would be here. Wisely, May kept that thought to herself.

Apparently C. Hunter Douglas wasn't going to take her estimation of the subject; he stormed off to the cubi-cle kitchen and began slamming cabinet doors open and shut. "Where are your food supplies? All I see here is this bag of apples."

"Try the refrigerator."

He opened up the fridge and found a box of Cheerios and a carton of Half-and-Half. He frowned. "Why do you have Cheerios in the refrigerator?"

"Just in case." This was relayed with the utmost seri-ousness.

Coming from New York City, Hunter understood. One could never be too careful until one checked out the premises. Uninvited surprises rustling over the breakfast cereal had a tendency to remove one's appetite.

He opened the freezer.

A row of Tiny Cuisine boxes greeted him.

He rubbed the bridge of his nose. Great. Midget food.

"There's not enough here for one person to eat. Tell me this is not all the food you have here."

"Okay, I won't."

May reached past him, opening the refrigerator to remove the box of cereal. Getting a small bowl for Benny, she poured the dachshund a bowl, moistening it with a little water and a drop of Half-and-Half. The dog eagerly began consuming, his small tail wagging happily.

"We probably should save the cereal for him."

That left the midget food. Hunter grimaced; his stomach was already growling. He grabbed an apple off the counter. "I'll go check out that generator. See what you can pick up on your radio."

May crossed her arms over her chest. Why do men feel they can barge in anywhere and start giving orders? As if she would pay heed to a man talking to her in a red velvet suit! "Excuse me, but there's something you seem to have forgotten."

Hunter paused at the head of the cellar stairs. "What's that?"

"This is *my* rental cabin—*you* are the intruder."

He raised one eyebrow. "Meaning?"

"Meaning I'll give the orders around here."

He exhaled. "I see." He leaned against the door jamb and, imitating her, crossed his arms over his chest.

May had to admit that, of the two of them, he probably looked the more authoritative.

"And what, pray tell, are your 'orders'?"

She notched her chin challengingly in the air. "I'll go check the generator and you listen to the radio." She wanted to slap her own face. *Why had she said that?* She *really* did not want to go in that creepy cellar. She tried to look brave.

Hunter grinned slowly. It was clear the woman did not want to go down there. She was rather cute . . . If only she weren't one of *them*. "Okay, green eyes, I'll check the generator while you listen to the radio."

"Right." She nodded briskly as if that were what she had actually said.

He whistled all the way down the stairs.

Which made May realize that C. Hunter Douglas was going to prove to be the irritating type.

CHAPTER NINE

It had taken him a couple of hours, but C. Hunter Douglas had gotten the old generator working, which moved him up considerably in May's estimation.

He had also managed to drag up the cumbersome radio from the cellar, placing it on the countertop in the kitchen. He had worked on the radio as well, with some rusty tools he had found down there.

May was impressed. She had figured him for a man who never saw the outside walls of an office and therefore assumed he would have no mechanical ability.

When she jokingly told him this, he smiled faintly. "I sometimes suffer from insomnia and often turn on a do-it-yourself cable station in the middle of the night, hoping it will knock me out. It hasn't cured my insomnia, but I have learned how to plant an asparagus bed, put up dry wall, wire an enclosed porch, decorate with style on a shoestring, and cook a Cornish game hen."

He paused, then added, "I hate Cornish game hens. They look like diminutive pigeons."

May chuckled, the word "diminutive" reminding her that they hadn't eaten the Tiny Cuisine yet. She offered to heat up their meals in the small microwave she had brought with her.

Hunter continued to fiddle with the radio. They both were surprised when a burst of static blasted the kitchen.

"It's working!" May beamed at him.

Douglas wore the expression most men wore when they'd managed to repair something. It was a look of demure caveman cockiness. May had often considered the look just short of a gorilla beating its chest.

Women never displayed that look when they did something considered traditionally "female"! Like managing to feed a family of five on a blue-collar budget. Now, there was an accomplishment!

She could just imagine a woman taking her masterpiece of a tuna casserole out of the oven, placing it on the table, only to throw back her shoulders and beat her chest with her fists while letting out a victorious Tarzan yell.

Her humorous fantasy was interrupted by a now familiar male voice angrily yelling into the radio receiver.

"What do you mean, a week? I can't stay here that long! I'm a publisher!"

Apparently Douglas had reached the sheriff's office in town.

The radio crackled and a tired-sounding voice responded, "Look pal, haven't you been listening to me? It's still snowing out there! And it's going to be snowing for the next two days. The whole Northeast has been paralyzed by this storm. We can't even keep up with the emergencies."

"This *is* an emergency! I have to get a manuscript!" Douglas started ranting about a million dollars and Sri Lanka, and May was sure the guy on the other end had chalked him up as New York City looney-tunes.

"Hey! Hey!" the guy was getting really irritated. "You have shelter and food and you're in no immediate danger—that's all I care about. I know where you are. In order to get you out of there, we're going to need some heavy equipment which I can't supply right now. I've got people in desperate situations all over the county. The roads are impassable. So you can just sit tight and wait." The man ended the transmission.

May banged Hunter's tray of food on the table.

"Congratulations, Mr. Congeniality. We should be dug out of here by next spring!"

Hunter roughly pulled his chair out, seating himself. "It wasn't my fault! He . . ." His gaze went to the food in front of him. A spoonful of rice. Two half-dollar-size slices of turkey swimming in a cup of brown water meant to be gravy. "Where's the rest of this?"

Even though she secretly agreed with him, had even been planning on getting some real food, there was no way she was going to admit the deficiencies of the meal to him. Better he think she was a woman with an agenda who stuck to her plans! Otherwise there would be no end to the complaining.

"That's it," she loftily informed him, making her voice sound slightly disdainful as if there were nothing lacking in her choice of fare. "And since it looks like we're going to be stuck here together for a week, we have to go easy on this stuff."

She licked the edge of her fork. "Eat up."

She remembered a cartoon in which Mickey Mouse, Donald Duck, and Goofy all sat down at an elegantly dressed table, complete with overhanging chandelier. Unfortunately, they had nothing to eat except one bean, which Mickey made a great show of slicing into see-thru-thin slices, placing one slice on each plate. Donald Duck watched Mickey silently, his temper slowly reaching the boiling point until suddenly he erupted. Pulling the feathers out of his head, he squawked his head off as he swung upside down from the chandelier.

C. Hunter Douglas had that same look on his face right now.

So she was surprised when, after he clenched and unclenched his fists several times, he quietly picked up his fork.

He took a bite of rice. "Not only is there nothing to eat here, but it tastes lousy."

May shrugged off the critique. "Dieters can't be choosers."

Hunter's silver gaze skimmed her figure. "Why are you dieting? You look fine to me."

She put down her fork in exasperation. "I have a deadline!"

Hunter stared at her unblinking for several moments. "And A is to B as C is to . . . ?"

"Oh, you wouldn't understand."

"Try me." He swallowed both slices of turkey in one gulp.

"It's sort of all tied in with a sense of accomplishment."

Hunter gestured at her with his fork. "It shouldn't be. I have never understood why women feel they have to starve themselves scrawny to feel good about themselves."

"I hardly starve myself, as you can see!"

Hunter's eyes twinkled. "Which makes it all the more confusing as to why you only brought these minuscule dinners with you."

Her cheeks flamed. She thought he might be insulting her but she wasn't sure. "Are you saying what I think you're saying?"

He smiled, revealing two curved dimples. "No, I am not." He let his gaze travel over her again, lingering on her rounded hips and full breasts. She really was a lovely woman. Now that his head wasn't pounding so bad, he was beginning to see some advantage to his situation.

"Just the opposite," he murmured.

Now she did blush. May reached for a glass of water rather shakily. He had better behave himself or he was going to get locked in the fruit cellar with Norman Bates's mother.

Hunter tossed his plastic dinner tray onto the floor for Benny, who gratefully licked up the soupy gravy.

"That won't upset his stomach, will it?"

"Nah. Dogs can eat anything."

"Are you sure? I now he's your dog, but—"

"He's not my dog. He was one of the gifts I—"

"Uh-huh. And how did you know I would even want a dog?"

Hunter sighed. There was no sense trying to explain that to her again. He stood, grabbing two apples off the table. "I'm going to scoop out a place for our friend here. I'm sure he needs to go. The back stoop isn't too bad because of the overhang; it'll have to do. C'mon, Benny." The dachshund trotted after Douglas, something akin to hero worship in his eyes.

C. Hunter Douglas might say that dog does not belong to him, May thought, but the wiener believed otherwise.

CHAPTER TEN

By late that afternoon May wanted to murder him.

In fact, she began to think up ways to do it.

She closed her eyes as he paced by the back of her chair for the thousandth time. He had been pacing for hours. Admittedly, there wasn't much for him to do—there was no TV, her radio wasn't picking up any stations, and there was no phone for "business chats." It was obvious that C. Hunter Douglas was completely at a loss.

She clenched her jaw at his next pass. "Mr. Douglas, *please!* I'm trying to work here."

"It's Hunter." He stopped pacing suddenly. "Hey, do you have any games on that laptop?"

She gritted her teeth. "No. Just word processing. As in manuscript."

He groaned, clutching his stomach. "Don't mention that word to me, it's making my stomach hurt."

"You don't think it could be the six apples you ate?" she said wryly.

He paused to look at her. "You think?" he asked seriously.

She smiled at the boyish expression. "It's a distinct possibility. You better lay off them, Hunter."

"I'm starving!"

"Oh, stop complaining! You'd have to pay a spa three thousand bucks a week for the same treatment you'll be getting here for free, and all they would add to the plate would be a little raddichio."

He threw her a dirty look.

"Don't think about it."

"And what would you suggest I do to take my mind off it?" His glance ran suggestively over her again. If he had met her under other circumstances he would have asked her out to dinner. And more.

May had no trouble reading his look. "*Forget it.* Men in moldy, baggy red velvet are not a major turn-on for me." She wondering if her nose was growing. Hunter was an extremely attractive man. Even in the Santa suit.

"If it'll make you feel better, I'd be happy to remove it." He grinned wickedly at her.

She exhaled. "You're just trying to annoy me because you're bored. Why don't you read?"

"*Read?* You've got books here? Why didn't you say so hours ago?"

She gave him an exasperated look. "What do you think has been staring at you in that open carton over there by the fireplace?"

He shrugged. "Oh, well, those are *romance* books. I thought you meant you had—"

That deserved a glare. "Don't say it if you value your red velvet hide."

"I didn't mean it like that. It's just that I've never—I mean they are women's books—"

"It's not like you have anything else to do—why don't you pick up one, you might be surprised."

He speculated on that, then walked over to the box of books. He knelt down, shuffling through the titles. "Is your book in here?"

"Why would I bring my own book?"

Hunter shrugged. "Why not? Is May Forrester your real name?"

"May is; Forrester is a nom de plume."

Hunter picked up one of her favorite books, opening the step-back cover. His eyes widened. "This guy doesn't have anything on but a towel!"

"Best towel I've ever seen," she agreed with a smile.

He threw her a look. "So what is your real last name?" He sat down on the floor near the fireplace, opening the book.

"Bea."

He read a few paragraphs, then stopped, capturing her in his gaze. "Your real name is May Bea?" Rich laughter filled the room.

"Stop that!"

"That must have been real interesting in high school—'May Bea she will and May Bea she won't.'" He chuckled, shaking his head. "No wonder you took a pen name."

May snapped the lid of her laptop shut. The man was not going to let her work! And he was too close to the mark; the kids had teased her mercilessly when she was young. Which was probably why she had become a writer; she had often run off by herself and daydreams had been her constant companions.

She placed her hands on her hips. "And who are you to talk? I can just guess what hideous first name is hidden by the initial C, Mr. C. Hunter Douglas!"

A dimple showed in his cheek. "Go ahead." His silver eyes flashed challengingly at her.

She hesitated, leery of the look on his provocative face. "Go ahead what?"

"Try and guess."

She narrowed a distrustful look at him. "You'll tell me if I guess correctly?"

"Sure."

"All right." She tapped her foot against the wooden floor. "Cecil."

"Nope."

"Clem."

He grinned. "Uh-uh." He went back to reading his book.

"Don't you worry, I have a whole week to come up with it."

"It's enough to give one pause," he said without looking up. Which was a good thing, because his eyes were definitely twinkling with humor.

And something else.

CHAPTER ELEVEN

"By the way, what *was* the name of your book?"

It was late evening. Hunter had moved up to the bed. The floor was drafty and, with the winds still howling from the unabated storm, May guessed, downright cold.

It was going to make sleeping difficult for him.

She had already decided to offer him the one and only quilt. She would have to try to keep herself warm with her jacket.

"You know very well what the name of it is."

He quirked his brow. "Let's pretend I don't."

"Love's Loose Canon."

He burst into laughter.

May was incensed. "It's a pirate story, so stop that right now! There were *lots* of people who loved it."

He stopped laughing; that had gotten the publisher's attention. "By 'lots' what are we talking about?"

"Romance is *very* popular." Translated for him, it meant profitable.

He suddenly became serious. "I know; I've been looking into it, actually. My uncle has some old-fashioned notions about what Fortuna should and should not publish."

"Well, this could turn out to be a very good opportunity for you! You have the time, I've got the books, not to mention my knowledge of the genre, which I am willing to let you pick at—you could make good use of your time here."

A tiny line formed across his brow as he considered it. "Mmm . . . that's not a bad idea."

"Just remember, I'm off limits."

He looked her questioningly.

"I—I mean as far as writing for your company," she stammered.

He smiled rather sexily, enjoying her discomfort. "Does that mean you're 'on limits' for anything else?"

"Don't be cute."

He batted his thick lashes at her. "I can't help it; I'm a publisher. We're naturally alluring to writers."

"You have a warped mind."

He winked at her. "I'm going to take a shower. Any chance of finding a razor?" He rubbed the dark shadow on his cheeks.

While May thought the shadowy beard very attractive, giving him a brooding, dangerous look, she also recognized the wisdom of removing it from her sight. Hunter was starting to look tempting.

"Check the medicine cabinet; I think Billy left some stuff in there."

"Billy?"

"My neighbor—this is his place."

Hunter nodded, whistling off to the bathroom.

Surely she had misread that brief flash of relief in his eyes?

Hunter lathered his thick hair with some shampoo he found. Along with razor, shaving cream, deodorant, and best of all, a new toothbrush, he didn't feel half bad. Good ole Billy. He'd have to thank the man personally for the supplies.

Earlier, Hunter had noticed a box of condoms on the top shelf behind a large bottle of mouthwash. It remained to be seen whether he would be thanking the man for those as well. Ms. May Bea was looking mighty tempting to him.

In fact, she had from the instant he had first seen her.

Admittedly, he had been momentarily turned off when he discovered she had almost cracked his skull. But once he found out she was a writer, he realized he couldn't hold the outlandish behavior against her.

She couldn't help it. The poor kid.

The hot water sluiced over his head.

It felt great. The cabin was drafty as hell, and the heating system didn't keep up with the nightly drop in temperature.

When he came out of the shower, he eyed the red velvet outfit distastefully. He was going to have to see what he could rustle up in the way of clothes. And he wasn't going to put on that moldy red suit again until he washed it.

Donning his T-shirt and boxers, he padded out of the bathroom.

May was leaning over the bed, and he had a very good view of her backside. She had changed into a heavy flannel nightgown; inexplicably the old-fashioned garment looked sexier than a lacy negligee to him.

Her derriere wiggled under the loose flannel as she tried to pull the quilt free from the top mattress. Hunter crossed his arms over his chest and, leaning against the fireplace mantel, considered the scenery. It was . . . picturesque.

And it worked for him.

He felt himself begin to harden.

When she turned around and saw him standing there, she jumped a little. Seemingly against her will, her sights drifted to his paisley boxers, hesitating slightly. He wasn't really erect but he was . . . bulging. A becoming blush stained her cheeks.

Which made him bulge more.

He stepped forward. "Ready to go to bed?" His voice held the slow drawl of suggestion.

May sucked in her breath. *He was gorgeous.* Even the wretched red suit had not been able to disguise that fact, but when he appeared fresh from his shower in a V-neck white T-shirt and silk boxers, May was nonplused. He had an exquisite physique. Perfectly toned.

Real contemporary hero material, she acknowledged to herself.

However, the heated look in his silver eyes said he had more on his mind than sleeping. Therefore, May did the only thing a romance writer could do in this situation: she stuffed the quilt into his arms and showed him the floor.

To say that C. Hunter Douglas was not a happy camper was an understatement.

He was even less happy when she allowed the wiener dog to get into bed with her.

The floor was hard, cold, and drafty. Hunter heard the dog rustling close to her under her jacket. He bit off an expletive.

For a dog, Benny was one lucky bastard.

CHAPTER TWELVE

Sometime in the middle of the night, May felt the bed dip.

Sleepily, she opened her eyes to the sight of Hunter crawling into bed with her.

She was instantly wide awake. "What do you think—" He placed a finger against her mouth.

"It's freezing on that floor. I'm sleeping here and I don't want to hear one word." That said, he covered them both with the quilt.

Then he turned his back to her.

May's lips curved in amusement. And didn't that sound just like a hero in a book? She'd have to remember that line.

The bed shook slightly and she realized he was shivering. So he really had been cold. Unaccountably, she felt bad for him. His T-shirt and boxers couldn't be providing him with much protection.

Turning her back to him, she scooted a little bit closer to give him some of her body heat. May heard a faint sigh of contentment coming from his side of the bed.

Benny wiggled under the quilt like a sand worm, heading to the foot of the bed. He covered Hunter's cold feet with his long, puppy-warm body, giving his ankle a little lick before settling in to sleep.

Hunter got the strangest impression that he had just come home.

It didn't make sense, but he was too comfortable to care.

CHAPTER THIRTEEN

"He threw back his head and roared with laughter."

May looked at the sentence she had just typed on her screen. Something about it bothered her.

She paused, brow furrowed. "He threw back his head and roared with laughter"? She read it again, this time picturing the strange scene in her mind. May wondered if the gesture didn't indicate a silent plea from her hero for Prozac . . .

What's the matter with me? Everyone loves it when the hero does that! I love it when the hero does that . . .

May sneaked a peek at Hunter, who was sitting on the floor by the fire, engrossed in one of her books.

Well, if Hunter started throwing back his head to roar with laughter she was going to radio that sheriff to have them parachute down some medication for him!

She shut off her laptop.

When this kind of stuff happened, May knew it was useless even to attempt to write. Yawning, she stretched her hands over her head to loosen stiff muscles, her mind going to that morning and how she had awakened in Hunter's arms.

He had been wrapped all over her, and to make matters worse, Benny was tangled up in there with them, too. The three of them lay there like a multi-tentacled lump of snoozing flesh.

The man might suffer insomnia on occasion, but when he did fall asleep, he slept like the dead.

"Hunter!" She jabbed an elbow in his side.

"Nnnn," he mumbled into the curve of her neck. The man was too comfortable.

"Claude?"

She felt him smile against the skin of her throat. "No." He snuggled in and went back to sleep. After a few minutes, May gave up on the idea of untangling herself and fell asleep again as well.

The next time she woke, Hunter was up and making coffee in the kitchenette.

That's when she discovered him draped over the refrigerator drinking the Half-and-Half. *From the carton.*

She let out an ear-piercing shriek.

Stupefied, Hunter stared at her, a mustache of white coating his upper lip.

May made a dive for the carton, rescuing what was left of her cream. "You fiend!" She clutched the carton to her bosom.

"What in the world is wrong with you?"

"I'm a writer; I have to have coffee! It's our lifeblood; our adrenaline!"

Having had a great deal of experience with the breed, Hunter calmly inquired, "Can't you drink it black?"

"No!" She clutched the carton tighter. "It's my one weakness. My God, you drank almost half the container!"

He gave her a patient look. "Your *one* weakness," he said dryly.

"And you were drinking right from the carton!" She screwed up her face. "Eew! I hate it when men do that! What is it—something genetic with you guys?"

She ranted on until he poured her a cup of coffee, pried

the cream lose from her, plopped some into her cup, and brought it to her lips, forcing her to drink.

Those silver eyes flashing all the while in amusement. She was fine after the first cup.

May glanced to where he was sitting by the fire. What was he reading that had him so engrossed? He hadn't lifted his nicely shaped nose from that book in hours.

She squinted her eyes to read the title. No wonder. It was one of her favorite authors and the woman wrote steam heat. Her love scenes could blister paint from a wall. Smiling, she went back to her own story.

Hunter closed the book and leaned his back against the wall of the cabin.

He had just had an incredible revelation.

He had just realized that all these years he had known next to nothing about women. Not according to these books, anyway.

Like most men, he had always assumed that women wanted the same things men did. Now, he realized, they wanted something *else*. Something completely different. Something more.

Did they really go for the swaggering, drag-them-by-the-hair, boy-next-door type? And what did that mean? How could one man be all those things?

Did a man with a heavy-lidded expression—whatever the hell *that* was—turn them into . . . He tried to recall how the last author had phrased it. "A bowl of mush."

And those love scenes.

Mama mia.

They were beyond even his imagination. Since Hunter had always prided himself as a man with an excellent imagination, especially in bed, he was impressed. *I've discovered something here.*

It was a blueprint! A set of directions. Waiting in every bookstore, supermarket, and airport for any man smart enough to find it.

His sights rested on May. Luscious, soft, sweet-smelling May. Totally-oblivious-to-her-own-appeal May. Who had made him stone hard with one sweep of those sexy green eyes.

Hunter smiled wickedly. The theory was at least worth a test run.

CHAPTER FOURTEEN

That night Hunter came out of his shower wrapped in the quilt.

He sat by the fireplace and pretended to read. Making doubly sure the quilt slipped over his shoulder and down one side of his chest.

May finished the last sentence in her chapter and gratefully closed down her computer. "Well, that does it for toni—"

Hunter was sitting by the fire dressed in nothing but that fluffy comforter. May swallowed. *Is he naked under there?*

Firelight bounced off the highlights in his rich brown hair, gilding his shoulder and chest. May noted that said shoulder was plenty muscular and said chest was nicely delineated.

Hunter shifted his attention from his book to her, gazing at her with a carefully constructed, boyishly sweet, totally innocent expression. Like the book said. "Were you saying something?"

She quaked a bit under that intense regard. "N-no, just that I'm finished working for the night."

"Oh. Were you going to take a shower? I washed all my clothes and hung them up over the tub, but I'll take them down if you need to use it."

"Thanks." Her voice cracked a bit. She was right; he was naked under there.

It was sweet of him to offer to clear the shower for her . . . although, she didn't want him to move just yet. He looked awfully cute sitting there quietly reading a book.

Naked.

But for the quilt.

"It'll just take me a minute." He stood up, clumsily gathering the quilt about him. A section accidentally parted, revealing a tantalizing glimpse of tanned, muscled thigh before his fist clenched the material closed.

May forced herself to look away. Unfortunately, the picture must have seared in her brain, for she could not seem to shake it.

Hunter exited the bathroom, his damp clothes draped over his arm.

"You *washed* the velvet suit?" she asked incredulously.

"Uh-huh. Why? Is something wrong?" He looked at her earnestly.

She didn't have the heart to tell him. He'd find out soon enough when it dried. And could stand on its own.

She straightened the stack of papers she had printed out, scanning them for typos. A voice came from right behind her chair and it sounded like a croaking bullfrog.

"You must be stiff from sitting here all day; would you like me to massage—"

She gaped at him over her shoulder. "What happened to your voice?"

He seemed surprised at her reaction. He frowned. "I'm speaking to you in a husky murmur."

"Well, don't. You sound like a foghorn at low tide."

Hunter stroked his freshly shaved jaw. "I must be doing it wrong. Can you demonstrate it for me?"

She put her hands on her hips. "Where did you ever get such a crazy idea? And why do you want to talk in a husky murmur?"

"I'm . . . testing out something. Go with me on this, okay?"

She expelled a gust of breath. The man was strange. "All right. Try this." She lowered her voice to a throaty, intimate drawl. *"The shower's ready and waiting . . ."*

Hunter's eyes glazed over. His heart kick-started. He leaned toward her . . .

"Your turn," she said in her normal voice.

Hunter pulled up short. Well, it sure worked on him! Positive that he could give as good as he got, he cleared his throat to try again.

Resting his forearm on the back of her chair, he bent close to her, whispering softly, "Your . . . shower is *ready* and I'm waiting . . ."

May's eyes widened. "Th-that's good." More than just good. Drooling good.

The corners of Hunter's mouth curved. He decided to move in a little closer to her. He wanted to kiss that little curve on the corner of her mouth that had been fascinating him since he met her.

May bounced out of her chair. "Guess I better take advantage of it then, huh?" She dashed to the bathroom.

Just before she closed the door, she called out, "Cedric?"

"No," he yelled back, smiling. *It was working.* He could feel it in his . . . bones.

The thought made him laugh. Huskily.

CHAPTER FIFTEEN

"My underwear is still damp. I guess I'll have to sleep like this."

Hunter gestured to the quilt covering his bronzed skin and gave her an apologetic "it's beyond my control—what can I do?" look which didn't quite pass muster.

May's black brow notched. The man was getting decidedly frisky. And if he thought he was crawling into bed with her buck naked, he had another think coming. There was no chance she was going to wake up in the morning wrapped up with an *in-the-raw* Hunter.

She marched to the bathroom, where he had slung the clothes he'd washed over the shower rod. Hunter followed behind warily. May looked like she meant business.

Spotting the paisley silk, she whipped the shorts off the rack and grabbed her blow dryer. Adjusting the heat setting to low, she held the very edge of the garment up between two fingers as if it might bite her at any moment and blasted the dampness right out of it.

Hunter's lips parted slightly. Now, why hadn't he ever thought of that? His second thought was: foiled.

May turned to him with his boxers dangling from her index finger. The arrangement of her features was definitely smug. "There you go—nice and dry."

Sheepishly, Hunter reached for them. "Ah, yeah. Thanks."

Once again, when they got into bed they turned their backs to each other.

Just before May drifted off, she asked him in the darkness, "Chester?"

Hunter smiled, drowsy. "Nope." He rubbed his silk-covered backside against her flannel-covered one before falling into a restful sleep.

CHAPTER SIXTEEN

Hunter tossed a piece of apple to Benny, then crunched into his fourth apple of the day. And it was only late afternoon. He was getting mighty sick of apples.

Well, beggars couldn't be choosers. Desultorily he wolfed down the fruit. He was starving.

Those frozen meals were not enough for him, even though May had been giving him two of the tiny cuisine meals every night.

His silver gaze wandered to the windows. It had stopped snowing this morning but it was a real mess out there. There was no chance of getting to his car. Not without boots and a plow.

He looked down at his wardrobe. May had dug out a pair of her black sweat pants this morning after he discovered that the red velvet suit was now a free-standing sculpture. They fit him like a second skin and only came to mid-calf on him, but he had been determined to ram down into them.

There was a faint floral perfume to the pants which evoked May. The fact that he was *inside* them, surrounded by the scent, made him . . . bulge. A situation made more blatant by the stretchy material.

He rubbed the bridge of his nose, wishing it were something else. Something May.

This morning she had been been draped over his back,

her cheek using his shoulder as a pillow. One of her small hands had found its way around his waist to rest flat against his lower stomach, just above the band of his shorts.

In his sleep his hand had come over hers, making sure she didn't leave the needy spot. He was uncomfortably aroused and had a hell of a time disengaging himself from her without waking her up.

The memory of it alone was enough to get him going again.

Frustrated, he grabbed up another book. *Rough Possession* was the title. Hunter quickly threw it down and picked up another. *Day for Knight.* That sounded innocuous enough.

He began to read.

Across the room, May furtively eyed Hunter.

He was engrossed in his book and he didn't seem to be paying any attention to her.

Good.

Her hand inched slowly to the stack of papers on her lap. The stack that was hiding the half-eaten package of M&M's she had found in the bottom of her purse this morning.

She was starving.

In desperation she had tackled her pocketbook for booty and had come up with a small treasure trove.

Covertly she rooted around in the little bag, her finger snagging the small candy-coated jewel. Glancing his way one more time to be certain the coast was clear, she secretively brought the nugget of heaven to her mouth where she sucked on it for five minutes, savoring every molecule.

When it was over, her eyes were dilated with chocolate satisfaction.

Hunter was still engaged in the book. And looking damn fine, she thought resentfully. Those black sweat pants had been a mistake. Instead of covering him up and removing temptation from her sight, they seemed to be doing the opposite. The clingy material delineated every muscle in his strong thighs.

Every muscle.

May fanned herself with a sheet of paper. Hunter was packing.

She rummaged around for another M&M.

"What are you eating?"

May's head snapped up, her face flaming guiltily. "What?"

Hunter's silver eyes narrowed. "Don't what me— you've got something stashed away under those papers. What is it?" He tossed his book down. Rising to his feet, he began stalking her.

She didn't know why she did what she did.

There must have been a little devil on her shoulder.

She looked the publisher square in the eye and, parting her lips, she stuck out her tongue and flaunted the yellow M&M at him.

It was like waving a red flag at a bull.

Hunter charged her.

Squealing, May bolted out of her chair and took off. The papers and the candy package which had been on her lap toppled to the floor.

Hunter stopped briefly to grab the empty M&M wrapper. Then he turned and sets his sights on her.

"Last one," May taunted around the candy in her mouth.

Hunter lunged for her.

If she hadn't backed herself against a wall she might have escaped.

His palms came down on either side. He pinned her in

place with the lower half of his body. Even through her jeans, May had no trouble feeling the hardness that pressed against her. Her breath caught in her throat.

She looked up into his face. A lock of mahogany hair had fallen over his forehead, giving his face a definite rakish cast.

As he bent his head, May noted that he didn't seem to be thinking about candy anymore. By the glint in those silvery eyes, it appeared that Hunter had decided to substitute one gratification for another.

May squeaked, the sound distorted by the candy in her mouth. "Hunter, you shouldn't—"

His mouth sizzled over hers.

There really was no other way to describe it.

A hot flame shot down the center of her body to her toes. Which began to wiggle.

May moaned into his mouth. There was only one other man who had ever made her toes wiggle . . . and not nearly this much.

Hunter removed one of his hands from the wall and cupped the back of her head, holding her to him. He strengthened the kiss, probing between her slightly parted lips with his tongue. Sinking deeper and deeper with every delving thrust, he forced her to open her mouth wider, to accept him . . .

He plunged into her with rough expertise, neither too naive nor too practised. His movements were honest and raw. He explored her thoroughly, leaving her totally breathless and wanting more Hunter.

May thought he tasted sweeter than any candy, and she clutched at his shoulders to bring him closer.

This time it was Hunter who groaned. His other hand left the wall to capture her waist, clasping her tight against him.

She didn't know how long the kiss went on but when they came up for air, May was feeling somewhat disoriented. She placed her palm against his chest to steady herself.

He was breathing heavily, but was curiously silent. Warily she glanced up at him.

His eyes glimmered with heat and . . . something akin to mischief. He quirked his brow in a cocky way, then slowly opened his mouth.

The yellow M&M dangled impudently from his tongue.

"Hunter!"

He grinned roguishly at her.

"That was a dirty trick!"

"Mmm . . . best M&M I ever had," he drawled. He made a great show of savoring the candy, even to the point of licking his lips when he was done.

May's face flamed.

He chuckled, leaning back into her. "Seconds?" he asked innocently.

"No!" She shoved his chest, pushing him away.

"You mean you don't like the heated press of my masculine lips against the soft fullness of your ripened mouth?" He spoke from behind her.

"Don't you dare!" she gritted out, refusing to look at him.

"Surely you felt the savage intensity of my raging hunger as I claimed you with the brand of my desire?"

"You are horrible!" She walked to the bathroom and slammed the door behind her.

His low laughter followed her.

May winced. The truth was she had felt all those things. She splashed cold water on her face.

CHAPTER SEVENTEEN

"What's wrong with Benny?"

Hunter had just come out of his nightly shower and when he bent down next to her, May caught a whiff of soap and after-shave. Old Spice. Billy's choice, she knew; Hunter was definitely not the type to buy Old Spice.

For some reason, the spicy scent reminded her that it was Christmas Eve.

She delicately inhaled more of the scent. It brought her back to her childhood when she had lived by the coast in a small New England fishing village. A lot of the men had worn Old Spice back then, and she rather liked the old-fashioned scent.

The word old-fashioned brought to mind how gentlemanly Hunter had been these last few nights, letting her shower first, giving her best crack at the hot water, which had a tendency to suddenly give out.

She adjusted her nightgown as she sat cross-legged on the floor.

"He has a tummy ache." She continued to rub the dachshund's belly.

Benny lay on his back, short feet up in the air, in what May was beginning to think of as his dead cockroach position. The wiener dog's expression was a carefully balanced blend of ecstasy at what she was doing combined

with the sad "I'm a poor puppy" face which instantly pro-
duced a feeling a guilt in humans.

"How did he get an upset stomach?" Hunter had the
nerve to ask that seriously.

May threw him a look. "How many pieces of apple did
you give him today?"

A dull bronze colored his cheekbones. "I . . . ah . . .
don't remember."

Benny gave a little whimper right on cue.

Hunter was consumed with remorse. "Hey, there, fellah." His hand joined hers on the dog's belly, rubbing.
"Will he be all right?"

With all the attention, Benny was in puppy heaven
and trying hard not to show it, while the man leaning
over him had an expression of concern which only comes
from an owner of a beloved pet. May smiled inwardly.
Hunter was as good as gotten.

"Yes, but you shouldn't keep tossing him food; he probably can't eat so many strange combinations."

Hunter nodded, continuing to rub the dog's stomach
with her. Every now and then their hands brushed against
each other.

"How come you didn't do this for me when I had a
tummy ache?" Hunter murmured next to her ear.

"Because you don't keep my feet warm at night," she
replied without thinking.

May realized her mistake as soon as she saw those dark
lashes lift languorously and those silvery eyes met her own.

There was such a frankly sexual look in them that her
breath stopped in her throat.

"I'd be happy to keep you warm at night."

He did it. He spoke in a husky murmur.

And it sounded exactly the way she had imagined a

perfectly executed husky murmur would sound. It even sent shivers down her spine.

He leaned toward her just a bit, and May knew he was going to kiss her. Instinctively she moved her head back a few inches.

His hand came over hers on top of Benny.

His other hand cupped the back of her neck, bringing her up against his descending mouth in a seamless move. She opened her mouth to attempt to object, but Hunter was already there.

His lips covered hers in a gentle press that was somehow persuasive at the same time. The tender act turned May into. . . . a bowl of mush.

Her mouth softened beneath his, returning his kiss.

Like any red-blooded man, Hunter took this as encouragement. He went from softly coaxing to "seize-the-moment fire" in the blink of an eye.

May gasped. What were they doing? She began to pull back.

"Hunter, stop!" She tried to speak between the molten imprint of his ongoing kisses. It was almost impossible; the man was definitely charged up.

"We shouldn't be doing this," she managed to croak just before he swept inside her mouth, staking a devastating claim. She moaned in response.

"Why not?" he whispered a few seconds later, not stopping in the least.

The question had been rhetorical, but May attempted to respond any way. "Be-because . . . you're only doing this because you're hungry! You're substituting—"

He chuckled, a low rumble against her lips. "I'm *hungry* all right." His mouth moved along her jawline to her throat.

May sucked in her breath. That was a very sensitive area. She closed her eyes, desperately trying again. "You see? You admitted it. You've been complaining how starving—"

He stopped. Raising his head, he looked at her, desire and something akin to amusement lighting his features.

With his lips a mere heartbeat away from hers, he purred, "I'm hungry for May."

Then his mouth seized hers and that was the end of that objection.

How did the man kiss like that? May was devastated and knew it. Especially since her toes were wiggling like mad under the hem of her nightgown.

His lips moved back to her throat, and May actually arched her throat to give him better access.

Hunter breathed in her flowery scent and went as hard as a brick.

Earlier, in the bathroom, he had opened her jar of floral scented cream and had inhaled deeply. It had not had the same effect on him and he realized that it needed the added factor of May. Her personal, sexy scent which had been driving him crazy since that first night.

His mouth closed over the spot of tender skin under her ear and he felt her tremble. She was responding to him.

"*Hunter* . . ." It was the sound of a woman in the throes of desire; however, there was the faintest hint of underlying protest.

He did not want her to stop him. Not now. Not ever. C. Hunter Douglas wanted May "Forrester" Bea.

So, clever strategist that he was, he decided to make absolutely sure of her compliance.

He was going to pull all the stops out and completely test his new theory. He was going to follow the directions that had been handed to him in the books he'd read. He was going to make love to her with *romance*.

He leaned over and, gathering her in his arms, he stood, without breaking the kiss. It was not an easy thing to do from a sitting position, but Hunter was a strong, large man. He hoped the small pop he heard in his back had been the settling of his joints and not a disc compressing.

Benny gave one bark of protest at the loss of his belly rub, then gave up, apparently recognizing when it was pointless for a dog to bid for attention.

Hunter carried her to the bed, gently depositing her in its center. He immediately came over her, his silk boxers sliding against the flannel of her gown.

His mouth fused with hers as he laced his fingers through her hair and kissed her senseless.

May's hands reached for his bare shoulders. They were muscular and hard, yet so very warm. . . . And the way the man kissed should be illegal!

He had carried her to the bed, actually carried her to the bed!

Her toes wiggled.

Hunter's knee wedged between her flannel-clad legs. He rubbed his thigh back and forth in a suggestive slide, inching higher and higher. The flannel of her gown pulled taut with his erotic motions and she gasped into his mouth.

How could she come to her senses when he wasn't giving her time to think?

One of his hands moved to the front of her gown and he cupped her breast, flicking his thumb slowly back and forth across the flannel-covered nipple. It hardened instantly.

He covered the jutting peak with his mouth, capturing it with his teeth.

When May felt the damp heat of his mouth through the material, a strangled sob seem to escape from her

throat. Without thinking, she sank her fingers in the rich
thickness of his mahogany hair. Drawing him closer.

He began to unbutton the front placket of her gown.

The feel of the tips of his fingers against the soft skin
of her breast suddenly made May realize what she was doing. "Hunter," she choked, "what—what are we doing?"

Hunter paused. She was starting to balk. Now what?
Time out for following the directions, he realized.

"You feel this, sweetheart?" He spoke against her lips as
he stroked his fingers around her breast.

May closed her eyes and nodded.

"I'm stroking my hand against your velvet skin—here.
And here." He brushed her lips with his mouth. "Does it
feel good?" he whispered.

"Yes . . . oh, yes, Hunter, it does," she whispered back
breathlessly.

Hmmm . . . it seemed to be working. "Do you know
what I'm going to do next?"

She watched him, eyes open wide. Slowly she shook
her head, indicating she had no idea.

"I'm going to dip my hot tongue into your luscious
mouth and then . . ." He paused purposely.

May swallowed. My god, the man was dangerous. And
he was very good with dialogue. "And then?" she asked
faintly.

The corner of his mouth lifted in a roguish grin. "And
then, lovely May, I'm going to *drink*."

She gasped, lips parting, and Hunter did exactly as he
said he would. He delved into her. And drank. May
writhed beneath him, caught up in the sensual storm he
was creating.

He reached down and methodically lifted her nightgown inch by inch up and over her head. She wore nothing underneath. When the entire six-foot length of his

flesh pressed against her, heavy and hot, she sighed into his mouth.

Hunter ran the palms of his hands over the curves of her body, marveling at how exquisite the touch of her skin was. He hadn't stopped to get a thorough look, but he had seen enough.

May was beautiful.

He expected she would be because . . . well, she had had that effect on him right from the beginning. In his eyes, she would always be beautiful.

He took her breast into his mouth and she arched up against him, a small, sexy moan of pleasure escaping her lips. The feminine sound shook him to his core.

"Hunter!"

"Easy, May . . . I'm just tasting you." He rolled his tongue around the jutting peak. "And teasing you." He flicked the nubbin several times, causing her to clutch at his shoulders.

"And taking you inside the burning dampness of my fiery mouth so I can draw on you with an untold hunger," he improvised.

May blinked. An untold hunger? That line needed a good editor. But then he drew on her voraciously, and in the next instant she didn't care what he was saying.

It was what he was *doing* that held her interest. And what he was doing was sending her over the roof. His hands were caressing her and molding her. Stroking and rubbing and stirring her up with each delicious sweep of his fingers.

Her palms found their way down his contoured back and of their own accord slipped under the elastic band of his shorts.

But no further.

May suddenly comprehended that there was only the thin silk of his boxers between the two of them.

And that item of clothing had a convenient slit in it.

May swallowed nervously. She couldn't do this! There was a very good reason why she couldn't do this. Suddenly scared, she desperately searched her brain for an excuse, *any* excuse that would . . .

She had it.

Grabbing a hank of his thick hair, she pulled his head up. Glazed silvery eyes tried to focus on her. "We can't do this, Hunter."

He stared at her, frozen to the spot. Then he nodded, as if he understood what she was saying. "It's okay—I'll deal with the fact that you're a writer."

May's eyes darkened. "No, you numbskull! I'm not talking about that. I mean we can't do this because we don't have . . . protection." There. That seemed an excellent reason. The best reason. She was very proud of herself.

Dazed, Hunter paused, his kiss-swollen lips parting a little.

The poor thing.

Then a slow, calculating smile creased his passion-etched face. She did not like that look. "What are you smiling for? Didn't you hear me? We have to stop and I—"

"May."

She stopped speaking to stare up at him.

"Don't you want to feel the driving thrust of my steely manhood between the petals of your tender femininity as I masterfully take you to a place where only the angels dwell?"

This he rasped in that perfected husky murmur of his.

"That is, until we float back down from the stars to the safe cushion of our entwined bodies."

Her face flamed. In some strange way she couldn't define, his words were having the oddest effect on her. It was as if . . . No.

In any case—despite the rather enticing image his words provoked—they could not go on.

Hunter didn't seem to share her opinion. Taking her silence (and flushed face) as interest, he winked rakishly at her.

Furthermore, the silk shorts were quickly dispensed with.

"Hunter!"

A whoosh of cold air crossed her body as he jumped off the bed. May got a brief flash of something rather . . . robust, before she was presented with his backside as he headed toward the bathroom.

Her sweat pants hadn't lied—Hunter's bulge was nothing less than impressive. His buns weren't bad, either, she clinically noted as he strutted through the door. Not bad a-tall . . .

Realizing she was lying on the bed buck naked, she dived under the covers. Then began to wring her hands. Was that it? Was he just . . . leaving?

Or was he coming back?

May didn't know whether to exhale or take a deep breath.

She soon found that Hunter was coming back.

And in his hands were *dozens* of foil packages. She decided to take a deep breath. Her brilliant excuse had just gone out the window. "Where did you get those?" she gasped.

He grinned at her. "Good ole Billy—your neighbor."

"Billy?" This was more bizarre than she thought. She cocked her head sideways, trying to come to terms with the idea. "He's in his sixties! *At least.*"

Hunter snorted. "So what?"

May plucked at the quilt. "Well, I just thought . . . men that old didn't . . . I mean. . . ."

"You thought wrong. My uncle is seventy-three and he's

still pounding his—" He stopped, realizing what he was saying. C. Hunter Douglas turned bright red. "Ah. . . . sorry."

Her lips twitched. He really was adorable. The perfect
combination of boyish charm and predatory "hunkiness."
She sighed demurely.

Unfortunately, her *nice* thoughts of him shifted to ap-
prehension when he tossed the mound of packets onto
the bedside table.

She swallowed. There were hundreds of the little bug-
gers. "You—you're being overly optimistic, don't you
think?"

"Nope." He lifted the quilt and climbed into bed.

Before she had time to think of something to say, he
scooped her in his arms and rolled on top of her, his lips
taking hers in swift possession.

Caught in her own sensuality, May succumbed to his
passion—until he began gently to probe between her thighs
with his erection, trying to get her to unlock her legs.

"Open for me, honey," He whispered the sweet words
against her mouth, and if anything was ever more perfectly done in her life, she hadn't known about it.
Still . . .

The wispy words rushed out. "Oh, Hunter, it's been . . .
such a long time and—"

"Don't worry, sweetheart, I'll be careful."

May unlocked her legs—a little—and squeezed her
eyes shut.

What was this all about? Hunter wondered. Since she
had only spread her legs the smallest space, he had to
wedge himself in there bit by bit until she finally opened
her thighs all the way for him.

Hunter pressed forward slightly.

She was very tight. A little bit more . . .

He felt the barrier.

Astonished, he looked down at the woman beneath him. Her face was drawn up anxiously and she was biting her bottom lip.

Despite the seriousness of the situation, his lips twitched. *Does she think I can't tell?* "May." His voice held a hint of laughter and a hint of reproach.

She did not change her expression or open her eyes. "Yes, Hunter?" she whispered haltingly.

He decided that what he was going to say could wait until later.

"Aren't you going to kiss me?" His mouth brushed her closed lids in a loving caress.

Her green eyes fluttered open. "Oh, yes, of course, I was just—"

His mouth covered hers and he sunk into her, rapidly piercing the thin membrane.

She flinched, then lay perfectly still.

"I'm sorry," he spoke quietly in her ear but May didn't even hear him. She was too wrapped up in the feel of Hunter. He was inside her and it was . . . it was . . . precisely as she had imagined.

Giving her time to adjust to him, he brushed his lips across her slightly parted mouth, back and forth, laving the seam with his tongue, gently suckling on her lower lip.

"*Hunter*," she uttered tremulously.

"I know, honey. I know." He kissed her deeply.

When he began to gently move in her, May cried into his mouth, small sounds of feminine pleasure that made it very difficult for him to maintain his control. She was driving him crazy. His body was telling him hard and fast, but his mind was cautioning him to slow and easy.

A sweat broke out across his brow but he held to his guarded tempo.

It was May who finally changed the pace.

Wrapping her arms tightly around his neck and her legs securely around his waist, she hugged him to her, her uneven voice shyly beseeching him, "More?"

It was the sexiest thing he had ever heard in his life. Hunter groaned out loud. And gave her more. Much more.

He drove into her with strength and power, releasing the passion he previously held in check for her sake. May went right along with him, encouraging him, begging him, commending him, in the unintelligible words of lovers which always spoke volumes.

A pounding, building tempest overtook her, lifting her higher and higher. It was extraordinary . . . she was pulsing everywhere and she wanted to—had to

"Let go, sweetheart, let it go," Hunter rasped, guiding her even as he took her.

May cried out and let go and everything simply exploded around her. He thrust into her *deep* and clutching her to him, he covered her mouth with his own, joining her in a powerful release. May was intensely aware of the moment, of Hunter, of their joining.

It was a special gift that she would treasure forever; he had given her what every woman dreams of, hopes for. He had made the reality of her first time a true fantasy. And she would love him forever for it.

Hunter smiled tenderly down at her. He kissed the edge of her temple, feathering her jawline with tiny nibbles. "It looks like my May Bea didn't." He teased her softly. "How did you write all those love scenes?"

May kissed his chin. "Writers don't do *everything* they write about, Hunter."

He thought about that. "True. If Rex Stevens did half the stuff he wrote about, he'd have gotten the electric chair twenty times over."

She nodded. "We only wish we could."

He laughed against her throat. Then nuzzled her collarbone.

May sighed contentedly. Lovemaking *was* all that it was cracked up to be. And it was exactly the way she had written it countless times.

Incongruously, a large grin broke across her face. "Mmm, Hunter?"

Expecting to see a sexy, satisfied look on her face, Hunter was amazed to see a ridiculously huge smile. Confounded, he gave her a questioning look.

"I *am* a terrific writer!" She beamed up at him.

Oh-oh. It was another of those "writer" references that had a tendency to be non sequiturs. He had always marveled when he had seen two writers talking together; they always seemed to understand each other. It was the damnedest thing.

Well, Hunter had no idea what her being a good writer had to do with *this*, but he nodded as if he understood just the same.

He snuggled back into her neck.

And reached for another foil packet.

"Champ?" she whispered teasingly a few minutes later.

"Uh-uh." Smiling, he nipped the curve of her neck.

CHAPTER EIGHTEEN

Benny woke them up Christmas morning.

The little dog was barking and dancing around the bed, trying desperately to get Hunter to pay attention to him.

They both groaned.

Hunter had made love to May the entire night and they were both exhausted.

"What's the matter with him?" May mumbled sleepily. "Does he have to go out?"

"I don't think so—I just let him out a few hours ago." Hunter yawned, then leaned over May so he could see Benny over the edge of the bed. "Wuzza matter, fellah?"

Benny wagged his tail and barked twice. Then he trotted to the front door, looking over his shoulder to see if Hunter was following him.

"I guess he does have to go out." Hunter rolled over May to get out of bed.

"Hunter!" she complained.

The corner of his mouth lifted crookedly in a smile and he bent over to kiss her nose. "Sorry." Naked, he padded after Benny.

May got a very nice view. She crossed her arms over her chest to watch the show. "Anytime," she murmured to herself.

"C'mon, Benny, we gotta go out the back door—too much snow out there." Hunter started for the door off the kitchen but the wiener dog wouldn't budge from the front door. He stuck his long nose near the bottom crack and sniffed all along the edge, his tail wagging excitedly.

"What is it do you suppose?" May asked.

Hunter scratched his chin. "I don't know. But he thinks there's something out there." Hunter walked over to where the dachshund was standing and carefully opened the front door.

As he suspected, snow was piled three feet deep on the porch and there was noplace to go.

"See, boy? Nothing there—"

Benny dived head first into the snowbank.

"Hey!" Hunter lunged after him, trying to retrieve him before he lost sight of the thumping tail.

He pulled Benny back out; the dog had a piece of cloth clamped in his jaws and was tugging furiously.

Curious, May squinted to get a better look. "What does he have in his mouth?"

"It's the sack!"

"What sack?"

"The sack of gifts I was carrying when I came up here. I forgot all about it. I must have dropped it on the porch." Hunter released Benny, putting him behind him; then he yanked the material, trying to loosen the large bag from under the snowdrift.

It came free suddenly, and both Hunter and the sack came hurtling into the room. May giggled.

Hunter regained his balance and gave her a look.

"Well, it is funny, Hunter; I mean, you are naked."

Shivering, he closed the door. "Not for long—it's c-o-o-l-d." He snatched up his shorts and T-shirt, putting them on.

Benny started circling the bag excitedly, yapping his head off.

"Now what?"

May found her nightgown scrunched down at the foot of the bed. She was still buttoning it when she came beside him. "What's in there?"

"Just gifts I was supposed to deliver." He reached into the bag and pulled out a red package with a big white bow. A small tag dangled from the top.

Benny barked louder.

"To Joanna," Hunter read the tag, "Merry Christmas from Santa Claus."

Benny sat up, waving his front paws madly.

"I think he wants you to open it."

Hunter shrugged. "Why not?" He unwrapped the gift. A huge grin filled his face.

"What is it?" May looked at him inquiringly.

Hunter reached in the box and held up a plate of candied sweet potatoes.

May's eyes glazed over. "*Hunter.*"

"*Woof!*" Benny concurred.

"That's why he was barking, he could smell the food."

"Do you think it's still okay?"

Hunter dipped his finger in the sauce and licked it off. "Mmmm-hmmm. Natural Maine refrigeration. It's perfect."

May rushed over. "Open up the others, quick!"

Hunter grabbed the next package. "To Alicia, Happy Holidays courtesy of Ingles Delicatessen, where Katya and Rolph say every bite of our food tastes like a little bit of magic." This one held a scrumptious-looking pecan pie.

May and Hunter's eyes met above the plate.

In the next instant they were both diving for the boxes, tearing the wrappings open.

"To Jennifer . . ." May opened a tray of assorted hors d'oeuvres.

"To Chris . . ." Hunter held up a tureen of creamed pearl onions.

"This one is to Ted . . ." May pulled out a pair of bayberry candles and holders.

"For Richard, Happy Chanukah . . ." A dish of giant potato pancakes. They both licked their lips.

Next came a box of dog biscuits with "Benny's favorite" taped to the box. Hunter tossed him one, then reached in the bag to get the biggest gift out.

"To Johnny . . ." They both held their breath as he unwrapped it. It was a big Christmas ham.

May ran into the kitchen to get some plates and silverware. Hunter took the quilt off the bed and spread it before the fire. They were going to have Christmas dinner.

Soon they were seated before the fire feasting on the riches they had found.

May looked at the wonderful food before her, the sweet puppy lying contentedly by the fire, chewing on his hambone, and the man next to her, who against all expectations had turned into a real-life hero.

Her eyes filled with moisture. "This is the best Christmas I've ever had, Hunter."

He put his fork down to cover her hand with his. "Me, too, May."

They came together to kiss.

"Casper?" She planted a soft kiss next to his dimple.

"No, honey."

May sat back on her haunches. "Then what *is* it?"

Hunter grinned at her. "Christopher," he said nonchalantly.

"*Christopher?* But that's a nice name!" She was indignant.

He laughed. "I never said it wasn't, Ms. Bea. That was your idea."

"No wonder you had on a Santa suit," she grumbled. "With that name you were a shoo-in. How come you don't use it?"

"My grandfather's name is also Christopher. It got too confusing at family get-togethers."

As simple as that. No wonder he wasn't a writer. A writer would have a much better story than that.

However, flights of fancy notwithstanding, she was absolutely crazy about the publisher.

Hunter reached over, his hand clasping her about the neck. "You know what?" Their noses were almost touching.

"What?" she purred.

"I think I'm in love with you."

May blinked, stunned.

"Know what else?" he went on unperturbed.

"N-no."

"I think you love me, too."

A *writer and a publisher? How existential* . . . May's thoughts were interrupted by his next question.

"Know what else?"

May shook her head.

"I predict that you and I will be here next Christmas and we'll be old married folks." He stopped to stare at her poignantly. "What do you think of that, May?"

She did not have to think. "Mmmm, I just love sequels . . ." May closed the small distance between them.

After they ate, May went to store the leftovers in the refrigerator and Hunter was picking up in the room. He had already replaced the quilt on the bed and was in the process of folding the large cloth sack when a small card floated out of the bag to fall at his feet.

Thinking it was a tag that had fallen off a gift, he bent

down to retrieve it and was about to throw it away when he spotted *his* name on the front of it.

Gingerly he opened it and read:

To Hunter,

It seems Benny and you are a perfect match. The other half of your gift is a lifelong one—something you've been needing for a long time. Remember, it only comes from following the "directions" exactly. Merry Christmas.

Your Friend, the Old Coot

P.S. It's a good thing I have an extra suit.

A cold sweat broke across Hunter's brow. He suddenly remembered the names of some of those nurses in the hospital. Nurse B. Litzen? Nurse Donner? And that little red-haired one . . . Rudy.

No way.

What about that deli that supplied all those gifts for the children? Katya and Rolph Ingles . . . K. & R. Ingles . . . Kringles?

It couldn't be.

At that moment May came back to the room. Seeing his ashen expression, she asked, "Is something wrong, Hunter?"

He rubbed his hand across his face. Who would believe it? "No, everything is fine, sweetheart. C'mere, Benny." He patted his leg so the dog would come to him.

Benny obediently left his mangled hambone and trotted Hunter's way.

When the dog was sitting by his feet, Hunter reached down and untied the blue ribbon around the dog's neck. "Welcome home, boy." He ruffled the fur on Benny's head.

Tongue hanging out, Benny gave his new master a look of pure adoration.

The burst of static from the radio surprised both of them. "Hey, Douglas, you there?" It was the sheriff's office.

Hunter went over to the radio, flicking the switch. "Yeah, go ahead."

"I have an urgent message from your editorial director."

Hunter took a deep breath. "Go ahead."

"She says, 'Rex's manuscript arrived last night from Sri Lanka. It's a knockout. Relax and enjoy the holiday.'"

Hunter was nonplused. Rex had come through. Big time. He actually felt his eyes get damp.

"We should be able to dig you out day after tomorrow," the sheriff continued.

"That's okay, Sheriff." He met May's eyes. "Take your time." He switched the radio off.

May beamed at him. "You got your manuscript!"

Hunter hugged her to him. "That and a whole lot more."

"*How romantic!*" May gazed up at him, love shining in her eyes. "Oh, Hunter, I absolutely adore you!"

He looked down at May and sighed. *Writers.* They were the best.

☐ YES!

Sign me up for the Love Spell Book Club and send my
FREE BOOKS! If I choose to stay in the club, I will pay only
$8.50* each month, a savings of $6.48!

NAME: _____

ADDRESS: _____

TELEPHONE: _____

EMAIL: _____

☐ I want to pay by credit card.

☐ **VISA**   ☐ **MasterCard**   ☐ **DISCOVER**

ACCOUNT #: _____

EXPIRATION DATE: _____

SIGNATURE: _____

Mail this page along with $2.00 shipping and handling to:
Love Spell Book Club
PO Box 6640
Wayne, PA 19087
Or fax (must include credit card information) to:
610-995-9274

You can also sign up online at **www.dorchesterpub.com.**

*Plus $2.00 for shipping. Offer open to residents of the U.S. and Canada only. Canadian
residents please call 1-800-481-9191 for pricing information.

If under 18, a parent or guardian must sign. Terms, prices and conditions subject to
change. Subscription subject to acceptance. Dorchester Publishing reserves the right to
reject any order or cancel any subscription.